QUEEN *of* DECEPTION

A grimy hand clamped onto Hela's elbow and halted her momentum. She stared fixedly at the man's hand on her arm until it slipped from the fine crimson silk of her sleeve, leaving a dark sweaty handprint in its wake.

"I am the warden of this part of London," he snarled with genuine anger that didn't quite overcome his bewilderment.

"I don't care," Hela said with a voice as deadly as her death touch. "You do not have the right to lay your hands on me. Step back."

The warden hesitated, as if expecting her to follow that with a threat or an excuse or even a plea. Yet Hela simply stood there resplendent in black armor and a fine velvet cloak with a sword on her hip, radiating threat. She dropped her voice to a growl. "I will not tell you again."

The man's throat bobbed as he swallowed convulsively, a shiver rippling through him at the death promised in her voice.

T0018593

MORE LEGENDS OF ASGARD FROM ACONYTE

The Sword of Surtur by C L Werner

The Serpent and the Dead by Anna Stephens

Three Swords by C L Werner

THE CHRONICLES OF HEIMDALL

The Head of Mimir by Richard Lee Byers

The Rebels of Vanaheim by Richard Lee Byers

The Prisoner of Tartarus by Richard Lee Byers

MARVEL LEGENDS OF ASGARD

QUEEN *of* DECEPTION

ANNA STEPHENS

ACONYTE

FOR MARVEL PUBLISHING

VP Production & Special Projects: Jeff Youngquist
Associate Editor, Special Projects: Sarah Singer
Manager, Licensed Publishing: Jeremy West
VP, Licensed Publishing: Sven Larsen
SVP Print, Sales & Marketing: David Gabriel
Editor in Chief: C B Cebulski

First published by Aconyte Books in 2023
ISBN 978 1 83908 203 0
Ebook ISBN 978 1 83908 204 7

Cover art by Grant Griffin

Distributed in North America by Simon & Schuster Inc, New York, USA
Printed in the United States of America
9 8 7 6 5 4 3 2 1

ACONYTE BOOKS

An imprint of Asmodee Entertainment Ltd
Mercury House, Shipstones Business Centre
North Gate, Nottingham NG7 7FN, UK
aconytebooks.com // twitter.com/aconytebooks

For my good friend Leife.
Thanks for always being there.

⊙NE

CRYSTAL AND BOOK

The marketplace was busy and loud under a vibrant sky, thronged with shoppers and merchants and cutpurses. Lord John Dee, nobleman, magician, and chief astronomer to the queen, strolled through the crowd with one hand close to his purse and the other ready to fend off unwelcome attention.

He was by far the richest man in the small town of Mortlake, and the one with the highest social standing, and everyone in the market knew his face and name. Still, that wouldn't stop an enterprising young thief from trying their luck, for not everyone had the same reverence for nobility as Dee's peers.

He stepped wide around a pair of squabbling youngsters and then nudged a panicking chicken away with his foot. The strident voices arguing to his right assured him its escape had been noticed and blame was being hotly contested. No one was actively seeking to recapture the bird, though.

Dee exchanged nods with the more well-to-do merchants and businessmen, gestured politely for a couple of elegant ladies to precede him, and ignored the rest. He'd only stepped out for some fresh air and to rest his eyes from the dimness of his study, for the thickly leaded windows didn't allow much in the way of light, especially on a day as gloomy as this one.

The sky was threatening rain when he reached the edge of the market without having seen anything to catch his fancy. There was a cloaked figure standing in the shade of the tavern's overhanging thatched roof. Their hood was pulled well forward so Dee couldn't see their face. They didn't have a stall or even a table. Instead, there was a tray hanging around their neck and on the tray was a beautiful, polished wooden box. Cherrywood, if Dee was any judge from this distance. Even in the gloom of late, cloudy spring, it gleamed.

To his surprise, the merchant beckoned to him with a gloved hand. Intrigued and wary, he stepped between the last market stalls and approached, checking the rest of the shadows for pickpockets or thugs. It was unlikely he'd be openly attacked this close to the edge of the market, but that didn't make it impossible. His cloak, doublet, and boots were valuable, let alone the contents of his purse. Dee carried a short dagger, but no sword. He wasn't much given to fighting anyway. He was a man of peace, a man of God, a magician.

"My lord, I've been waiting for a distinguished customer such as yourself to come along. What I have here is not for common eyes but you, I think, will appreciate it."

Dee scoffed. He'd heard such nonsense from countless

merchants before, all of whom were far better at it than this man who wouldn't even show his face.

And then the merchant lifted the lid on the – yes, it was cherrywood – box. Despite himself, Dee inhaled sharply and stepped closer still, angling his body so that his shadow didn't add to the gloom and obscure the objects further.

The box was large and lined in plush red velvet, thick and rich, but what nestled upon its softness was extraordinary. A leatherbound book longer than Dee's forearm and thick enough to contain hundreds of pages. And beside it, spherical and exquisitely made, sat a crystal almost the size of his fist. Its center was veined with lines like a starburst or the flecks of green in a hazel eye, and it was polished to a high sheen.

"Do not touch," the merchant warned. "If you wish to handle the artifacts, you must put on gloves. They are rare and expensive, and their power is not to be trifled with."

Dee looked up at that. Somehow, despite being so close he could hear the trader breathe, he still couldn't see his face beneath his hood.

"Power?"

"They are magical in nature, milord. Why do you think I waited here for your approach instead of displaying them openly in the market for all to inquire about and run greedy, ungloved fingers across? They would have been stolen within the hour, even if no one knew what to do with them. You are the queen's magician though, milord, and as such the only man qualified to own and use these things."

"You are correct, of course," Dee said, drawing himself up proudly while having no idea what the book and crystal actually did. "They would be wasted on another. That said, I would have your knowledge of them first – where they are from, these powers you claim they possess, and anything else you know. Who wrote the book?"

Despite not being able to see a single scrap of the merchant's flesh, Dee got the sudden sense the man was aware of his ignorance and amused by it. Something in the shift of shoulders beneath the cloak, perhaps. Still, he spread his gloved hands as if in apology. "I am but a merchant, milord. I cannot say what they might do together. They came into my possession from a far-off land and the man who gifted them to me was dying. He said they were to be given to someone who could change the world with them, but who would never underestimate their power or use them for personal gain. All know you are a man of good conscience and are trusted by Her Majesty herself. There was no other I would consider showing these precious items to. I have traveled a long way to meet you, milord."

Dee didn't believe a word of the story – if the man who'd given them to him was dying, that was probably because this villain had killed him before stealing the box and its contents. Nevertheless, he pulled his gloves from his belt and slipped them on. They were fine, supple calfskin, but even they seemed too cumbersome a barrier between his hands and the crystal. He itched to cup it in his bare palms and press it to his cheek. Was it as cool and solid as it looked?

Despite his desire, he reached first for the book. He didn't want to seem too keen and he needed to know everything he could about the objects before they set to haggling. Dee weighed the heavy book in his hand and then opened it randomly a few pages in. The vellum was thick and creamy, of good quality, but the markings made no sense, the language unlike any he'd ever seen. Was it even language that accompanied the dozens of pictures of flowers, herbs, and other plants? He flicked further on and came across what were clearly astronomical illustrations. His pulse jumped. But again, the notes accompanying them were meaningless. Not just the language itself but the shape of the letters – if such they were – was indecipherable.

Dee flicked back to the plant illustrations: they weren't native to any forest, field, or garden he'd ever seen. Gently, he replaced it in the box and allowed his gloved fingertips to brush over the crystal. It was truly exquisite.

"I will take the crystal," he said, "but I fear you've been misled about the book. It is worthless."

"It is not," the merchant insisted. "The items belong together. The magic comes from using them both. I cannot sell you just the crystal."

Dee stepped back and folded his arms, affecting surprise. Even that small distance between him and the veined stone seemed too much, seemed a heresy. He wanted it. He needed it. This would restore his waning fortunes with the queen, he was convinced of it. How, he didn't know yet, but there was something compelling about it and, if nothing else, he could gift it to her as a pretty bauble … even if the thought of it being dismissed as such made the back of his neck itch.

But first things first. "You said you have traveled a long way to bring me these objects. You admitted they were a gift to you. Why then should I pay for them?"

The merchant snapped the box lid shut, cutting off Dee's view of the crystal. His stomach lurched.

"I am a merchant, my lord. If you do not wish to purchase the scrying stone and its book of ritual, I will take them elsewhere."

Scrying stone. Book of ritual?

Dee's heart thundered in his ears. He already had two scrying crystals, both of limited power and dubious results. If he could attune this one to scrying, this crystal whose power he'd felt from a mere brush of gloved fingertips, his reputation and standing at court would both be restored.

And I wouldn't have to give it away as a trinket, but respect and keep it as it deserves.

"What is your price?" he asked, letting none of his sudden excitement into his voice. He strove to keep it level, long-suffering. "You've woven a pretty tale of dying men and distant lands, but you won't let me touch the objects with my bare hands, as if I'm some grubby stableboy, and I've already told you the book is worthless. So…"

"It isn't worthless. If you can't learn to read it with the crystal's aid, I must take it to someone who can."

"With the crystal's aid?" Dee snorted. "Does it contain an imp who will translate for me?" He chewed his lip, eyeing the burnished sheen of the cherrywood on the tray, and then glanced in each direction again, suspecting his interest might be held in order to allow others to approach and rob him. A clever bit of trickery.

The space around them remained empty and cool in the shadows.

"An old book that can't be read and an alleged scrying crystal I'm not allowed to touch? I will give you two sovereigns, and that's mostly for the prettiness of the box."

The merchant sighed, the edges of his draped hood flickering. "Twenty sovereigns and you have a sale, milord," he said calmly.

Dee choked. Twenty was an outrageous sum and they both knew it. "Good day, sir," he said, furious at having his interest piqued and then abused in such a way. He didn't have time for this. He spun on his heel, cloak flaring, and began to stride away.

"You haven't even held the crystal, milord."

Dee stopped. "And nor will I," he said, even as he inwardly rejoiced at having pressed the merchant to change his approach. His palms sweated within his gloves. "You have wasted enough of my morning as it is. I should point you out to the town wardens to ensure you are not welcomed to Mortlake's market ever again."

"Please, milord, no need for threats." He proffered the tray again. "Hold the crystal and all will be clear. You'll see that twenty sovereigns isn't so much. You'll understand why you need it and the book both. Why you are the only one who should possess them. Please, milord. A single moment of your time to weigh the scrying stone in your hands, no more. You may remove one glove, but not both. If you are unconvinced, then I will leave you to your day."

Dee hesitated a moment longer, for looks, and then stripped off one glove with an air of skeptical impatience.

Feigning extreme reluctance, Dee let the merchant draw him slowly back within reach. Some of those glimpsed astronomical illustrations tickled the edges of his mind, hinting at understanding. When the box's lid was opened once more, he lost his breath all over again. Even in the building's shadow, among the reek of urine and stale beer, the stone was beautiful and the book intriguing for all its plain cover and nonsense words.

This time Dee didn't hesitate. It would be his only chance to touch the crystal because he wasn't going to pay the merchant's...

The stone was smooth and round, slightly flatter at its base so that it would sit easily and not roll away. It was cool and far heavier than it had any right to be. *Loaded with the weight of history, of lore and magic,* his mind supplied. He blinked away the nonsensical thought but couldn't deny the romance of the idea.

And it almost seemed to vibrate, like a bell after it was struck, but if it emitted a tone, he could not hear it.

Dee stepped backwards, into the glare of the sun, and the crystal took its brightness and shattered it, casting rainbows across the muddy, filth-strewn track between the tavern and the market green. The merchant moved with him, alert in case Dee tried to run off with the scrying stone, but he didn't. He couldn't. Because there was something...

Experimentally, he swung the crystal away from and then towards the box still holding the mysterious book.

The merchant chuckled from within his hood. "You begin to understand," he said approvingly.

"They... react to each other?"

The nameless figure made a thoughtful sound. "They work in harmony together," he corrected. "They like each other, want to be close together at all times."

"What happens when they are separated?"

"Ask the dying man who gave them to me," the merchant

said, and Dee startled, then tried again – still unsuccessfully – to see beneath his hood.

"Who are you?"

"Just someone selling magic to those who can best use it. Twenty sovereigns."

"Five," Dee said as he tightened his grip on the precious object and strove for a casual, dismissive tone. "And that's generous. Just because it has a few curious properties doesn't mean it's worth so much. It is not a philosopher's stone."

"Isn't it?" the merchant asked. "Fifteen."

"Eight."

"For the ability to see the future? Twelve."

"Ten," Dee said, still clutching the crystal to his chest.

"Done." The man took the box off the tray around his neck and held it out.

Dee put the stone inside it and then hefted his purse. "Come to the house," he said. "No sane man walks through a market carrying ten sovereigns."

"As milord commands," the merchant said, bowing his head. He followed as Dee strode briskly through the thinning market crowd to the river side of Mortlake, where his property nestled against the bank of the Thames. His manservant, Fletcher, opened the door as they approached and raised one eyebrow in silent enquiry.

"Fetch my strongbox and Francois. We'll be in my study."

Fletcher nodded and hurried away, and Dee led the trader into his study – a cozy, book-lined room – and paced before the fireplace, laid ready to light his scholarly pursuits into the evening.

"Will you tell me your name?" Dee asked the merchant

when his personal guard stepped quietly into the room a moment later. Francois was tall, broad, and armed, wearing a thickly padded gambeson in lieu of armor, but it would still provide decent protection against knives or arrows. Well, not arrows while they were here indoors, he supposed. And the merchant couldn't conceal a bow beneath his voluminous cloak anyway. Could he?

"The items I sell are rare and often otherworldly," the man said, still in that calm and even tone as if this was a casual conversation. "It is a dangerous business and I have no wish to be accused of witchcraft. Therefore, better that my name be left unspoken and my appearance unknown."

"You don't want the people you've swindled to be able to find you again, you mean," Dee said, but without much heat. Francois stirred at that and Dee sent him a quelling look. No doubt most of what the man sold was lead-painted to look like gold, but not this. He was almost sure not this.

"I can tell you a name if you insist, milord, but it won't be real. What is real are the crystal and the book. What is real is the gold you're paying me for them. Let us focus on that."

Dee paced some more until Fletcher returned with his strongbox. Francois was a comforting presence beside the door, and he'd ensure the nameless purveyor of magical artifacts didn't escape with both the crystal and the money.

Dee pulled the key for the strongbox from where it hung around his neck beneath his doublet and shirt and unlocked it, taking care to keep the lid raised to block the man's view of the contents.

He counted ten sovereigns onto the desk one at a time, then closed and locked the box and slid it to the other end of the desk. Fletcher took up his place in front of it, a barrier.

The merchant – whose face was still hidden after all this time – placed the cherrywood box on the table with great reverence. "Keep them together and use them to change the world," he said with great solemnity.

Dee snorted again. "Open it," he ordered, because he had to be sure no sleight of hand had been involved. The man did so, revealing the red velvet, the leatherbound book, and the starburst crystal. The fine hairs on the back of the magician's arms rose, and he suppressed a shiver.

He nodded, once, and the man promptly scooped the sovereigns into his hand, jingling them together. "Pleasure doing business with you, milord," he said and turned away.

Dee checked the box once more – yes, the items were still there, tingling along his nerve endings – and then gestured for Fletcher to escort him out with Francois keeping a watchful eye over them both.

The study door shut behind them and Dee was finally alone with the scrying stone and its book of ritual. Hands trembling, he stripped off his other glove and cast them both on top of his strongbox. Then very, very gently, he touched one fingertip to the crystal.

Nothing happened. The surface of the crystal was as cool and smooth as it had been the first time he'd touched it, but that was it. There was an oath already burning his tongue when the side of his other hand grazed the edge of the book.

The finger touching the crystal began to tingle, as if a fine tremor or vibration ran through the stone. Dee snatched away his hand on instinct and immediately the tingling ceased. Carefully, he reached out again, this time using the back of his fingers to touch the crystal. Again, the tingle. The fine hairs on his knuckles stirred and stood up. The magician straightened and stared at the objects still nestled on the red velvet inside their box.

Then, excitement bubbling in his veins, he hurried to the study door, slammed it, and locked it. Hastening back to his desk, he pulled the candlesticks close and lit all of them despite the afternoon still being young. Then he shrugged out of his fine velvet doublet and dragged a chair to the desk and sat. Finally, reverently, he removed the book from the box and placed it on a clear space on his desk. Shifting to the edge of his seat, he opened the book to the first page and stared again at the incomprehensible language in which it was written. This time, though, he placed the palm of his hand against the page and, steeling himself with a deep breath, picked up the crystal in the other.

What had been a mere buzz in the fingertips before was far more now. The vibration was so strong it was almost shuddering apart the bones of his hand and traveling quickly up his arm into his shoulder. The hand touching the book became warm and Dee stared at it in alarm, half expecting the pages to burst into flames. Neither it nor the stone seemed affected, but the ever-strengthening vibration was accelerating through his body, buzzing through his jaw and teeth and up into his brain where, in a burst of light and sound and the distant chiming as of bells, a voice began to speak. Dee didn't recognize the language although the intention was quite clear. The meaning behind it spoke to his very soul, as if God Himself were talking to him. He knew things, saw things, understood the secrets of the world and God's plan for it.

And then it was gone.

Dee opened his eyes to find himself slumped over his desk with the crystal clenched in his fist and his fingers bloodless from the force of his grip. His other hand had parted company with the book of ritual, which he supposed was the cause for the cessation of his communion with… whatever it had been. There were tears on his face and running down into his beard, but they were tears of joy and spiritual ecstasy rather than pain or fear.

Well, the merchant had said that twenty sovereigns was a fair deal. "And yet I got this wonder, this miracle, for only ten," Dee muttered to himself. He was both delighted at the bargain and strangely shamefaced at having haggled over something that was clearly priceless.

Then the magician realized, with a lurch of horror, that he could remember nothing he had learned or seen or who he had spoken with during the trance induced by the scrying stone. He would need to write it down while in the trance. He hesitated and then groaned.

"And yet I need both hands on the objects to activate this ritual." He paused to think about that for a moment and a slow smile spread across his face. "How very clever. Only someone with a vast intellect and the ability to learn and retain information will be capable of understanding everything they are shown. I flatter myself that I am such a man, and I will not squander this mighty gift that I have been given."

Dee placed the stone back on its velvet cushion and then slid off his chair onto his knees, cramped between the desk and the window behind it. He put his hands together and closed his eyes. "Dear God, thank you for this mighty gift. I swear to dedicate myself to learning the mysteries contained herein that I might know your will and bring it to the world. I pray the merchant was right to choose me and that I have both the strength and knowledge to interpret the mysteries that are presented to me. Amen."

Despite his eagerness, the magician paused to drink a cup of water and kick off his shoes for comfortable slippers. He checked again that the door was locked and then placed parchment, quill, and ink on the table next to the book. He was determined to scribble down every impression he had the moment the trance lifted. It didn't matter how long it took, it didn't matter how tiring the process, Lord John Dee was going to translate this magical, mystical language and learn the secrets that he had known in the trance, but which now eluded him.

Fascinated, his veins singing with promise, Dee sat himself comfortably back in his chair and cradled the stone in his palm against his chest. He took a deep breath and picked up the book.

Two

The Summons

"My lord? My lord Dee?"

"I'm busy," Dee roared for what felt like the twentieth time that day. Who were these ignorant servants to keep on bothering him so?

"My lord, it is most urgent," Fletcher hissed through the heavy oak door of the study. "There is a summons from–"

"I care not!"

There was a long silence and Dee breathed a sigh of relief and bent once more to the book and the crystal. It had been a week and he was so close, *so close*. Already he had learned part of the angelic speech, for that was what he now knew it to be. The nameless merchant had been a fool to part with the gift for ten sovereigns, but wise to deliver it to John Dee. No other had the ability that he did; no other had the queen's ear, albeit more distantly these days. But no more, not once he'd fully understood what he was being told by the angels. He'd take his marvels to–

"–Whitehall, my lord!"

Yes, to Whitehall… Dee paused and looked up from the book, open to the astronomy pages, which was what the voice spoke of most often. A path from the earth to Heaven, a way to speak with the angels. Perhaps more.

"What?" he asked his desk blankly.

"There is a summons from the Palace of Whitehall, my lord. The queen requires your presence!"

"What?" he repeated and then shook himself. "When?"

"Upon the hour, my lord!" And the urgency in Fletcher's voice told Dee that that hour was almost nigh.

"Hell's teeth," he swore and closed the book, placing it back upon its velvet cushion. The scrying stone sat on his desk and, despite the need to hurry, he took a fine silk cloth and carefully polished it until no finger smudges remained and it was pristine once more. Then he replaced it in the cherrywood box and snapped it shut.

Dee pushed himself up to standing and his knees and most of his back popped and clicked as he did, testament to the hours he'd spent hunched over his desk learning the language of the seraphs. His stomach was empty, his mouth dry, his eyes sore and gritty. A dull throbbing assailed his temples. He locked the cherrywood box in the secret compartment behind the bookcase in his study, replaced the volumes of Greek philosophy and medicine that hid it – all original, of course – and hung the key around his neck to clink and jingle with the key to the strongbox. Much more of this and he'd begin to sound like a badly tuned harpsichord.

He crossed the room on aching legs and unbolted the study door. Fletcher's look of naked relief as he straightened up reinforced how little time he had. "I was worried, my lord. I'd been shouting at the door for a quarter of an hour. I was about to ask Francois to fetch an axe."

"Don't be ridiculous," Dee said, but inside he quailed. This wasn't the first time he'd been so consumed by the secrets of the crystal that he hadn't heard his manservant's call. "The work I am doing is of the utmost importance and secrecy. Her Majesty is the only one permitted to draw me from my studies, is that clear? I will not be interrupted for anyone else."

"As you say, my lord. I have taken the liberty of laying out a change of clothes and there is a pitcher of milk and some bread and butter in your chamber. You missed luncheon," he added pointedly.

Dee paused to pat Fletcher on the back. "And you do make an excellent luncheon, I know. I will have it for supper instead, supposing I am back from seeing Her Majesty by then. Leave it out for me anyway as no doubt I shall be famished. And thank you, Fletcher," he added. The man nodded, startled, and then a pleased flush rose into his cheeks. It gave Dee pause. If his servants were reacting so obviously to scant praise, then what would Lady Dee think of his seclusion in the study for so long? He winced and then glanced back reflexively at the bookcase and its hidden compartment. Concerns about Jane's state vanished from his mind, to be replaced by other, deeper fears.

"I want Francois armed and armored and guarding this door," he said severely. "No one is to so much as approach, do you understand? No one."

Fletcher nodded again, bewildered this time, but he'd

been in Dee's employ for twenty years and Dee had no fears his manservant's curiosity would get the better of him. His hand went to the keys around his neck just to check, though, and then he locked the study door and pocketed that key as well.

Dee hurried to his bedchamber to change. And eat. And drink. And then to the queen of England. Her Majesty Elizabeth, by the grace of God.

It was a long ride, and quicker on horseback than by carriage, so Dee pushed his mare into a canter and pounded along the riverbank towards the ferry and the outskirts of London. His progress would be impeded once he was in the winding, narrow streets, so best to make time while he could.

The countryside passed in a green blur on one side and the Thames in a brown smear on the other, both busy with people working, shouting, and living. It was another fine day, much like the one when he'd met the merchant and purchased the book and crystal, and Dee squinted against its blustery brightness. He hadn't set foot outside his house in Mortlake since the moment he'd first touched the scrying stone. The stone itself hadn't shown him a vision, but he'd seen one nonetheless: his waning fortunes at court restored, his stone and knowledge and abilities sought after and revered, the queen's ear his to whisper into once more.

The afternoon was waning by the time he clattered into the outskirts of Whitehall Palace and was challenged by the guard. He dismounted and identified himself, then straightened his doublet and hose and followed a page into the palace. Ruffled and sweaty from the ride and from cursing his way through the roads, as expected, he made surreptitious efforts to neaten his hair as he hurried through the echoing stone passages.

The queen was in the great hall, which was full to bursting with courtiers and their wives, other notables, clergymen, and soldiers. Her Majesty sat upon a throne and watched, with no great enthusiasm, as a juggler performed a series of tricks involving brightly colored balls. Dee winced. The man had been here a month and didn't seem to have added to his repertoire. From the sheen of sweat on his face, he knew his days entertaining the court were all but over.

A servant murmured in her ear as Dee waited in the doorway, and he was heartened to see her sit up straighter and then look over in his direction. Her Majesty beckoned him forward and he plastered a look of grateful humility on his face and hastened into the royal presence, sweeping into an elaborate bow at the foot of the dais.

"Lord John, it is about time," Queen Elizabeth said. "We had almost quite forgotten your looks, you have been missing so long."

There was a dutiful ripple of mirth from those courtiers within earshot and Dee resisted curling his lip in disdain. They'd be laughing on the other sides of their faces before long.

"Forgive my absence, Your Majesty. I have been working on a most intriguing project. Most intriguing indeed. If I might beg a private audience at some point to discuss the finer details?"

"Will it put an end to Philip of Spain's endless posturing? I swear he is more peacock than man."

Another titter and Dee joined in this time. "In fact, my queen, I believe that it may." That got her attention. "My work is only in its infancy but, Your Majesty, I believe it may have the power to change our standing in Europe – in the world – for good."

"Change our standing?" someone asked, and Dee looked around to see Sir Francis Drake – of course – leaning against a nearby pillar. He was newly elevated to his knighthood and had evidently decided that gave him, a commoner, the right to address his betters. "Are we not already the foremost power in Europe, thanks to Her Majesty's diligence, foresight, and formidable intelligence? What more could we hope for?"

"Divine approval," Dee said bluntly and was gratified to see Drake's mouth drop open. The man spluttered.

"Do we not already have that?" asked Walsingham, the queen's principal secretary known to all as her spymaster. "Her Majesty not only enjoys primogeniture but was avowed by God Himself when she took the throne."

Dee inclined his head. "Forgive my vagueness, my queen, but all I can say at the moment–" he looked around meaningfully at the crowded chamber and the courtiers gathering close to listen "–is that I have in my possession items of rare and magical ability and which I believe are of," he paused and dared to put a foot on the lowest step of the dais and lean closer, "angelic origin."

Elizabeth was suitably awed by his pronouncement. "My dear Lord Dee, would you join me for supper and tell me all about these wondrous objects? Walsingham, attend us. And ensure Lord Dee's house is secure," she added in a low voice as the spymaster ushered Dee up the steps to the dais and through the door behind it that led into the innards of Whitehall Palace.

Dee smiled humbly in acquiescence, while inside he crowed at his achievement.

His place at the queen's side: restored.

"What an extraordinary tale," Her Majesty said at the conclusion of supper and Dee's enthusiastic rambling. "And where did you acquire such wondrous items?"

Dee hesitated. He didn't have the merchant's name, but he wasn't sure that was what the queen was asking. He suspected she was wondering why he hadn't turned the objects over to her immediately.

"The merchant was most secretive with his identity, Your Majesty. I have spent the entirety of the last week researching and experimenting with these items so that I could bring you real evidence rather than supposition as to their abilities. If you would like me to arrange a viewing, I would be delighted to bring them to you. The language of the angels is particularly difficult to understand and record, but I am making some progress and hope that this will continue at an accelerated speed now that I have a basic grasp of it."

There, that should do it. The queen could see and even handle the items but should not expect to be able to understand anything that was said to her. The magician hesitated: her reign was blessed by God Himself, perhaps she would have an innate understanding that he lacked. Dee fought down his sudden panic, visions of his bright future at the queen's side vanishing when she claimed the items and their power for herself.

"Yes, I should like to see these magical artifacts for myself. Bring them to me tomorrow at four in the afternoon and we shall experiment together."

"Please exercise the utmost caution, Your Majesty," said Walsingham. "We do not wish for there to be any rumors of impropriety or Papism, especially not with his grace the duke of Alencon due to visit soon to negotiate Your Majesty's marriage."

The queen gave her secretary an unimpressed look. "Even though his grace the duke of Alencon is himself a Papist?" she asked tartly. Walsingham bowed his head in acknowledgment of the rebuke, but his point was well made and Dee seized on it with relief.

"Lord Walsingham has a point, Your Majesty. Although I am supremely confident in the conclusions I have drawn so far, I cannot guarantee that there is no danger to what I am attempting. Perhaps I could offer you a demonstration first and then you could handle each of the objects separately so as not to begin the mysterious process of communion."

The queen's unimpressed look switched from her spymaster to Dee with celerity and he bowed his head in abject humility over the remains of his supper. "Perhaps you are both right," she conceded with ill grace. "My body is but that of a weak and feeble woman after all. Still, I should like to see and touch these objects and so you will present yourself to me with them tomorrow at four as commanded."

"It would be my absolute honor, Your Majesty. I hope to provide a worthy demonstration and perhaps together we may discover some new understanding of the angelic language and the message the seraphs have for you."

Elizabeth dismissed him soon afterwards and Dee retrieved his horse from the stables and rode slowly home in the dark to Mortlake, his mind spinning with possibilities and the bright dancing motes of his dazzling future.

The house was much as he left it and Fletcher had been as good as his word and left a late supper – or rather the luncheon he'd prepared – in the dining hall. Dee stared at it in over-full dismay and then seized half a bottle of wine and some cheese and cold meat and loaded it all onto a platter to take back to his study. The middle of the night might be approaching but there was work to do. There were angels with whom to converse. And there was a world to change for himself and for the queen of England.

A world of wonders to create. A world of empire.

THREE

ELJUDNIR

Hela lounged in her throne with one leg thrown over the arm and her cheek pillowed on her fist. She was barely listening as her seneschal, Eirik, related something he'd already dealt with and therefore she probably didn't need to know. His voice was a comforting drone in the background as she stared moodily down the length of the audience hall and thought upon her latest failure.

Hela's palace was gray and gloomy, with expansive marble columns holding up an enormous roof and the hall floored with thousands upon thousands of highly polished, worn smooth skulls. The only colors to lighten the paleness were the scarlet sashes on the palace guards and the gold lining of her own cloak.

Eirik wore a red sash slashed with gold to denote his position, though as his monotone continued to echo through the hall with no signs of stopping, it was one Hela was tempted to take from him. She sighed and shifted to a more comfortable position in her throne and then stilled, the breath catching in her chest. There was something... something somewhere, tingling at the very edges of her senses.

"Quiet."

Eirik cut himself off mid-sentence and the palace guards snapped to attention, bringing their long spears to bear and their helmed heads swiveling as they checked for danger. Hela swung her leg off the arm of her throne and sat up straight, then raised one hand to quiet the room.

"What is this I feel?" she murmured to herself. "Someone somewhere is playing with a magic they do not understand. A magic they... cannot understand." She opened her eyes, intrigued, and fixed Eirik with a glare. "I will discover the source of this magic. Guard me while I journey."

"As my goddess commands," Eirik said and drew his sword. He climbed the steps onto the dais and turned to face out into the audience chamber, the last line of defense if her palace guards should fall.

Hela put them from her mind: whoever was wielding the magic – or being wielded by it, more likely – they weren't directing it at her, nor were they anywhere within Helheim's bounds. She didn't tell her guards that, though. Better to give them something else to concentrate on. It was good for them to remember their allegiance and what it meant to be battle-ready.

Resting her head back against her throne, the goddess of Hel gripped the arms to anchor herself and shut her eyes. Although she was sure the magic's origin was nowhere within her Realm, she conducted a thorough sweep anyway. Hela had many enemies and not all of them were incompetent. It was conceivable that someone was hidden in a distant region of Helheim and weaving a magic against her. It was a common enough tale, though never one she approached with any less than the required caution. Usually, the magic had a scent and taste familiar to her: the burnt ash and heat of the fire demons of Muspelheim or the metallic earthy tang of Nidavellir, land of the dwarves.

Not this, though. This was different. Intriguing.

The millions of souls under her command felt the brush of Hela's sentience and responded with the adoration that was her due. There was no subterfuge in any of them and so she cast her mind further, sending a part of her spirit soaring out of her Realm in search.

Asgard was, of course, the most likely culprit for a move against her and she hovered close to that Realm to feel for the tendrils of strange magic that had first attracted her. They had faded now, as if whatever ritual or spell had been underway was concluded. If it had been aimed at her it had caused no ill effect – she had barely felt it, let alone been damaged by it. Yet the aftertaste lingered.

Hela swooped as close as she dared to the palace in Asgardia, for the All-Father's protections were strong and they would register her presence if she ventured too close. If it was them planning a move against her, she didn't want to alert them that she knew about it.

Hela could sense nothing directed towards her or her Realm. The magic embracing and surrounding Asgard appeared purely defensive, while what she had sensed, however distantly, was more than that. She hadn't quite managed to identify it before the connection had failed, but it had seemed to be searching. For what, she didn't know but was determined to find out. Hela reeled in her consciousness and directed it further out, to Muspelheim first, as the most next likely antagonist. She searched the Realm of the fire giants and found no clue. Irritated, she sped even further, weaving around the great World Tree, Yggdrasil, from which the Realms were suspended. It took time, and more effort than she had realized, but eventually Hela found the source of the magic. Back in her palace of bones, one finely plucked eyebrow rose on her otherwise still face. Interesting. Most interesting.

Almost as if the wielder of the magic wanted her to know of it, the elusive wisp suddenly strengthened into a beacon and this time Hela saw towards where the magic was reaching. Her other eyebrow rose to join the first, because both origin and destination were not what she'd expected. She sped towards the magic's origins first, and then followed the thread all the way to where it reached. She was far from her physical form now and the hours and the strain were beginning to tell even on her formidable strength, so she assured herself of the general location and then raced back into her body.

Back in herself, on her throne and within the strength of her palace, Hela opened her eyes and swallowed. Her throat was dry and the shadows through the windows had shifted far across the floor. She had journeyed for hours and most of the day was gone. "Eirik," she said in a hoarse rasp and her seneschal jumped and spun to face her.

"My lady, you are back. Are you quite well?" He waited for her nod before sheathing his sword and snapping his fingers for a servant to bring refreshments. Hela drank deeply from a goblet of mead before selecting a few choice cuts of meat from a platter. Hunger gnawed at her belly, but excitement consumed her mind.

"I have business to attend to outside of Helheim. You will administer my Realm in my place and Fenris will ensure the safety of my throne – against any who think to take it," she added meaningfully.

Eirik bowed hastily. "I will do all that you require, my goddess," he promised.

Hela rose from her throne and stretched luxuriously, glad to be back in her body again. She gestured for Eirik to fall in behind her and then strode down the dais steps and across to a niche in the wall, hidden between two columns and behind a statue of Hela herself. She gestured to dispel the magical barrier that both concealed and protected the niche, exposing a shelf carved from the wall which held the preserved skull of a mountain giant. Hela reached into the left-hand eye socket and retrieved a heavy, ornate gold torc which she wound around her neck. The metal was smooth and cool against her collarbones. From the right-hand eye socket, she retrieved a second, far smaller and simpler torc, which she handed to Eirik.

"We can communicate through these. You will not make a single decision without clearing it with me first. I will check in with you thrice a day, at dawn, noon, and dusk. Contact me in between those times only if there is an emergency. I will have other eyes watching," she added and Eirik bowed yet again.

She turned in a swirl of cloak and faced the enormous colonnade that made up one end of the audience chamber and through which she could see the distant city and hills of Helheim. She waved her hands again in another, more complex piece of magic, and the central columns bent like saplings in the wind to allow Fenris to squeeze his enormous bulk into the audience chamber. All around the walls, palace guards and servants shifted and shrank back, giving the wolf the respect and space he deserved.

Eirik slipped on the torc, and Hela checked the connection between their minds as she approached Fenris. The wolf loped up the steps and curled himself around her throne and she leaned against his massive jaw to stroke between his ears. "Guard well my palace, my friend. Watch the seneschal for me. Watch everyone."

Fenris rumbled an agreeable growl that echoed down the chamber and made the bone floor shiver. Hela felt the vibrations through the soles of her boots and smiled. Between the wolf and Eirik, her Realm was well protected.

"I need armor for wearing – subtle and practical – and silver for spending. And bring me the Nightsword," she said to a servant, who curtsied and hurried away. She turned to Eirik, who waited at the base of the dais near Fenris's lolling hind leg. "I will be gone no more than three days," she said and saw him pale. Hela grinned without amusement and tapped the torc at her throat. "Stay in touch, seneschal. And stay loyal."

Fenris added a rumbling growl of his own and lifted his upper lip away from canines longer than Hela's forearm.

"I shall do all that my goddess requires, that and no more. I am your most devoted servant," Eirik hastened to promise.

Hela pushed herself upright from where she had leant against the wolf's jaw to allow her servants to dress her in her armor: a black breastplate with matching greaves and vambraces. They were all made of supple leather with toughened steel scales sewn on, and they were imbued with magic and with curses against any who should touch them. As her cloak fell from her shoulders for the few moments necessary to buckle on the armor, Hela's true appearance was revealed: the left half of her body, from scalp to soles, was blackened, rotting and skeletal.

The armor went on over tight black breeches and a deep crimson shirt. Her helmet was shaped into a jet and onyx diadem and secured across her brow. Cloak and beauty restored, Hela fastened on the Nightsword and tied a coin pouch bulging with silver to her belt. Anything else she needed, she would simply buy. Hela preferred to travel light. She swept the audience chamber with her eyes, cold threat promised to all who came beneath her gaze if they should fail her. One by one, guards and servants, seneschal and even the wolf, bowed their heads. "Three days," she reminded Eirik. "Three days, no mistakes."

Hela didn't wait for his response. She strode down off the dais and into the center of the audience chamber. When she could be sure she had all eyes watching in appropriate awe, she Realm-jumped, transporting herself instantly from Helheim to the Realm from where the magic originated.

Midgard.

Hela had targeted her jump to come out as close to the wavering source of the magic as she could manage. There was a moment of dislocation and intense disarray and then she stood in a narrow alley between crooked buildings that leaned towards each other so that only a faint strip of blue sky showed between the roofs. She was immediately assailed by the stench of sewage and rotting garbage. To her left, the alley twisted away around a corner from whence came the distant sounds of commerce. To her right she found a group of ragged, filthy Midgardians who stared at her in openmouthed astonishment. Hela threw back her shoulders and tossed her hair out of her face and gave them a haughty glare.

She'd never bothered to learn much about Midgard itself, having no interest in Midgardian souls, but she was unsurprised by her surroundings and the general state of the humans gawping at her. They were favored by Odin, after all: what else could they be but pathetic?

The one closest eyed her deliberately up and down and then let out an unpleasant bark of laughter. "Lady in trews, is it, whatever next?" He squinted and then nudged his companion. "Is that armor? You wearing armor? Who are you supposed to be, Joan of Arc? Is there a mummers play happening we haven't heard about?"

Hela had no idea what any of that meant so she ignored it. "There is magic being practiced nearby. Tell me what you know of it," she demanded.

"Ooh, got a sword as well, have you? You should be careful you don't hurt yourself – or get yourself into trouble you don't know how to get out of," he added meaningfully and began advancing down the alley, making no effort to answer her as he should. He trod heedlessly through the piles of trash, seemingly unaware of the unspeakable mess clogging his shoes and stockings. The stink increased the closer he got, and Hela realized with horror that some of it drifted from him rather than the ground.

She folded her arms across her breastplate and glowered. "I said: tell me what you know of magic."

The rest of the group were advancing now, and rods and short knives appeared in their hands. At their rear was a woman with straw-colored hair wearing a grubby, floor-length dress that dragged through the dirt. "Get her, lads," she screeched. "Armor and sword like that will see us fed for the rest of the year. That coin purse looks fat, too. Take it all from her."

Hela threw back her head and laughed. "You think your little sticks and knives can hurt me? You think to intimidate me – do you have any idea who I am?"

"Could be Philip of Spain himself for all I care," the man at the front snarled and hefted his heavy stick. He was only a few strides away now. Hela contemplated drawing her sword. No. It would be much more fun to deal with them unarmed. "Probably a Papist seeing as you want a magician. No magicians round here in this good Protestant town. Her Majesty saw to that, as did blessed King Henry before her. Now, how about you start with handing over that fancy sword and then–" he grinned back at the others "–you strip off that armor, too?"

There was a sudden strengthening of the magic that had drawn Hela here in the first place, a low tingle rushing up into a vibration that grabbed at her like a fishhook beneath the ribs. West and south, a couple of leagues at most perhaps. Oily and dark and different. But powerful and full of promise. She grinned. She had no need to deal with these commoners, after all.

The goddess looked left towards the unoccupied end of

the alley. It wasn't quite the right direction but if it got her out into a main street then she could orient herself properly. A sudden whistle through the air alerted her and Hela raised her right arm. The heavy stick arcing towards her shattered across the fish scales of her vambrace and triggered a curse that would turn his bones to dust within him.

His bones did not turn to dust. The curse didn't work on Midgardians, it seemed. Hela turned her deflection into a grab about the man's throat, lifting him off his feet and pinning him to the wall. She let him hang there, feet kicking and helpless, while she glared at his cronies who'd come to a disbelieving halt a few steps away.

"I wouldn't if I were you," she said pleasantly. "Though if you do want to, I won't stop you. It's been a while since I've enjoyed myself."

The four men and one woman screeched and pelted back down the alleyway, leaving their leader in Hela's grip. She squeezed a little harder just to enjoy the purpling of his face, and then leaned in close. "Like I said, you have no idea who I am. I suggest you run away, now. And I also suggest that you tell no one what you saw, or I might come back here and rip off your arms. Understood?"

Her hand around his throat made it impossible for him to nod, but he wheezed something she took for assent and so she let go. The man crumpled to the floor, his hands at his neck, coughing and choking for air. Hela turned in a swirl of cloak and stalked away.

If this was the best Midgard had to offer, she'd find this magic-user and return with them to Helheim by this Realm's sunset. Better to have them secure in her grasp and her Realm than to demand their secrets here. That way, Hela could take her time extracting everything they knew. Not just the magic itself, but where they'd learned it, was of profound interest.

Because it was a magic not native to Midgard.

It quickly became apparent that the ragged beggars in the alleyway weren't the only ones to find Hela's attire a source of both amusement and alarm. She strode out of the alley's mouth into a busy street thronged with hurrying Midgardians and dirty children, all of whom halted upon seeing her in order to stare. Hela was used to being the center of attention wherever she went, but that attention was usually accompanied by respect and even outright fear.

What she was hearing now, beneath the growing murmur of whispered conversation, was amusement. As if Hela was a source of ridicule for these poor miserable creatures. She was tempted to throw off her cloak and show them exactly what she was, wielding her death touch on any who stepped within range until the street – perhaps even the entire city – was a silent mass grave of tangled limbs and screaming mouths. If she didn't have better things to do, she might have enjoyed such sport.

Instead, Hela straightened her back and placed one hand very deliberately upon the pommel of the Nightsword, drawing all eyes to the weapon. Her gaze swept those closest to her with challenge and she was gratified to see how quickly they backed down. A moment later she noticed how every single woman and girl was wearing a variation on the beggar-woman's gown, varying only in color and the amount of grime soaked into its hem. This then was a difference to Asgard, it seemed: it was uncommon, perhaps even forbidden, for women and girls to dress practically and comfortably. The man from before had commented on her... trews, as he'd called them, first, and only her armor and sword second.

Hela could fight in a gown – exceptionally well, in fact – she just didn't see the point in handing her enemies any advantage. Trousers were warm and sensible and made fighting and horse riding both much easier. She stared back at the mostly silent crowd and noticed that of the few weapons on display, every one belonged to a man. She arched a contemptuous eyebrow and stared down the biggest and nearest without effort.

Didn't women fight in Midgard? Perhaps magic was their path to power, and the magician she was searching for was a woman. Hela stared at the women she passed as she strode down the center of the street, forcing the crowd to part for her. Even the occasional horse and rider had to detour around her assured and predatory walk.

None of them seemed particularly powerful. She sensed no aura of magic, no whiff of sorcery, from any of them, whether it was magic native to Midgard or this other, darker power she'd felt. They seemed as humbled and meek as the majority of men. Hela was pulled from her rumination by a strident voice bellowing for someone to stop. She would have ignored it if not for the sudden wariness in the crowd, which hurried away and left her in an expanding pool of silence and solitude.

"You there. Woman in the... the *trousers*. Halt and turn around, in the name of Her Majesty, Queen Elizabeth."

Hela came to a halt and stared up into the sky for a long moment. Then she sighed and turned to face the speaker in a swirl of cloak. The sun glinted black from her breastplate and diadem. She folded her arms across her chest. "Yes, little man? Why do you seek to delay me? I have urgent business in the south. If you're not here to act as my escort, I suggest you don't delay me further."

A short man in dull and battered armor of his own puffed towards her, his face red and sweaty beneath a round helmet. He tapped a finger against his breastplate in a meaningful way that caused one of Hela's eyebrows to rise slowly. "Where do you think you're going dressed like that?" he demanded. Hela stared down her nose at him, at least a head taller than he was, until the red of his face was darkened by a blush. "My lady," he added belatedly. "Is it perhaps a masked ball?" he asked hopefully. "A joke among the nobility?"

Hela wasn't sure who he was trying to convince, himself or her. She waved away his prattling. "I have just told you, I have urgent business in the south. What is the business you think you have with me? I'd advise you to make it good, for I have very little patience and none at all for time wasters. Are you a time waster, little man?"

The man goggled at her and spluttered something she didn't understand out of a mouth mostly hidden by an over-long mustache. He slapped his breastplate again. "Don't you have any idea what this is?" he demanded, petulant now. Was he going to stamp his foot next?

Hela presumed he meant the badge carved in leather and fastened to the top of his breastplate. She leaned close and inspected it. "No," she said without much interest, "I have no idea what it is other than filthy. Your armor too. Has no one taught you how to care for it? It's practically rusting, man. Primitives," she added under her breath. "No wonder your magician hasn't the faintest idea how to harness the magic in which they dabble."

The man before her spluttered some more, flailing for words he clearly didn't have the wit to utter, and Hela's patience ran out. "I am looking for a magic-user who lives south of here. Do you know where I might find them? Speak quickly or leave me be."

"Magic? Are you perhaps referring to Lord John Dee, the queen's astronomer?" The man seemed to remember himself as soon as the words were out, for he bristled some more and began to say something about stating her name and place of origin. There was a threat in there, too, something about theft.

Hela ignored all of it. Lord John Dee, astronomer to the queen. Not a woman, then. Still, it was more than she'd had before – it was all she needed – and she turned away to resume her journey. A grimy hand clamped onto her elbow, above her vambrace, and halted her momentum. The man had the gall to pull her back around to face him. Well, he tried: Hela dug in her heels and refused to move and so he pulled himself to her instead of the other way around. She heard a ripple of laughter from the watching crowd, which had gathered at a greater distance to see how the altercation would play out.

She ignored it and stared fixedly at the man's hand on her arm – dirt under his fingernails, dirt in the creases of his hairy knuckles – until it slipped from the fine crimson silk of her sleeve, leaving a dark sweaty handprint in its wake.

Hela began to gather power. He would die, agonized and protracted and screaming, until this insult was avenged. As would any whose laughter might be directed at her.

"I am the warden of this part of London," he snarled with genuine anger that didn't quite overcome his bewilderment. He looked like a man out of his depth and struggling to pretend he wasn't paddling madly under the surface to stay afloat. He indicated the badge on his breastplate yet again, but whatever status it conferred on him was as meaningless this time as the last. In Helheim, authority was conveyed through strength and cunning and loyalty to her, its goddess, not grubby bits of leather.

"I don't care," Hela said with a voice as deadly as her death touch. "You do not have the right to lay your hands on me. Step back."

The warden hesitated, as if expecting her to follow that with a threat or an excuse or even a plea. A bribe, maybe. He seemed the sort who'd turn a blind eye. She did none of those things. Instead, she simply stood there resplendent in black armor and a fine velvet cloak with a sword on her hip, radiating threat. She dropped her voice to a growl. "I *will not* tell you again."

The man's throat bobbed as he swallowed convulsively, a shiver rippling through him at the death promised in her voice. He stepped to one side.

Hela felt yet another pulse of magic from the south, and it was all that saved him. She let the curse die unspoken and strode past and on down the street. He called something after her that she didn't bother to hear, too busy wondering how it was the men who apparently had dominion over the women here. She couldn't understand why they hadn't all been stabbed long ago. Perhaps she'd have a word with one or two of these cowed creatures before taking Dee and his magic back to the comfort of Eljudnir in Hel. Perhaps she'd have a word with Dee himself. It was likely the man would need to learn his place – and that of women – if he was to serve her appropriately.

Four

Mortlake

The repeated activations of magic had finally ceased a few hours before and dusk was falling when Hela reached the bank of an enormous river. Despite the magic quietening, she had enough of a lock on its direction to know that she needed to be on the other side.

Her march through the teeming, stinking city had been an education, both for her and for the people she passed. The warm sun and soft breeze had made tightening her cloak to cover her armor a ridiculous notion, though not as ridiculous as the idea of the Goddess of Hel hiding away from these impoverished peasants.

Hela had decided not to pander to their notions of who got to wear armor and trousers, or who got to walk through a city unmolested. The next person to lay a finger on her would find it lying in the mud next to their teeth. She hadn't had any further run-ins with either desperate thieves or pompous so-called officials, but gossip had followed in her wake much like the seagulls following the fishing boats on the river before her. None of it was worthy of her attention and so she paid it no mind. She'd find this John Dee and be back in Hel with him before this Realm's midnight was a promise in the sky.

Hela looked in both directions along the riverbank. There was a small boat bobbing in the gentle swell on the end of a rope with a young man lounging in the mud nearby. He was scribbling furiously in a book, squinting against the dying light.

"I need to cross the river," Hela stated as she strode over. "You will take me."

The boy looked up, and then further up as she loomed over him. His mouth dropped open when his gaze reached her face and he scrambled onto his feet, a blush already darkening his cheeks. "I am no boatman, my lady, but it would be my honor to take you wherever you need to go. The boatmen generally charge a sovereign per journey," he added, and the lie was so transparent Hela almost laughed.

She had no idea what a sovereign was, but she knew it was far too much. No doubt the lad thought her a foreigner and expected her to be stupid enough to pay up. She was a foreigner, but she wasn't stupid. "What is your name, child?"

"William, milady, and I'm sixteen. A man."

Hela snorted.

"What's yours?" he asked and gave her a cocky grin, though it was tempered by the youthful adoration in his gaze. He blinked and checked their surroundings, and she wondered if he thought to rob her, too.

Hela spread her arms to part her cloak, revealing the shimmering black armor in all its glory and leaned in close to his face. "Hela, goddess of Helheim and ruler of the dead. If you do not wish to join my subjects, you will take me across the river."

The boy's bottom lip disappeared into his mouth as he considered her face and her words. He put his head on one side. "Prove it."

It startled a laugh out of Hela. "If I do, you take me across the river for free and wait for my return," she said, not to haggle but just to see how far this boy's curiosity would stretch.

William shrugged and then nodded. "As God is my witness, my lady."

Hela grinned. "I'm your god now, boy," she said, and checked their surroundings for privacy. "Are you ready?"

William nodded, his eyes wide and excited. There was no one close enough to see what she was about to do, so she brought her hands together and conjured a light between them. At the same time, she commanded her diadem to reform into her great spiked helm. Hela shattered the globe of light between her palms and let each spark drift upwards to nestle among the spikes until she was crowned with a living wreath of lights.

The boy's mouth fell open on a soundless gasp and he fell backwards into the mud, flailing to get away from her. Hela clapped her hands once and the lights winked out. Her helm reformed into a simple, elegant diadem again. "Now take me across the river, lad, as you promised," she said and gave him a toothy grin.

The boy was lying in the mud, his clothes and even his hair caked with it. He was pale in the last of the daylight and tears sparkled in his eyes. He clutched his hands together. "Don't hurt me, devil, please don't hurt me. I've done nothing wrong. Please, Jesus, don't let the devil hurt me."

Hela hauled the boy to his feet by his shirt front. She patted his shoulder and then gave him a gentle shove towards the rope anchoring the boat to shore. "Take me across and wait on the other side for me," she repeated with the sort of patience for which she was not at all famous. Eirik would have been stunned to hear her speak so.

"And I told you, William, I am a god, not a devil," she breathed against the back of his neck, making him shudder. "Your god now and don't you forget it. You will give me the respect I deserve and demand. I will not tell you again – and you will not survive further disobedience."

To his credit, William wiped his face on his sleeve and took a breath. Then he turned determinedly to the rope and hauled his boat to shore. It was clear he didn't know how to address her now, so he gestured mutely. Hela decided that was good enough. She didn't actually have any desire to take this boy's soul, not unless he annoyed her again. She climbed into the boat and waited while William pushed them off and jumped aboard. He let them drift for a moment while he fitted the oars into the row locks and then he spun them with a deftness she hadn't quite expected and began to row. They traveled downriver as well as across and the sun had almost entirely set before they finally crunched in among the weeds on the other side.

William leapt out and grabbed the little boat to haul onto the bank. Hela walked up the shore. "Not a boatman, you say?"

He flushed. "This belongs to an acquaintance. I begged the loan of it for my stay in London."

"And how long are you staying?"

"A month, mighty goddess."

Hela paused, unsure if she was being mocked, but William's face remained terrified and earnest, the mix of emotions familiar and comforting. "'Your Highness' in private, 'my lady' in public," she said generously. "And I should only be a few hours," she added. He nodded miserably. "What are you crying about now?" she demanded.

The boy wiped his face again. "Nothing, Your Highness."

Hela folded her arms and tapped her foot in the mud.

"My lodgings are the other side of the Thames, and they lock the door at eight of the clock," he said mournfully.

Hela waved away his concern. "So sleep in the boat. Now, where does Lord Dee live?"

William shrugged. "I don't know, Your Highness. Sorry."

Hela pinched the bridge of her nose and then tossed him a silver coin from her purse. "Take me to the nearest tavern or farmhouse and find out for me. I'll wait outside. Don't even think about telling them who I am. Just say you've a message for the lord."

The boy looked up from biting the coin, all fear of the dark and being on the wrong side of the river having left him. "At once, my lady, sorry, Your Highness," he babbled and beckoned her forward. "There's a tavern up yonder a little way. They'll know where Lord Dee is, I'm sure of it. This way, Your Highness, watch your step there."

Hela wondered vaguely if she had in fact paid a sovereign to cross the river, for the boy's enthusiasm was acute. Not that it mattered: she'd grab Dee and his magical artifacts and Realm-jump home soon enough. What was a silver coin to the Goddess of Hel anyway?

They scrambled up the bank onto a path and followed it towards the distant lights of a tavern with a wide stable yard. Conversation and raucous laughter drifted from the screen-covered windows, which glowed yellow with lamplight. The boy looked to her for confirmation and Hela nodded and gestured him forward. He hurried to the door, dragged it open, and disappeared inside. Clearly, a silver coin bought quite a lot of cooperation in this land. Hela waited in the shadows on the far side of the stable yard until William returned, grinning widely and flushed with obvious triumph. He hesitated outside the door, scanning the darkness with growing worry until she shifted and revealed her location.

They moved back down the path before he spoke. "Lord John Dee is the queen's own astronomer. He lives in the village of Mortlake upriver a few miles. If you follow this road, it should take you all the way there or there are beds in the tavern here if you'd rather spend the night and go in the morning, Your Highness." He let her process the information for a moment, before bursting out with, "Are you going to visit Her Majesty the queen? Can I come? You shouldn't be wandering around London without a footman at least, Your Highness, and I should be honored to escort you about your business."

"Take your boat and your silver coin and go home, boy," Hela said instead of replying. "Tell no one you met me or where I am going or I will rip your soul out of your body and eat it. Do you understand?"

William skipped backwards out of range and then sketched a bow. He was smiling when he straightened up, as if her threat meant nothing to him. Hela narrowed her eyes. "I'll tell no one about you, Your Highness, if you promise not to kill Good Queen Bess." He dashed away before she could respond, vanishing down the bank towards the river and his little boat.

Hela stared after him for a few seconds, almost charmed by his cocksure impishness. Almost.

Then she put him out of her mind and set off in the direction he'd indicated. The village of Mortlake, where Lord John Dee and his mysterious magic awaited.

It was deep night by the time Hela reached the small village, which she presumed was Mortlake. A man on a horse had galloped past some time before, spattering her cloak and the side of her face with mud. The goddess had hurled a compulsion at the animal to rear and throw its rider, but they'd disappeared around a bend before she could see if it had done so. There was no one there by the time she reached the corner herself, so she chose to believe it had happened and that he was either dead in the dark somewhere or at least unconscious.

It had been a long day full of idiots, and Hela's patience was at an end.

There was a big house set back a little from the river with the rest of the village extending into the fields beyond. The house loomed tall and black against the nighttime sky. It had three chimneys, two of which spewed smoke and sparks into the air, although only one window at the front of the house showed the rich yellow glow of fire and candlelight. Even if the soft tendril of magic hadn't confirmed it, Hela would have guessed this to be Dee's home. It was, she supposed, grand enough for a Midgardian lord, even if it wasn't somewhere she'd bother stabling her horses.

She was halfway up the path leading to the grand front door when the magic blasted out at her again. Stronger by far this time, beckoning and writhing. Untethered but seeking an anchor point. A magic to which the Goddess of Death herself was intimately attuned, despite its foreign origin.

Hela paused on the path, breathing deep of the ozone tang of magic, and then stepped off the flagstones to stride through the rose bushes towards the lit window. Within sat a tall man of middle years with a neatly trimmed white mustache and long beard. He was hunched over an ornate desk with his face scrunched up and his eyes closed. The forefinger of one hand traced over lines of text in a leatherbound book; in the other he cradled a glowing, swirling orb. His lips moved as he muttered in time with his moving finger, the orb casting weird shadows across his face until he looked like a troll stooped over a piece of arcane magic.

Hela flicked her hand at the leaded window, sending a flare of power to shatter the glass. Nothing happened.

"What?" She stared blankly at her hand for a moment and then repeated the gesture, with more force and more intent. The window remained stubbornly intact.

There was a low cry from within the room, dragging at her attention. Dee slumped, babbling louder in a language he couldn't possibly understand but one Hela knew, and the orb in his hand was brightening, the swirls of magic growing faster and bigger until the flesh of his hand glowed with it. For the third time, Hela flung magic at the window, and for the third time nothing happened except that the man within let out another cry, this one sharp and pained, and he let go of the book. Instantly, the glow faded, but Dee paid it no mind, scrawling hastily on a piece of parchment in charcoal, as if desperate to record his observations as quickly as possible.

"Angels," Hela heard. "Holy seraphim, I am your instrument upon Earth. I will do all that you command. I will turn this England into a garden for you. I will fashion you a bridge to bless our great nation with your presence. O angels, that you should come to me, choose me!"

He was enraptured for another moment, and then the light in the orb – the crystal, Hela now saw – winked out. Dee's hand stuttered to a halt on the page. "No," he whimpered. "No, there was so much more. I learned so much this time. That can't be all. Think, you fool, think! Remember it." He stared at the crystal as if willing the glow to return, but he wrote no more.

With a frustrated groan, Dee placed the crystal carefully on to a red velvet cushion in a box and reread his scribbled notes. Wonder returned to his face and his eyes widened, his free hand pressed to his cheek. "Angels? God above, can it be true? Am I speaking with your holy choir, Lord? Will I be the one to greet you when the path between Heaven and Earth is opened?"

The man slumped back in his chair with his hands over his face, giggling madly, and then scrambled onto his knees behind the desk and began to pray, his face screwed up in a paroxysm of belief and the prayers babbled with as much fervor as the earlier language had been. The language he couldn't possibly understand.

Hela tapped her forefinger against her lip. So, he couldn't remember anything once the glow faded, and he needed to be touching both items at once in order to trigger what he thought was communion with some supposed angel of this Realm, preventing him from recording his notes at the time. No doubt he'd experimented with holding both objects in the same hand to no avail and only someone who understood the tongue he spoke would be able to translate it and make a record. There was no one on Midgard other than Hela herself who could do that.

The goddess was intrigued. The magic was created specifically to be difficult to use or remember, requiring... ah. She smiled. Clever. It wouldn't work on her, she was far too powerful with magic of her own, but yes, such a simple glamour was more than enough to encourage Dee to experiment with the crystal and the book over and over. Leaving Dee with hints but wiping his memory of all else ensured he remained fascinated, almost obsessed, with uncovering all the book's secrets, and those repeated experiments would build the magic layer by layer until it reached enough strength to trigger the connection across Realms.

Though it wouldn't be Heaven to which he opened a path.

Hela's gaze was drawn to the window again – the unbroken window. She rubbed her fingertips together, uneasy. Might the crystal, activated by Dee's chanting, have dampened her magic somehow? And if so, what might happen if she Realm-jumped with the crystal in her possession? Perhaps she should spend more time observing Dee with the artifacts before seizing them and him and returning home.

There was the clunk of a door opening followed by the crunch of boots on the path to her right, the distinctive rasp of a sword being drawn. She'd been noticed. Hela contemplated brazening it out and demanding an audience with Dee before deciding against it. She furled her cloak more tightly around herself and cast a glamour that would keep her from being seen.

An armed figure strode around the corner and raised their sword. "What are you doing?" he demanded to her. Hela blinked. "Go on, off with you. His lordship isn't receiving guests, supplicants, or beggars. Be about your business."

Beggars and supplicants? Hela's fingers dropped to her sword hilt, but she didn't have time to waste sparring with the soldier – verbally or physically. Her glamour hadn't worked, either. Someone or something was interfering with her magic use, and she needed to find out what.

The goddess of Hel turned her back on the soldier and strode into the darkness.

It was late by the time Hela reached the coaching inn where the boy had enquired as to Dee's residence. She'd seen several such places on her long walk through London, but been inside none of them. She'd as soon not be inside this one, but she demanded their best room and a late supper with a bottle of their finest wine, anyway. The place was at least somewhat familiar. The innkeeper took one look at her silver and fell over himself to comply.

"Your best room," she emphasized.

"Of course, milady, of course," he assured her, bobbing his head like an arthritic pigeon. He led her to a room and opened the door with a flourish. Hela's nose wrinkled. "This is your best room?"

"None finer this side of London, milady."

"Really? Show me yours."

The man paused a moment and then smiled obsequiously. "At once, milady. This way." He led her the opposite side of the inn and opened a door on a room twice the size and twice as clean. "Yes," she said and flipped him another coin. "I'll take my supper in here. And bring me a bath. And I want to see your wife's finest gowns. She can measure me and alter whatever I choose to fit." Hela waved her fingers in dismissal. The innkeeper gaped for another instant and then bowed again and fled.

"See how you enjoy sleeping in your so-called best room," she muttered as the door closed behind him. Then she proceeded to strip out of her armor and pile it on a chair under a spare blanket. While she'd been prepared to buy whatever she needed while here, Hela hadn't truly wanted to spend even a single night in this primitive Realm, secretly hoping to finish her task swiftly. On the other hand, the interference with her powers was enough of a concern that she had no interest in fending off outraged comments about her attire while she dealt with that matter: if the simple application of a gown would shut up the gabbling peasants around her, it was a sacrifice she was prepared to make.

The innkeeper's wife – Hela didn't ask her name and the woman didn't offer it – arrived with supper and the bottle of wine, and nervously pulled three gowns out of a trunk for

Hela's inspection. She chose the least offensive – a pale green with some rudimentary embroidery on the cuffs and bodice. It would do nothing for her complexion, but the other two were hideous, so pale green it was. Still, she could hear her teeth grinding together as she pointed at it.

"Would you let me measure you, milady, for the alterations?" the woman asked meekly when Hela had finished eating. She pushed back from the table and stood, then unclasped the cloak and let it fall, keeping hold of one edge in her fingertips.

"It will be ready for dawn," Hela said as the woman measured, and it wasn't a question.

"Of course, milady," the woman said, though there was a quaver in her voice. "And I'll have a boy bring the tub for your bath directly."

It was nearing midnight when she had bathed and was finally ready for bed. The sheets and blanket were grimy and Hela shuddered and stripped them from the feather mattress, then spread her cloak over it and slept on top of that. Or tried to sleep, at least.

What had happened back at Dee's house? Why hadn't her magic shattered the glass? And how had the soldier seen through her glamour? When she could no longer still the whirl of her thoughts, she contacted Eirik.

"How is my Realm?" she demanded as soon as the torcs linked their minds. Eirik startled at the sudden voice and her lips curved in a dangerous smile. "You are nervous, seneschal. Why is that?"

"Not nervous, my goddess, merely sensible of the vast honor you have conferred upon me. Helheim and Niffleheim are well and peaceful, my queen. Your borders are secure and there is no unrest among your subjects. Fenris guards your throne and palace."

Though Eirik didn't know it, the torc prevented him from lying, so she merely grunted her approval and terminated their link. Then, fitfully, she attempted to sleep.

FIVE

BRIGHT-BATTLE

The dead were calling. The dead were crying.

Endless voices, from whispers up to screams, begging for aid and an end to their torment.

Brunnhilde the Valkyrie woke with a gasp and her hand already reaching for Dragonfang, her sword. The room was still and dark, night pressing in through the windows. No threats lingered within the deep shadows. She was at home, she was safe, and her heart was hammering against her ribs. The back of her neck was damp with sweat against the pillow, but at least the sword's hilt was cool in her palm.

Brunnhilde sat up. She took no reassurance from the blade. This was the third time tonight she'd been woken by nightmares and she knew, instinctively, that she wouldn't get back to sleep again. Even the Valkyrie's great strength was being taxed by these nightmares and the regularity with which they struck. She quested outwards with her mind for Aragorn, her winged steed. He was asleep in his stable. She didn't disturb him. At least one of them should get some proper rest.

Brunnhilde rose and dressed and splashed her face and neck with water before braiding back her hair. She settled Dragonfang on her hip and left her house, walking through the dark fields until the burst of magic needed to jump to Valhalla wouldn't disturb Aragorn. There was always someone awake in the Hall of Heroes. Mead and stories were the only things that might soothe her now.

As ever, the dream had faded quickly after she awoke, and all the Valkyrie was left with by the time she reached the Hall was a vague, nameless dread – and a bone-deep weariness not even her goddess nature could overcome. This had been going on for too long, and she needed some way to break the cycle, but for now, she was too weary to come up with a plan. Perhaps the tales of heroes would lull her into a better rest, or at least a longer one before the nightmares gripped her again. Just a few hours' uninterrupted sleep, that was all she wanted.

The vast Hall was shrouded in darkness, the sun not even a suggestion at the edge of the world. The sky was black velvet scattered with stars, the air cool and still. The waters of the fjord lapped gently against the shore, peaceful and rhythmic.

Brunnhilde paused at the threshold, arrested as ever by the sight – limned in starlight – of the carved oak doors. The work was intricate and detailed, battles and hunts and duels, warriors and shield-maidens stalking its panels while gods fought giants and elves, dragons and trolls. In the carven sky, Valkyrior flew on winged horses, delivering the souls of the glorious dead to Valhalla. Carved into the lintel and looking down on it all were the three Norns and Odin All-Father, the former setting, weaving, and cutting fates, while the latter judged and defended and ruled the living.

The Valkyrie traced her fingertips across a stag fleeing hunters, the carving so detailed she could almost feel the flick of hooves against the whorls on the pads of her fingers. The sight of the door, of the Hall itself, settled something within, easing a nameless fear that was all that lingered from the dream. Instead, a fresh layer of concern and self-doubt fell on top of all the others, laid by each successive nightmare until they were as thick and cloying as a grave-shroud.

Mead and stories and the company of warriors, she reminded herself, and pushed open the door. Within the Hall itself, most of the torches were doused, though there were small, intimate pockets of light scattered amid the gloom. Heads turned at her entrance and there was the flash of teeth as warriors grinned in welcome and acknowledgment.

"Bright-Battle," they murmured, and she reached out to grip wrists or squeeze shoulders as she passed. She wasn't looking for anyone in particular and settled with the first group who invited her to sit and sloshed a full horn of mead into her hand.

"You honor us, Bright-Battle," a grizzled Einherjar said. "Though it is an ill night that drives a Valkyrie from her bed. Is aught amiss?"

Brunnhilde gave the man a weary smile. "It is not a night where sleep will visit," she said. "So I seek the company of those who are likewise wakeful." She nudged him in the ribs. "Such as yourself, Harald. What stories are you telling this night?"

Harald laughed unselfconsciously and pointed to a young

shield-maiden. "We are welcoming Solveig to Valhalla. She joined us just recently."

"I honor your bravery and dedication, shield-maiden Solveig," Brunnhilde said warmly. "Your sacrifice will never be forgotten."

"The honor is mine, Bright-Battle," Solveig said, her eyes wide and shining.

"I trust you don't believe every story Harald weaves for you," the Valkyrie added, to soft-voiced protests and muted laughter. "The one about the dragon I can promise you is false."

"You–" Harald began as Solveig startled and then turned a murderous glare on the old warrior. He held up his hands, grinning. "I'd have told you the truth eventually," he said. "In a few years or so."

Solveig crossed her arms and sniffed, but there was laughter tucked in the corner of her mouth. The clear affection she already had for these warriors who'd taken her in as one of their own during the first, confusing days of her afterlife, loosened something in the Valkyrie's chest. She gulped mead and listened to Harald weave another story, winking when Solveig glanced over in unspoken question of this tale's veracity. She was a quick learner, it seemed.

Brunnhilde drank more and let the peace and quiet humor soothe her troubled heart.

The Valkyrie was gritty-eyed when dawn broke over Valhalla and the other einherjar began to wake. Harald had stumbled off to sleep a few hours before. Brunnhilde and Solveig had talked through the rest of the night. The warrior was young and fearless, but she missed her first life and the family she'd left behind. It was always so, and Brunnhilde had done what she could to soothe the warrior's regrets.

When the sun rose, they went to the practice fields to spar and the Valkyrie made sure to give Solveig a real test, to focus her in body and skill and take her mind away from what she'd lost. They were both grinning and sweaty by the time the fields filled up with warriors and Brunnhilde was pleasantly sore from the rigors of the combat.

"Truly, you will be an asset to the All-Father when the last battle is fought," she said, clapping Solveig on the arm. "Thank you for the test. It's been many a week since I've been pushed so hard."

Solveig flushed under the praise. "Thank you, Bright-Battle, for the lessons and the talk. It has helped."

Brunnhilde nodded. "It is my duty and my privilege. Send for me or one of my sisters if you have need. For now, I must away to Asgardia on business. Stay well, shield-maiden."

She left Solveig in a ring of her new friends, all praising her performance against the leader of the Valkyrior, and Realm-jumped back home to wash and change. Aragorn was awake and whickered an imperious demand to be let out of his stall as soon as he sensed her arrival.

"We're going to Asgardia soon," she said, "so don't stray far." The winged horse flicked his tail in disdain and trotted across the field before breaking into a canter and then spreading his wings and leaping into the sky. Brunnhilde watched him cavort for a while, a small smile tugging at her mouth. He was a dear friend and an unrepentant troublemaker in the way of all horses: the grooms attached to the All-Father's stables drew straws to determine who'd care for him when she brought him to the city. Aragorn knew this and enjoyed it.

"The Loki of horses," she muttered as she turned into her house. Above her, Aragorn trumpeted his outrage. Brunnhilde smiled again and went to clean up.

The horse consented to being saddled and bridled and then they flew together towards Asgardia, over farmland and wild land, rivers, and woods. The city appeared at the horizon, all great towers and airy turrets and wide gardens and rivers. Tamed wilderness, molded by the will of the gods. It never failed to steal Brunnhilde's breath, it was so beautiful, and she waved down to the warriors guarding the walls and then landed in a courtyard to give her name to another.

She dismounted and a groom hurried over to take Aragorn's bridle. "Be good," she said sternly, patting his neck. The horse flared his wing, forcing her to skip sideways, and she narrowed her eyes at him. "Awful creature," she muttered, and Aragorn's eyes danced with amusement. The groom reached for the bridle, and he tossed his head, lifting it out of range.

"I'm sorry," Brunnhilde said, swallowing her laughter as the groom did his best to herd the horse towards the stables. Aragorn pranced on his hind legs and then condescended to do as he was asked. She watched him step proudly through the courtyard with his head and tail high. Oh, but he was going to run them ragged while she was here.

"I don't have an appointment, but I would like to request an audience with Frigga, if she is available," the Valkyrie said when she reached the vast audience chamber in the All-Father's palace. Her voice was calm despite the nerves fluttering in her belly. This was ridiculous... there was nothing to actually wrong with her and bothering Odin's wife over her inability to sleep was a huge overreaction. Still, she led the Choosers of her Slain and that duty was sacred: the All-Father needed to be able to trust her and, right now, Brunnhilde didn't know if he could.

She followed the servant who led her to Frigga's private chambers and then slipped inside with her request.

Brunnhilde didn't meet the eyes of the warriors guarding the door, worried they'd see her inner turmoil and mistake it for threat. Or, worse, that they'd know somehow of this new and unsettling weakness that plagued her. If the servant hadn't already disturbed the goddess, she would have turned on her heel and fled, but then the door was opening again, and she was gestured inside.

Frigga sat in a large room with a wide, open balcony overlooking the city and the distant sweep of green hills. She rose at Brunnhilde's entrance and held out both hands in welcome. The Valkyrie crossed the marble floor and saluted, then hesitantly took Frigga's hands in hers. "Thank you for seeing me, my lady," she said. "I know this is most unusual and I must apologize–"

"There is no need," Frigga interrupted smoothly. "You would not seek a private audience if there wasn't something worrying you. Tell me how I can help."

Brunnhilde chewed her lip for a moment. "I think I'm sick," she admitted eventually. "Or maybe cursed. I don't know. Something's happening to me, but I can't tell what it is. I don't... I'm plagued with nightmares, three or four times a night, every night. But I can never remember them when I wake, just a sense of despair and some formless dread that leads me to Valhalla again and again. But I don't know what I'm doing there, what I'm checking for." She paused and took a breath, then let go of Frigga's hands. "Forgive me for wasting your time."

The goddess put her head on one side and looked up into the Valkyrie's face. "You are doing no such thing," she scolded gently. "You are clearly worried enough to seek out help. What sort of person would I be if I denied that help? Is there anything that makes you think this is a curse or an attack specifically?"

"I don't believe so, but I've never had my body out of control before. I am, perhaps, overreacting."

Frigga clicked her tongue in reprimand. "Let me be the judge of that," she said and gestured for Brunnhilde to sit. "Would you allow me to examine you?" At the Valkyrie's agreement, she sat beside her and placed one cool hand on Brunnhilde's temple and the other over her heart. "I will search for the curse first," she murmured and Brunnhilde closed her eyes.

Frigga's healing magic was as cool as her hands, like slipping into a still pool shaded by trees. Brunnhilde shivered delicately as it moved through her limbs and veins, seeking signs of evil magic or the traces of a spell left behind when the curse was activated.

The Valkyrie sat still and open, letting the magic and Frigga's consciousness sweep through her for what seemed like hours. She blinked hazily when the hands left her body.

"You are not cursed," Frigga said, and tension she hadn't even known was there slid from Brunnhilde's muscles. She gusted a relieved sigh.

"An illness then?" she asked. "I should arrange to see a physician."

"Let me see if I can determine that first," Frigga said. "It is no trouble, nor is it an imposition," she insisted at Brunnhilde's instinctive protest. "You are dear to the All-Father, and to me. I should like to set your mind at ease if I can. Besides," she added with a hint of mischief, "I'd like to think I know at least as much about healing as Asgardia's physicians."

Brunnhilde managed a small smile. "Thank you, my lady."

The tests Frigga administered were both arcane and mundane and took up much of the morning. Finally, she sat back and poured honeyed water for them both. "Well, you're exhausted, Bright-Battle," she said, frowning, "but other than that I can find nothing wrong with you. My fear is that this is an illness of the mind, not the body, which is why it haunts your sleep. We will visit my husband and ask for his advice."

"My lady–"

"If anyone can help you, it's the All-Father," Frigga said firmly. "And he will want to know about this."

"Thank you, my lady," she mumbled and followed Frigga out of her chambers and back towards the audience chamber, where the All-Father sat in his throne and dispensed justice.

Would he think Brunnhilde weak? Would Odin take her duty from her, the thing that defined Brunnhilde's very existence? Fear gripped her in its icy fist, bringing clammy sweat to her palms.

A tall, lithe warrior with wild black hair stood at the base of the dais giving a report when they entered. Brunnhilde recognized her immediately. At the opposite end of the hall, the God of Thunder was deep in conversation with three other warriors. He looked over, distracted, and offered them both a small smile before returning to his conversation. As Frigga and the Valkyrie walked between the vast stone pillars framing the entrance, the guards lining the walls snapped to attention. The movement drew Odin's gaze, and he raised a hand to pause the speaker when he saw them approaching.

Brunnhilde's heart beat in her throat as Frigga crossed the echoing marble vault and climbed the steps onto the dais to whisper in his ear. Lady Sif, the warrior giving her report, bowed and retreated to the edge of the hall to await a further summons. The Valkyrie nodded at her and Sif nodded back, a small line between her eyebrows at the interruption. Not of annoyance so much as curiosity and concern. It didn't make the Valkyrie feel any better. She had no wish for an audience for this.

Odin made an interested sound and then fixed Brunnhilde with his single-eyed stare. She swallowed and bowed her head. "My lord, forgive the interruption."

Frigga took her seat in the throne next to her husband's and waved her hand in dismissal. "Tell the All-Father what you told me," she commanded, and Brunnhilde swallowed again. Here? In front of the court and Sif and Thor?

The Valkyrie took a deep breath and told the story again, of the nightmares she couldn't quite remember and the worry – the dread – that seeped within her like slow poison with each day. She did her best not to glance at Sif. She could feel Thor's gaze as heavy as storm clouds on her and had to fight to keep her voice steady.

"And how long has this been going on?" Odin asked, and to her surprise, he didn't seem dismissive.

"Twelve nights, my lord. Once a night to begin with. Last night I was woken by fear–" she almost choked on the admission "–four times before I gave up on sleep and visited the Hall of Heroes to check again that there was no danger to the einherjar. There was not," she emphasized, just in case.

The ring of bootheels on marble told her the God of Thunder had heard enough to be curious. He came to stand at her shoulder and pressed her arm briefly, reassurance and greeting both. "Asgard is safe from our enemies, Father," he said. "Whatever is attacking Bright-Battle is subtle. I have sensed nothing similar – nor heard similar reports – from anywhere across the Realm."

Brunnhilde bit the inside of her cheek. Thor believed her with the same simple trust as Frigga. Like mother, like son. She let out a slow, controlled breath that wasn't in any way the gust of relief it wanted to be.

"And there is no curse on her?" Odin asked.

"None I could sense," Frigga confirmed. "Bright-Battle's fears concern the glorious dead, so perhaps there is some magic targeting them of which we are unaware?"

"If there is, my lady, it is beyond my skill to detect," Brunnhilde admitted. "Hence my coming here."

"Approach, Bright-Battle. Let me see you," Odin commanded. Thor patted her arm again and Sif, when Brunnhilde glanced over reflexively, gave her an encouraging nod. She strode forward, doing her best to hide her anxiety. Almost, she'd be relieved if the All-Father found a curse upon her: her bigger fear was that there was nothing and she was wasting everyone's time.

She bowed again at the foot of the dais, and at his signal,

approached and knelt beside Odin's chair. The All-Father put both hands on her head, fingers cupping gently over her ears and the points of his thumbs resting below her eyes. His magic, when it poured into her, was nothing like the cool river of Frigga's.

The All-Father's magic was a raging storm, a volcano's eruption, a wildfire, but all held under tight restraint, chained and well fed, but never really tamed. It swept through Brunnhilde and, if not for his anchoring hands, might even have swept her away. Swept her soul out of her body to roam between the Realms.

The magic drained out of her like the tide fleeing a fjord and left her kneeling, gasping, and gripping the arm of the All-Father's throne to stay upright. She blanched and let go hurriedly, swaying and then holding herself still through will more than balance. She was unsteady, scoured out, and even more weary than before.

"There is no curse," Odin confirmed. "But there is… something. Something is calling to you, Bright-Battle. Another Realm. Name it."

Brunnhilde startled and then scrambled backwards to put distance between them. "I thought… I thought I was imagining it," she whispered. He gestured and she took a deep breath. "Midgard. I keep thinking it, keep thinking I hear people speak its name. But I don't know why. It's not in my dreams, or I don't believe so. Forgive me for not making better sense."

"You cannot be expected to make sense of something that contains none," Odin said. "But there is more to this than meets the eye. Even my eye. I fear these dreams signal that trouble is stirring on Midgard, and I would have you investigate it. It is likely traveling there will clarify what plagues you when you sleep."

"The dreams may also become harder to bear," Thor said from behind her. "Someone should go with her. I–"

"Not you, son. If there is a threat, especially if it is one we struggle to understand, then I want you here. Lady Sif can accompany Bright-Battle. You have worked well together in the past."

Brunnhilde didn't look over at the raven-haired warrior. While it was true their enmity was long past and their friendship and trust strong, it was also true that Sif had no liking for Midgard or its inhabitants. Yet she was as famous for her loyalty and dedication to duty as for the story behind her black hair. The Valkyrie was not surprised to hear her immediate agreement to his proposal.

"Leave at dawn. Prepare what you need and take no risks. I would rather you return here with information than stay there and try and solve something for which you need reinforcements."

"I… forgive me, All-Father, but I would prefer to leave as soon as Lady Sif is ready. There is a weight on my soul, and it shames me to admit, but the worry and the lack of sleep are blunting my edges. I would prefer to be sharp and as ready as possible to face whatever threat this is. Another night of torn sleep…"

Sif's eyes widened and then narrowed in appraisal, but not in contempt. "I stand ready to do your bidding, All-Father, and Bright-Battle's, too. We can leave this evening."

"This evening then," Odin agreed. "And there is no shame

in such an admission," he added as Brunnhilde bowed. "It does you credit to know your limitations and voice them."

Brunnhilde held the bow longer than necessary as she fought against the blush rising in her cheeks. "Thank you for your trust – and for your belief in me," she said as she straightened up, though she hadn't meant to add that last.

Finally, Odin's face softened out of the stern lines of command into something gentler. "You have never let us down, Bright-Battle," he said. "I do not think you will do so now. Either of you," he said, flicking a glance at Sif, who had pushed away from the wall to take her place at Brunnhilde's side. "Be wise, be careful, be thorough."

"We will," they said, and bowed.

"Take this, Bright-Battle," Frigga said, and pulled a bracelet from her wrist. Warily, Brunnhilde advanced and took it from her, bowing again. Frigga stood and clasped the Valkyrie by her shoulders. "Each jewel contains a store of magic. Not a huge amount, but in Midgard's magic-free environment, it should stand you in good stead. With this, you will be able to master small spells – you already have your glamour, of course, but you could glamour Lady Sif, or cast silence, or something similar." She smiled warmly. "Each stone will crack when its magic is used up, so take note of how much is left."

Brunnhilde gasped, for the bracelet was exquisite. "My lady…"

"It is of no matter. You and Sif are jewels in Asgard's crown, and I would have you both shine brighter than all the bracelets in the Nine Realms."

"You honor us, my lady," Sif said from behind Brunnhile. The Valkyrie nodded her mute agreement and then backed carefully down the steps, slipping the bracelet over her non-dominant hand to settle against her vambrace. Incongruous and beautiful.

She took a deep breath and looked at her one-time rival and now friend. "This evening?"

"Dusk at Bifrost," Sif confirmed. "Don't be late."

"No chance of that," the Valkyrie said as they bowed again to Odin, and then to Frigga and Thor before making their way out of the great, echoing hall. "I want this over and done with and then I plan on sleeping for a week."

Sif chuckled. "Ever the laziest of us," she teased and then softened it with a squeeze of Brunnhilde's hand. "We'll figure this out and be home by dusk tomorrow. And then I'll tuck you into bed myself."

The Valkyrie managed a laugh of her own. "Aragorn would treat me with more tenderness," she countered, "and he's got hooves."

Sif's laugh was unrestrained as they exited the palace to a bright afternoon and warm sun. It was beautiful, the city gleaming under its rays, her friend's joy echoing from the high walls.

None of it could lift the shadow from Brunnhilde's heart.

SIX

To Dress in Silver

The tavern keep's wife was gray with exhaustion when she knocked on the door a little past dawn. The gown had been altered, washed, and was still warm from being hung over the fire to dry. It smelled a little of smoke, but that was far better from how it had smelled before.

"I'll need a large basket," Hela said instead of thanking the woman. "I'm going to the market at Mortlake today."

The woman's mouth opened and closed a few times. "It is Sunday, milady. There are no markets on a Sunday," she clarified at Hela's blank expression.

"I need a basket anyway."

"Of course, milady." The woman had obviously decided to not ask questions, which made things easier for everyone, as Hela had no intention of answering any.

She dressed and then piled her armor in the large basket provided and covered it with her shirt and trousers. She wrapped her sword's hilt in a spare scarf taken from the woman's trunk and wedged the scabbard into the basket with the rest, then slung it over her arm – *as if I'm a peasant!* – and set out again for Mortlake.

"This is getting ridiculous," she muttered as she walked the now familiar path along the side of the river towards the village. If not for the value she could sense in the magic – and its interference with her own – she'd have Realm-jumped home by now. As it was, she wouldn't take that particular risk until she knew for sure what repercussions there might be for her. All she needed was a meeting with Dee and she could be back in Eljudnir by the time the sun set on Hel.

And once there, with Dee and the stone and the book, she could pick apart the magic at her leisure and not have to deal with any of these... people.

The sun was well risen by the time she reached Mortlake and a bell tolled a solemn, regular note. She was just in time to see the magician leave home in the company of an elegant young lady and several men and a woman dressed in more humble attire: servants, she guessed. One of the men was the soldier or guard who'd confronted her the previous night. Everyone in the village seemed to be heading in the same direction, towards the only other stone building. This one had a tall tower at one end: the source of the ringing bell.

Curious, Hela followed and slipped into the cool echoing structure after the last of the hurrying stragglers, staying well back in the crowd. There were rows of hard benches near the front where the best dressed villagers sat, Dee and the young lady – his daughter? – prominently in the very front row. There was a statue of a man sacrificed on a scaffold at the front and Hela nodded her approval when she saw it. It was a wise ruler who made the consequences of disobedience clear to their subjects.

What followed, though, didn't conform to those expectations. Instead, she was subjected to a tedious hour in which a man in a severe black robe told them various stories about a god and his son, neither of which Hela had ever heard of among the true pantheon. It appeared the criminal hanging from the cross was actually this son and that, rather than being a warning against rebellion or treason, the villagers were encouraged to follow his example.

Hela hadn't seen any other crosses during her journey through London. Perhaps there was another room in this building where they chose someone and sacrificed them. She was tempted to ask if she could see the performance, but then the ritual was abruptly over, and everyone was filing out of the place, and no one was sacrificing anyone.

Disgruntled and bored, Hela slipped out of the door and lingered in the hot sun as the villagers scattered in every direction back to their homes. She'd wasted enough time and spent a thoroughly uncomfortable night in an inferior bed. She was dressed in badly dyed wool on a hot summer morning and had run out of patience.

"Finally," she growled as Dee emerged from the building, talking with the man in black who'd told the stories and preached about being content in one's station in life. As well he might when it was obvious he and Dee were the most important, and wealthiest, men in the village. It was easy to tell people to be resigned to their lives when your own was comfortable, well fed, and well paid.

"...hard to believe, Father, I know, but I believe it to be true.

And if the voice is that of an angel, surely it can only be Uriel, archangel of wisdom? That is what it is promising, and it even requires me to touch the sacred book."

The priest or father, despite appearing at least a decade younger than the tall, slender, white-bearded John Dee, looked at him sharply. "Sacred book?" he asked. "There is only one holy book, my lord, and I beg you not to forget its teachings."

Hela had been about to interrupt, but she was intrigued. Her Asgardian hearing meant that every word reached her ears clearly despite the distance between them. She pretended to fiddle with the contents of her basket as an excuse to loiter.

"Father, I am a good Christian man and a follower of Her Majesty's faith. I rejected Papist ways many years ago and, I would venture to claim, my wife's recent delivery of a fine son is testament to the righteousness of our lives." He gestured to the young woman Hela had taken to be his daughter. The goddess's lip curled.

"The queen herself has inspected the magical items, and as head of the Church as well as our sovereign, I trust her judgment in this. All that being said," he continued as the man tried to interrupt, "I should like to invite you to a demonstration of my communion with the archangel this afternoon. You have been a wise counsel to the village and to me for many years, Father, and latterly to my good lady wife. Your attendance and approval would mean much. I do not wish to do anything against the will of the Church, and I believe the bishop of London may attend to give his blessing, as well as a few close friends from court."

"The bishop?" the father asked, and Hela snorted quietly

at the naked ambition blazing through the sudden cracks in his humility.

"Indeed. There will be a light supper afterwards, and some music. Guests are welcome from two of the clock onwards, if you would do me the honor of attending."

Someone tugged at the basket. "Your Highness, you shouldn't – gah!"

Hela spun and grabbed the thief around the throat, lifting and slamming them into the side of the stone building. Dee and the father looked up at the scuffle and Hela dropped the squirming figure and vanished around the corner, then hooked the boy by his collar and dragged him into the shadows.

"How dare you?" she snarled. William was watery eyed and wheezing, massaging his throat. "What are you doing here?"

"Hello? Is everything all right?" came a voice – the voice of the father.

An instant change came over the boy. He grabbed for the basket again, his shoulders hunched and his voice quavering. "I'm sorry I missed church, mother. I'm sorry, please let me carry the basket. Please, mother!"

Hela recoiled, letting go of the handle and stepping away from his teary performance just as Dee and the father rounded the corner.

"Missing church?" the man in black asked severely and William cowered some more. "You'd do well to beat him, mistress, and see he gets no supper."

Hela recovered her poise. "I shall do more than that," she threatened, and the boy shrank back, pleading for forgiveness. She glared at him, and he made a tiny motion with his head, beckoning her away. But Dee was right here. She could end this farce in a moment. She needed only to convince him to show her the book and the stone.

"Then I bid you good day, mistress," the father said and he and the lord ambled away.

Hela made to follow, and William dared to grab her arm. "Not now, Your Highness. Not dressed like that," he hissed. She paused. "I don't know what's happened since last night, but if you're confronting him–" he straightened and puffed out his chest and gave her a surprisingly imperious glare "– then you need to be better dressed. Come on."

"The markets are closed on Sundays." She scowled at repeating the innkeeper's wife's words.

"There will be places open if you've the coin to pay, Your Highness." William winked. "If you want to get yourself invited to that fancy party he's holding later, you'll need to look the part."

Hela recoiled that he knew her plans. "How do you know about that?"

The lad shrugged. "Came to find you this morning and hung around the church. I heard what his lordship and the good father said."

The goddess stared at him for several seconds too long, until the cocksure grin had faded. "You, boy, are going to get yourself into serious trouble one day," she said eventually. His grin returned as she asked, "Now, where are we going?"

Hela followed William along London's winding lanes until they came to an area that clearly catered only to the wealthy.

She'd considered how she'd spent the journey – in William's boat, quizzing him on what she'd learned in the church and about Lord Dee, and then she insisted on visiting three more churches before heading to the tailor's. She wanted options as to how she should appear.

There had been several examples of angels painted on walls and screens. None seemed to agree on much other than the wings, which would be easy enough to reproduce through illusion – supposing her magic was under her control this time. Some angels were armored, others in flowing drapery. Some, inexplicably, were fat, naked babies.

William gestured at a door and Hela shook herself from her reverie. She stared at him until he stepped forward and rapped on the wood on her behalf. It was answered by a thin, grumpy man of middle years and a squint that no doubt came from sewing by candlelight.

"What?" he demanded.

She swung her coin purse in his face.

"I am dining with the bishop of London at two o'clock and find myself inconvenienced for suitable attire." She stepped forward and the tailor, shocked, scrambled backwards to let her in. The bolts of material lining the shelves on the back wall were rich and jewel toned. Silk and wool, lace and taffeta, and wide stiff collars. Shoes and petticoats and more.

"Something in–" she began.

"My lady, forgive me and welcome to my business. You grace this establishment with your patronage, and I can of course alter some existing finery to your measurements in the time available. The fashion at court is currently for gray and silver," he added, "or I have a half-finished gown in pink damask that you can view. Might I offer you some refreshment while we consider your options?"

Hela smiled, relaxing. This was a man who knew how to treat his betters. "I'm not sure pink is really my color," she said. "Something richer, perhaps, more vibrant?" She let one edge of the cloak fall back to reveal its gold inner lining. The tailor's eyes widened appreciatively. "And something to match for my servant here," she added, indicating William who gazed at the blue velvets with covetous eyes.

He spun to face her. "Truly, my lady?"

"Of course, of course," the tailor burbled. "He will be easy to outfit. Please, take a seat or browse. I shall be back directly with some samples and a goblet of watered wine."

Hela gestured at the boy. "You. Go away for a while. I'll find you later." She put her coin purse down with a thump and jingle and smirked. The tailor was practically salivating. "The people you're making these gowns for won't mind if I take them instead?" she asked as William, his heart showing in his eyes – and not for the coin – bowed and slipped from the shop.

The tailor waved away her concern. "My patrons will understand if there is a delay," he said confidently. "I serve them faithfully and they reward me generously." His eyes strayed to the purse again. "Please. Examine whatever you like. If I might suggest, due to the time constraint, that you choose between these four? All of them can be finished and altered by this afternoon. Forgive me that the colors are not more vibrant. If your heart is truly set on vividness, might I suggest the silver skirt there? It is only loosely joined to the bodice and won't take much to separate. Then I will sew you a new bodice in your preferred material and color."

It was an excellent compromise. Hela nodded her

agreement. The skirt was a shimmering gray-silver silk, heavily embroidered with more silver thread and encrusted with tiny beads and seed pearls. It was paler than the colors she normally wore, but it was superior in every way to the green monstrosity currently clinging to her back and hips.

As she had done with the innkeeper's wife the evening before, Hela slipped off her cloak and held an edge in one hand as the tailor measured her. He suggested – and she agreed – to a full new wardrobe including underclothes, stockings, and shoes, and then she left him to his stitching.

With hours to kill and nothing but curiosity fueling her, Hela visited a few more churches to look at the artwork and ask questions that would have been blasphemous coming from someone less obviously wealthy. She sat in a great, ornate cathedral to listen to another interminable sermon that advised its listeners not to take vengeance for wrongs done them, and she snorted so loudly at that that several people turned to glare at her.

When she tired of Midgard's religious offerings, she wandered back to the riverbank and made her way east along it to where William had tied up his boat. The city was quiet in comparison with how it had been during her arrival, but the marketplaces were busy with playing children instead of merchants and the river was thronged with boats carrying people enjoying the sun. Mudlarkers combed the muddy shore looking for lost or discarded treasure.

The boy was dozing in the shade of his boat when she found him, and he grunted when she kicked at his foot. "Wake up."

He opened one eye and squinted up at her. Then he grinned and shoved up onto his feet to sketch a bow. "O mighty goddess," he said with delight. "Have you come to give me those fine clothes you promised?"

"That depends. Look at the state of the ones you're wearing," she said sourly. "Can I trust you to take care of them?"

William looked down at himself and then brushed half-heartedly at the mud on his trousers and the cuff of his sleeve. "You were gone a long time. I had a nap. To prepare myself for what's to come," he added, sensing correctly that his words had made the wrong impact. "Though the people I'm staying with would prefer it if I were home for supper."

"You'll be home when I'm done with you and you'll be a good sight richer, too, so be quiet and show some manners."

Hela grabbed the boy by the arm and began walking back to the tailor's shop. Her lip curled when he spat into his palm and tried to use the moisture to slick down his hair. It was a futile task and unless the tailor had a comb and a lot of patience, she was going to have to buy him a hat, too.

"You're not really a god, are you?" William asked suddenly when they were only steps from the tailor's door. Hela pulled up sharply. "I mean, it was just magic you did, wasn't it?"

The goddess of Hel stared down at him. "Maybe I'm a god. Maybe I'm an angel." She flipped him a silver penny and he snatched it out of the air in an instant. "Does it matter?"

"I just… I don't want to go to Hell," he mumbled, though she noticed he didn't offer the coin back.

Hela threw back her head and laughed. "I can promise you, boy, Hel has no desire for you whatsoever. Now go on, we don't have much time."

He frowned but pushed open the door obediently.

"Ah, my lady, you are here. I am pleased to say your gown is finished," the tailor said from his place behind a long table. He appeared to be sewing madly but paused long enough to wave at a corner. "If I could trouble you to try it on while I finish up your servant's doublet, and the boy can scrub himself down in the yard out back before he dresses. When you are clothed, my lady, I can check the fit and make any final alterations. There is a changing screen just there."

Hela turned to William. "What will I do if you disobey me or betray me?"

"Eat my soul," the boy said dutifully, and with a small smile. Hela snapped her fingers and sent a shower of sparks whirling towards his face. They stung where they landed against his skin, and he yelped and batted them away. When he lowered his hands, the smile was gone.

"Don't think me merciful, boy," Hela told him softly. "And don't think I like you."

"No, Your Highness," he said. "Sorry, Your Highness."

"'My lady' when we're in public," she reminded him.

"Yes, my lady."

"Go and wash yourself," she ordered, and he scampered into the back of the shop after the tailor.

Hela had to admit the man had done an exceptional job in the amount of time he'd had. The bodice was a vivid crimson embroidered with silver thread and more of the beads and pearls. The patterning was simple but flowing and the bodice fitted seamlessly to the skirt so it appeared as if this had been its intended look all along.

The silk was stiff but cool and while the silver jarred slightly with the gold lining of Hela's cloak, it would serve admirably. For the first time since her arrival, the goddess felt herself again.

The tailor, for a miracle, had finished a doublet and hose in a darker red that complemented her gown perfectly and made it seem as if the boy really was her servant. He stared between the pair of them with evident pride.

"Exquisite, my lady. Truly beautiful. And now, ah…"

Hela counted out ten silver coins, large and fat and clearly foreign, not that that seemed to matter judging by the look in the tailor's eyes. And then one more, which made his breath hitch. She handed them over with a smile. "I shall ensure everyone this evening knows your name," she said and he reddened with pleasure. "Come now, boy, we haven't long."

She swept out before the tailor could give her his name, but Hela didn't think he'd remember that for some time, mesmerized by her promise and the coins. By the time he did, she'd be long gone.

Things were different with William trotting along in her wake, lugging her basket of armor and dressed in a complementary color, albeit of lesser quality. The curious, assessing looks she'd received since her arrival were gone, replaced with polite nods from the best-dressed Londoners and bows and curtseys from the rest.

It was as if Hela suddenly made sense to the Midgardians, as if her native divinity had not been enough to command their respect because she hadn't *looked right*. The insult stung, like salt in a wound, but she pushed it away. For now. Once she'd secured the objects and ensured she and her magic were safe from them, well, then she'd make sure these Midgardians knew exactly who and what she was.

She forced William to remove his new doublet before rowing them back across the river, fighting the current that wanted to send them downriver. He was breathing hard when they reached the other bank, and he soaked his shoes and hose jumping into the shallows and pulling the boat to shore.

Hela led the boy towards Dees's house, red brick with three chimneys and tiny, leaded windows with their sweeping view of the river. He hurried along behind her, basket in one hand and craning his neck back and further back the closer they got to the house, trying to see it all at once and nearly walking into Hela when she halted.

"Sorry, Your Highness," he said as he stumbled, but it was distracted. "I can't believe I'm going to see the queen's own astronomer do magic."

Hela rolled her eyes. "You aren't," she said shortly and pulled the basket out of his grasp and then hurried into the gardens behind the house. Her senses told her there was no one there to see her, so she pulled her old clothes from off the top of her armor and quickly strapped her breastplate and backplate over the crimson of her bodice, vambraces covering the sleeves from wrists to elbows, and the greaves beneath her skirt.

Lastly, she took her sword from the basket and unwrapped the scarf from the hilt. William's eyes had nearly popped from his head. "Who are you killing?" he demanded in a squeak. "My lady, Your Highness, I don't think–"

"I don't need you to think," Hela snapped. "You're going to find somewhere to sit and you're going to wait for me. Take the basket."

She didn't expect to see him again, but her time on Midgard had been so strange that she'd rather have him nearby just in case. Hela didn't wait for his reaction. Instead, she made her way to the nearest door, this one small and plain – a servant's entrance – and then glamoured herself into invisibility, breathing a sigh of relief when the magic tingled reassuringly over her skin.

She pushed open the door and stepped into a kitchen bustling with life. Everyone looked up at the door and for a second, Hela thought they could see her, but then someone hurried over to push it closed again, muttering about the wind and ill omens.

She followed a servant down a wood-paneled corridor with a tiled floor, cool and gloomy and faintly redolent of smoke, until she reached a room bright with firelight, candles, and conversation. It wasn't the same room Hela had seen from outside the night before, but that didn't matter. She slipped inside, avoiding touching any of the guests, and concealed herself in a corner. Then she settled down to wait for the magic show to start.

And the archangel Uriel, clad in silver and scarlet, to make her appearance.

Seven

The Archangel Uriel

John Dee was tense with nervous excitement, tugging fretfully at the ends of his long beard and sucking the edge of his mustache into his mouth to chew. Jane, his beautiful, demure, and accomplished young bride, who only a few months before had delivered him his first child – a son, no less! – gave him a mildly reproving look. Dee spat out his mustache and sipped hurriedly from his goblet instead.

Father Michael from Mortlake's parish church had already arrived, and shifted nervously from foot to foot, smoothing his cassock and waiting with ill-concealed impatience for his grace the bishop of London. Dee had invited a few others, and Walsingham had invited himself of course, to report back to the queen on the events of the afternoon.

Dee suspected that, although he had renounced Papism when he became the queen's astronomer, some still viewed his beliefs askance and deemed his actions the product of ambition rather than faith. Father Michael was young and zealous, having been born into an England already divided and brought up in the new – true – belief and his skepticism drifted from him like bad breath.

By inviting Father Michael but also Bishop Aylmer, Dee hoped to alleviate any further suspicions of Papism or, worse, witchcraft. He knew what his detractors at court whispered behind his back. They'd been the ones to seduce the queen away from his counsel and now they wanted him gone completely, his star fallen into the sea and extinguished.

This afternoon would prove them all wrong. This afternoon, he would speak with the archangel Uriel in the presence of his wife and friends, his peers, a prince of the Church, and the queen's own spymaster, under the light of God's sun where no lies could be told. No one would doubt his value to the crown or his faith after this.

The repetition of his convictions did little to soothe him, and he tugged at his beard again. Jane took his hand. "Be calm, husband. I have watched you commune with the crystal before. Well do I know its power and your mastery over it. And it may be that his grace the bishop understands the seraphic tongue as you speak it. Think what a boon that would be, and how quickly progress would be made if it were the case."

Dee forced a smile for her, but in truth, that was one of his greatest fears, that he would be relegated merely to the *conduit* through which the angels spoke, not with him, but with another. His fame would still be assured and yet he wanted to be the one – the only one, the *chosen one* – with whom the angels spoke.

It was a sin to be so covetous, but really, why had the

merchant come to him instead of a churchman if he wasn't the man destined to make this great revelation? Jane's words seemed to act as a conjuring trick, for Fletcher opened the door at that moment and allowed John Aylmer to precede him into the library. The bishop was dressed in fine robes and had dark hawk's eyes which latched onto Dee immediately, passing over Father Michael as if the young priest wasn't even there.

Dee swallowed and mustered a smile, as fake as the last one had been. Aylmer was a great scholar but a poor bishop and a vicious opponent of all who disagreed with his personal interpretation of scripture and the statutes of the Church of England. As a scholar, Dee was keen for his interest and approval, but as a bishop, the magician both feared and needed his attendance.

Jane appeared at his side again as Aylmer approached and he felt himself steady under her presence. The bishop was unlikely to cause a scene in front of a lady and especially not one as well connected as she, who retained many friendships and ties from her time as lady-in-waiting to the countess of Lincoln.

And so it proved. Aylmer greeted them amiably enough, congratulated them on Arthur's birth, and expressed interest in the forthcoming experiment, effectively soothing Dee's ruffled feathers. He began to relax for the first time, for although the gathering had been his idea, and despite having already performed for the queen, he now knew so much more, including with whom he was communicating. What he'd shown Her Majesty and what he was going to do today were markedly different.

Wine flowed freely for the guests, and while Dee wanted its rich heady soothing, he kept himself to a single goblet. He would need all his wiles and wills for this. He sipped moodily and examined the room: Walsingham was deep in conversation with Aylmer, to Father Michael's ongoing distress, and the other guests chatted excitedly with Jane.

For one long, seductive moment, he thought seriously about putting it off, pleading illness or that the angels did not wish to be disturbed, but he knew he couldn't. He'd pulled in several favors at court, including using Jane's connections, to arrange this gathering. His wife had described to him the events of his scrying sessions, though of course, not understanding the language he spoke, she could not aid him other than through observations of his actions. She'd assured him, though, that he seemed both rational and in control during the communions. He needn't fear the ravings and convulsions that commonly claimed the mad and those devil-touched.

All would be well. It had to be.

"My lords and ladies, my dear wife, your grace," Dee said, pushing away from the table where he'd been sitting. The murmur of conversation ceased at once and avid faces turned in his direction. "Allow my servants to refill your cups once more while I make ready for the communion. Jane, my dear, will you draw the curtain?"

In preparation for this event, he'd had a heavy velvet curtain commissioned and installed at one end of the library. Behind it he would prepare, including testing the connection between himself and the seraphic realm.

Jane gave him a gentle, reassuring smile, and ushered him away from the table, which servants swiftly set for supper while others poured rich burgundy into proffered cups. "All will be well, husband," she said and stretched on to her toes to peck his cheek. Then she untied the curtain rope and let the rich fabric fall across the nook at the end of the library, concealing him from view.

Taking a deep breath, Dee sat at the small table and unlocked the cherrywood box. It was time.

Hela was on the wrong side of the curtain when it closed, cutting off her view of Lord Dee. It was likely he was simply hiding back there to calm his nerves, but she couldn't be sure that he wasn't performing some initial ritual to activate the crystal or attune himself to the book. She needed to see what was happening to understand the magic, and while the glamour hid her from view, it would do nothing to conceal the movement of the curtain as she slipped beyond it.

Fortunately, her powers were vast and those of hypnosis and illusion were particularly strong. Despite the warmth of the early summer that had drenched the countryside on her walk here, the thick stone walls of the mansion meant that it was cool inside and so a fire crackled in the hearth to keep the chill out of the guests. Hela directed will and intention towards the flames and then clicked her fingers. One of the guests flinched at the noise and turned towards the corner where she stood, but then someone else exclaimed in surprise, drawing his attention away. The fire burned brightly. The edges of the flames were green.

"What is this?" demanded the bishop. "This is not the spectacle we were promised. Where is your husband, my lady? Back there working black sorcery, perhaps?"

Lady Dee stepped forward with a small smile. "It is but a green branch cracking in the heat, your grace. Or perhaps that one came from the tidal marshes and is salt-ridden. I can assure you, my lord husband's magic needs no such childish trickery."

Hela paused halfway behind the curtain to glance back, irritated and a little surprised at the woman's poise. She was very young and had seemed to be firmly in her husband's grip and the queen of Helheim had not expected such a quick and cutting response. She was tempted to cast another illusion, one that would make the flames burn blood-red just to spite her, but resisted. She'd have her chance to play with them all soon enough.

Assuming nothing interferes with my powers again.

She'd already decided that if she felt anything too untoward, Hela would reveal herself and simply claim the items. Let these puny humans try and stop her if they dared.

Ducking behind the curtain, Hela held her glamour tightly around her. Dee was looking at the other end of the curtain with a frown, as if trying to see through the thick velvet to what might be happening on the other side. If he noticed the ripple in the material, he paid it no mind and a moment later, his wife stuck her head around the other end. "Nothing to concern yourself with, my dear," she said softly. "Are you about ready?"

He nodded and stroked his beard until it lay flat and smooth against his chest. The book and crystal were laid out precisely before him, while the polished box they were kept in was out of sight. As before, there was a sheet of parchment and a stick of charcoal to one side. Dee sipped from his goblet and gave his wife another nod, this one firmer.

"My lords and ladies, honored guests, please approach close to witness my husband, Lord John Dee, in his communion with the angels."

With a flourish, Jane dragged the curtain to one side and resecured it with the rope, revealing her husband sitting in state behind the desk. The guests crowded forward eagerly, though all gave space to both the bishop and another man who had been treated with respect all afternoon. Hela suspected he was the one called Walsingham and that he was close to their queen.

She herself stepped forward, maintaining her glamour, until she was in a place that would allow her to manifest with the most drama. A small smile played around her lips as she wondered how they would react. Believing in gods and angels was one thing, but it was quite another to be confronted with one in your own library. She'd debated drawing her sword before she entered the house so as not to have to muffle the sound with magic but ultimately decided that to unsheathe the blade with a flourish in the moment of her appearance would create a greater reaction in her audience.

She looked forward to their stunned surprise and hasty worship and contemplated what it was they would think when she swept up Dee and his artifacts and whisked them all away to Hel. Perhaps she'd even Realm-jump back again an instant later just to watch their reactions. The more she thought of it, the more confident she became that whatever had happened to her magic here the night before had been some strange anomaly.

Dee held up the book so that his audience could see it. "This book I believe to be written in the seraphic language," he began with the slightest quaver in his voice. He paused to clear his throat and flicked through a few different pages. "As you can see, the language is indecipherable in the eyes of man, though many of the pictures are clearly comprehensible. The plants and flowers pictured here I believe to be depictions of the Garden of Eden, or perhaps of Paradise itself. If we continue further into the book–" he flicked through several more pages as the guests leaned closer "–you will see that we come to astronomical symbols and constellations. My lord bishop, you perhaps will find these familiar?"

Aylmer took a reluctant step forward and squinted at the book. He grunted something that might have been acknowledgment. Hela grinned at his pettiness. By contrast, Dee couldn't help the flash of triumph that crossed his features before he smoothed them into scholarly superiority once again.

"When I commune with the angels, I speak the language written in this book. A language no mortal can understand, and yet each communion teaches me a little more, to the point where I have learned to read some of these words. To understand these symbols that were not written by man." Murmurs rose from the assembled guests and Dee straightened a further. "The symbols, the words, that are most clear to me are the ones in this astronomy section, but not just because of my own expertise in the area. No, I believe it is because the seraph with whom I speak is instructing me in how to build a bridge. A bridge linking our England to Heaven itself."

Hela rolled her eyes at the exclamations of awe and disbelief that greeted this pronouncement. The young priest began a prayer of thanks, calling on someone to lend their aid to Dee, while Bishop Aylmer looked flabbergasted. Jane watched her husband with quiet pride.

If only you knew where that bridge really leads, Hela thought wryly. *It's best for everyone if I take this temptation from you. You will not enjoy the consequences of success.*

The magician didn't wait for the furor to die down. He placed the book on the desk, open at the first page – Hela was pleased and surprised to note he didn't intend to just read the bits he proclaimed to understand – and then reverently hovered his fingers above the crystal.

"This is the shew stone that channels the power of the words to reach the ears of the angels," he said and the room fell silent once more. The group pressed even closer until Jane murmured a request for them to give her dear husband the space to concentrate. The withering contempt on Aylmer's face was something to behold, but he grudgingly edged backwards a pace.

"I will need to examine that," he said shortly.

Jane bobbed a short curtsey. "That is for Lord Dee to decide, your grace."

The bishop was about to respond when Dee flourished his arms to get his voluminous sleeves out of the way, loudly proclaimed a prayer begging contact with the angels and asserting his own humility, and then laid his forefinger against the book and took up the stone in his other hand.

The change was instant: the old man's eyes rolled back in his head, and he jolted as if struck with a bolt from that cursed Thor's hammer. There was a collective gasp from the observers, and a pained wince from Jane Dee. Distantly, upstairs somewhere, a baby began to cry. Hela nodded. Infants were often the most sensitive to magic.

And this was magic indeed. Foul and dark and alien as it had been before, but so much stronger now. She could feel it sucking at the Realm, at Dee and all living creatures, and at herself. Hela tightened her defenses and fed strength to her glamour – and felt an immediate tug in her core.

She twitched in uncertainty as Dee began to speak. The words were grated and growled and disharmonious – how could anyone believe this was the tongue of a benevolent being? – but almost as soon as the thought occurred, they smoothed into something softer and almost pleasant to the ear. But only if you didn't understand what the syllables and phrases actually meant. What was being asked, and worked, and built.

And what was being promised in the language of Svartalfheim.

The Dark Elven language poured from Dee with increasing vigor. "With each repetition of this spell, the bridge binding these two Realms grows stronger. Each time the focal stone is spoken over, the link binding us to thee is laid anew. From here to there and there to here, we build a road that cannot sunder. A path through stars and a path through time, a path unobserved until portals open."

A path unobserved?

This was even better than Hela had hoped for. Everything she had suffered in this cursed Realm was worth it if she obtained this magic. The wording itself was ambiguous enough that once she possessed the book and the stone, she could manipulate the spell to open a bridge of her own, a rival to Bifrost. A bridge from Helheim straight to Asgard.

And from there, conquest and my rightful place as ruler over all the Nine Realms.

Though I confess to some curiosity about what the Dark Elves want with Midgard. Why come here, knowing as they must that humans manipulate and wield the iron they hate so much?

Dee spoke on and Hela put aside her speculations. He drew power from all living creatures and centered it in the stone to fuel the spell. Hela sent another burst of energy into her glamour. She wanted to see how far through the book Dee could read before exhaustion hit him.

"We speak now to the creature reading this spell. Know that we will come to you soon from beyond the stars. The answer to your dreams. The answer to your nightmares. A bridge will open, and you will see us in our glory and our strength. You will aid us in our endeavors. You will—"

The observers were rapt and silent, Father Michael's lips moving in soundless prayer. Hela sent another flick of magic into her weakening glamour. The time was nearly right for Hela to reveal herself as this archangel Uriel and seize the stone, the book, and the man himself. What a story these poor Midgardians would have to tell when it was over. What a—

Her attention was dragged away from the room and Dee's theatrics by a vast and powerful burst of magic – alien and yet intimately, horrifyingly familiar – that battered her senses. The magic of Asgard. Specifically, the magic of Bifrost opening… and opening to here, to this Realm, to the northeast.

To London.

She gritted her teeth and clenched her fists. "No," she growled, making no attempt to mask the word. Lady Jane looked around, confused, but then her husband let out a pained whine like a kicked dog and all her attention snapped back to him.

It seemed Hela wasn't alone in sensing the elven stone's power. And she wasn't alone in coming to investigate it, either. She had enemies arriving on Midgard now, and they'd be looking for Dee and his artifacts. If they found her at the same time...

No. It didn't matter. She'd take Dee and the stone now without bothering to reveal herself. That had been merely a whim to amuse herself. She would forego it rather than risk discovery. Let whoever Odin had sent flail around this Realm looking for something that was no longer here. The thought was amusement enough.

Decided, Hela began to gather up her magic ready to Realm-jump. She reached out to touch Dee and take him with her when the man's voice rose into a pained screech and the Elvish words came faster, the crystal glowing brighter until it outshone the firelight and drowned the candles in its blaze.

The room erupted into chaos. The bishop and Father Michael shouted words she didn't bother to listen to. Dee screamed and dropped the crystal. The building magic – the spell he was unwittingly weaving that would draw Midgard and Svartalfheim into alignment and allow the bridge to open – blasted outwards from the stone in a wave of light so bright none could withstand it. The shockwave guttered every candle, blew out the fire, knocked the guests to their knees and shattered the tiny panes of glass in the leaded windows.

The darkened room, made even darker by the after-images imprinted on their eyeballs, fell into a stunned silence, and then became suddenly loud with screams for help, shouts of fear and alarm, and prayers shrieked in wavering voices.

Hela herself had been shoved backwards by the force of the magic. She blinked but couldn't see Dee, the stone, or the book. Couldn't see much of anything as the room filled with smoke from the doused fire.

Rubbing at her eyes, she lunged towards the desk, but the shattered spell had disoriented her and instead she knocked into someone, who flinched at the contact and then gaped up at her. Young, clean-shaven, and clutching at his head, he nevertheless had the presence of mind to grab her sleeve.

"Who are you?" he demanded. "Were you… I didn't see you here before."

The priest.

She saw the dawning suspicion in his face, but her appetite for the ruse of being the archangel Uriel had left her with both Bifrost's opening and the spell's splintering. Hela gathered her magic and channeled her death touch into him, grabbing his face. There was a great wrenching pull at her core, at the seat of her magic, and, just like the previous night, nothing happened.

Hela snarled her frustration and hurled the man across the room into a knot of hurrying servants, sending them all down in a tangle. More shouts erupted, of surprise and confusion, and she cast around once more for the book or the crystal. Seeing neither, she flung her cloak up over her head and fled before anyone else thought to accost her.

Her magic was compromised. *Hela* was compromised. And Odin, curse him, had sent some of his pet hounds to interfere.

The aftereffects of the spell breaking had left her nauseous and dizzy with a strange lethargy pulling at her limbs. Had Bifrost's manifestation inadvertently powered the ritual enough to open a second bridge, the one to Svartalfheim?

She needed to find out before she did anything else, because if so, she was about to be confronted by both Asgardians and Dark Elves and her magic was–

The boy popped up from where he'd been sitting at the base of a low wall and Hela startled. "Your Highness! What was that bright light? Nearly lit up–"

"Get the boat ready to take me to London. *Now*," she snarled, and William swallowed his questions and did as he was bid without another word, vanishing ahead of her towards the river.

EIGHT

MIDGARD

How Brunnhilde wished they hadn't even waited for dusk. Even after she'd coordinated with Sif, wrangled Aragorn back out of the palace stables and away from the relieved grooms, returned home and packed, there were still a few hours to sit and think and brood before making her way to Bifrost.

It had seemed like the perfect opportunity to take a nap and restore a little strength and clarity. She'd tried not to overthink it as she lay in bed and stared into the roof beams. When that didn't work, she'd meditated until her heart eased and her eyes grew heavy. She'd slept and woken within minutes with fear clawing at her chest and a scream trapped in her throat.

Jittery with adrenaline and the same nameless, formless, ever-present worry, the Valkyrie went into the field and ran sword forms until she was dripping with sweat. Went in and washed and changed and slept – and woke gasping. Went into the field and shot arrows at a target. Slept – woke shouting.

Didn't sleep again.

As dusk began to color the edges of the sky, Brunnhilde felt only relief at not having to pretend that sleep meant anything other than fear for her. She strapped on her armor and weapons and covered them with a cloak. She slung her pack over her shoulder and went into the stable. Aragorn was resting a rear hoof and dozing upright. She scratched gently at one ear and reminded him in a whisper to find one of her sisters to care for him the next morning. The ear flicked acknowledgment and Brunnhilde smiled and then opened his stall door so he could leave. She put an apple in the manger full of hay near his soft muzzle and smiled as his twitched – even mostly asleep, apples were worth appreciating.

Brunnhilde met Sif outside the grand arched gate leading to Bifrost's temple. The rainbow bridge wasn't active when they arrived, cutting Asgard off from the other Realms, but Sif's brother, Heimdall the Far-Seeing, guarded its end and stood ever ready to magic it into existence.

The raven-haired warrior looked fit and well rested, scowling at their destination, perhaps, but otherwise disciplined and ready to do her duty. "Valkyrie," she said when she noticed Brunnhilde's arrival, hefting her pack more comfortably onto her back.

"Lady." Brunnhilde paused, narrow-eyed, and then grinned, and Sif returned it, slapping her on the shoulder in welcome.

"You look even worse than when I saw you this morning, if that's possible."

Brunnhilde arched an eyebrow. "Thank you. I feel it. Tried to sleep this afternoon. It didn't go well."

Sif winced. "Well, with luck, we'll discover whatever trouble is brewing on Midgard and put a stop to it so you can rest. Not that we have any idea what we're looking for or even what the problem is," she added, mostly to herself.

The Valkyrie smarted, but it was true. She rubbed the heel of her hand against her stinging eyes and then swallowed a yawn. Her indignation might fit her better if everything she did didn't highlight how fatigued she truly felt. At least by crossing Bifrost, she wouldn't have to expend energy Realm-jumping herself and Sif to Midgard.

"Are you ready?" the shield-maiden asked gently. Brunnhilde found a smile for her. Sif was known for her impatience and tendency towards recklessness, yet here she was prepared to let the Valkyrie take the lead.

"I really must look bad for you to be this nice to me," she said and elbowed her. "Come on. Let's get this over with."

"With pleasure," Sif said grimly and shook herself like a cat dropped in a bath. "I hate Midgardians."

Brunnhilde's smile grew more genuine. "Really?" she teased, compelled to make the effort to hide her exhaustion. "I didn't know that. You've never mentioned it. Tell me more."

Sif huffed a laugh and launched into a long, rambling explanation of the myriad failings of the human Realm as they walked through into Heimdall's domain, the cool stone walls bringing gooseflesh to arms.

Lady Sif's brother stood guard at Bifrost's end, staring across the Realms and searching for threats to Asgard's borders, people and freedom. He turned at their approach. "Bright-Battle," he said and inclined his head, then shifted his unsettling gaze to Sif. "Little sister."

Sif scowled but allowed herself to be drawn into a brief embrace, her armor clanging against his. "Less of the little," she muttered, but without heat, affection bringing a faint blush to her cheeks.

"Be safe, both of you," Heimdall replied, and then summoned Bifrost, which shimmered into being before them. "Destination?"

"Midgard," Sif grunted, and her brother smirked and completed the magic that sent the other end of the bridge to the human world. "Have fun," he added as they stepped on to the rainbow. He winked at Brunnhilde. Sif rolled her eyes in exasperation.

Traveling by Bifrost was both similar and different to Realm-jumping. They didn't need to make the same effort – holding their destination in mind as they physically transported themselves – but the weird between-space that wasn't quite the sky or the stars was the same. All around the edges of Bifrost was... nothing. Absence. Void. And the potential for everything.

There was no concept of time on Bifrost, but Brunnhilde counted her footsteps as they walked: fifty-six. It didn't seem possible that they had walked to another Realm in only fifty-six steps, yet the weird void that hurt to look at, that was empty and yet full was replaced, between one blink and the next, with a loud, thronging city scene.

Colors and scents assailed them, swamping their senses as they blinked at the bright sunlight. Sounds of people and animals pressed against their ears, warm sunlight stroking their skin. Amid it all, shocked gasps and a few muted screams.

Sif reached for her sword on instinct and Brunnhilde grabbed her arm. "We're already, ah, attracting attention," she hissed, and it was true.

They'd arrived in a clear space surrounded by buildings where entertainers were performing for the crowd. A garishly dressed acrobat was staring at them in shock, the balls he'd been juggling bouncing down around his feet. His audience were likewise dumbfounded, and then applause broke out, wild and raucous. A shower of tiny silver coins were scattered at their feet.

"What do we do?" Sif hissed even as she swept her arms wide and bowed from the waist, a big, false smile plastered across her face. Brunnhilde was impressed at the speed of her reactions, and even more so at her acting. Sif wasn't exactly known for playfulness.

"What we're good at," the Valkyrie said as she realized the juggler wasn't alone: there was a man breathing fire a hundred paces away and a girl with a dog dancing on its hind feet in the opposite corner. All of them had an audience. "It's a festival, I think, or some sort of public entertainment. We need to give them a show and then get out of here without too many questions. We're the only ones in armor, so… Fight me."

Sif's smile turned sharp, feral. "With pleasure," she said. Together, they dropped their packs and threw off their cloaks.

The crowd gasped again as their armor was revealed and then there were shouts of confusion and alarm when the pair drew steel. Their reaction seemed worried rather than approving, but then Sif was lunging and the sun was reflecting off her blade into Brunnhilde's eyes and the Valkyrie blinked and side-stepped, Dragonfang meeting Sif's sword with a clang and a shower of sparks.

They traded blows and then the Valkyrie back-flipped away. Give them a show, she meant, and Sif took her meaning.

They fought, not to win, but to impress and astound, using every flashy trick they could think of. Painting themselves firmly as entertainers and acrobats rather than the warriors they were.

Brunnhilde ran up the side of a wall to head height before leaping back at Sif. Sif responded by vaulting onto a wooden platform where a play was happening, disrupting the actors and the audience, and emerging on the other side wearing a blond wig made of straw and a crooked, painted-wood crown.

There was laughter as well as gasps as she cartwheeled off the stage with one hand, flinging the wig at Brunnhilde with the other and then retrieving her sword from the edge of the stage to battle on.

They came to a halt after several minutes, chests heaving for breath and the audience awestruck around them. A second round of applause, far louder than the first, rose as the crowd shook off the spell. Even the juggler and the actors were clapping, their own performances forgotten in light of the Asgardians' spectacle. The scattering of coins this time was bigger, and then several well-dressed men were pushing through the crowd towards them, calling out in imperious voices.

"Get the money," Brunnhilde hissed, because that's what entertainers would do, and several raggedy children were eyeing the coins with open covetousness.

"Extraordinary, most extraordinary," a man was saying the moment he was in range. "I simply must have you entertain for me privately. My name is–"

Sif flipped a couple of the smallest coins to the wide-eyed girls in the crowd. "Practice hard and you could be this good when you're grown up," she said, ignoring the man, who came to an affronted halt mid-command.

"Girls don't fight," a boy shouted and then wilted when Sif glared at him. She sheathed her sword without breaking eye contact, and then smirked when he turned and fled into the dispersing crowd.

The man cleared his throat pointedly. "As I was saying," he began again.

"Forgive us, we don't give private demonstrations," Brunnhilde said. She hadn't been paying attention and had missed the man's name, not that it would have meant anything. "Our skills are for all to enjoy, not just those of, ah, superior means, shall we say. Now, we are new to the city and have become a little lost. Can you tell me the name of this area and a reputable place to stay?"

"But I could expose you to the choicest members of the nobility," he tried. "Your earnings could be triple what you have made here today."

"Generous indeed," Sif interrupted as she dropped the last coins into her pouch and stood entirely too close to the man for comfort. "Just the area and a place to stay. Perhaps we'll visit you another day. A man of means such as yourself, you must be well known in the city, yes? Then it will be no hardship for us to locate your residence. But for now, we prefer to show our skills to those with less to enjoy in their lives than you." She gestured at the starry-eyed girls and crowd of people whose clothes were ragged, dirty and patched and hung from frames with far less flesh on them than the ruddy-faced, scrubbed-clean nobleman accosting them.

"Ah. Ah, of course, how noble of you." He rallied

magnificently and it took all Brunnhilde's willpower not to check Sif's expression or she knew she'd dissolve into laughter. "Beauty and talent and charitable hearts. Perhaps you are angels, or wild creatures escaped from the fairy realm." There was a hint of a question in there, but the Asgardians stood stoic and patient until he slumped, accepting defeat. "This is Clerkenwell, of course, and the Roan Horse is a very good inn and I expect will be within your means. It is but a quarter mile that way. Ask anyone if you get lost. But please, glorious Amazons, will you at least tell me where and when your next performance will be?" he begged. "I should love to bring my son and–"

"You should bring your daughter," Sif interrupted and Brunnhilde was interested to see how he recoiled. "Ah, well. We prefer to be mysterious, anyway," the shield-maiden finished, also reading his expression. She grabbed Brunnhilde by the elbow. "Let's go."

They wrapped themselves in their cloaks and shouldered their packs once more, then hurried away in the direction the man had pointed them, ignoring his forlorn cries. News of their performance had preceded them, and everywhere they went, people stopped to whisper and watch. Young men who obviously hadn't seen their performance themselves openly scoffed at their so-called prowess; some even had swords strapped to their hips and made a show of flexing their hands on their hilts, as if contemplating offering a match. Every one of them backed down when the Asgardians made slow, steady, inviting eye contact accompanied by smiles containing entirely too many teeth.

Not that they wanted to duel, but often the best way to

get out of a fight was to be openly prepared to fight. Make the invite obvious, make it clear they weren't afraid or even impressed, and let the other fighter's doubt and nerves get the better of them.

As expected, the approach led to zero accepted invitations, but muttered derision was thrown their way once they were at a safe distance. Derision Brunnhilde could live with.

"You see?" Sif hissed as they hurried down the middle of a street, the buildings pressing together overhead until there was only a thin strip of sky showing its blue above them. "This is why I don't like Midgardians. Disrespectful, arrogant, smelly–"

"Yes, yes," the Valkyrie said absently. "Let's just find the inn, shall we?"

They were both jumpy and on edge by the time they reached their destination, and Brunnhilde paused to wrap her cloak more tightly around her despite the heat of the afternoon, concealing her armor. Neither of them wanted to be identifiable as the women who'd fought in the square once they entered the building, knowing it was better to leave those disguises behind, to be resumed far from here if necessary.

The inn was situated on one side of an open courtyard with room for riders and carts to halt out the front. There was a stable attached to the building's side and a cat slept on a mounting block, black and white fur soaking up the sun. A distant dog barked.

The sun was brassy and unrelenting above them and there was little shade. The heat bounced back up from the beaten dirt and cobbles beneath their feet.

The cloaks were a poor disguise, and not just because of

the warm weather. Brunnhilde and Sif were taller than most Midgardians, including the men, and even though the thick material hid their armor and clothes, they both had their hair unbound and uncovered, which again seemed unusual. The Valkyrie realized she hadn't seen any women carrying packs like theirs, either. They looked more than foreign, they looked exotic. Perhaps they could use that to their advantage somewhere else, but here, they just wanted to blend in and couldn't.

"Do we have enough Midgardian coin for this?" Sif whispered as they ducked under the low lintel and entered the inn. It was smoky and hot, the tables crowded with patrons.

"The rich man assured me it was reasonable."

Sif snorted. "Reasonable for a rich man isn't the same as reasonable for everyone else," she pointed out.

Their Asgardian silver was of a size and quality far superior to that which had been thrown to them for their performance. They'd arouse even more attention if they started using that, but surely what they'd been given for the fight couldn't amount to much.

At least having their own coin was a backup. Brunnhilde didn't fancy having to perform for the crowd on a daily basis just to eat. They weren't here to attract attention. Or any more attention than their sudden arrival already had, at least.

They approached the long bar and asked for a shared room.

"Sixpence a night, extra if you've got horses. Tuppence a night for supper. Penny if you want a bath."

Sif dug out the handful of grubby coins she'd rescued from the floor and counted out six. The innkeep raised an eyebrow.

"Sixpence," Sif said, pointing.

The man folded his arms across his chest. "Foreign, are you? That's thruppence. Those are ha'pennies."

Sif narrowed her eyes but counted out six more. "Sixpence."

The man scooped them across the bar and made them disappear. "And two each for supper, one for a bath," he reminded them. "You want supper?"

"Not for hours, no," Brunnhilde said. "We'll see our room first."

"Aye, if you like. Name's Peter, and you can ask for me or Sal – that's Sal there, getting her rump pinched by one of the sots – if you've need of anything. This way, then."

He led them through a door by the side of the bar and up a narrow flight of stairs and down a dimly lit corridor. Their room was small but well appointed, with a single large bed, a chest for personal belongings, and a pitcher and ewer for washing. "I'll get a cot brought in, less you're sharing."

"Does a cot cost a penny?" Sif asked sourly and Peter grinned. "Ha'penny, milady."

"We'll share."

"As you will, milady. Peter and Sal, if you need anything. We serve supper until it's dark. After that, you'll be on bread and cheese, maybe a little pork if there's any left."

"Thank you, Peter. We'll bear that in mind." Brunnhilde glanced at Sif. "Now, we're new to town. What can you tell us about your fair city?"

Peter sucked his teeth and then waggled his eyebrows. "I thought you was foreign. German, is it?"

"No," Sif said and Brunnhilde bit back a frustrated groan.

Peter, however, didn't seem put out by her shortness. "Buy a glass or two of wine downstairs and I'll talk your ear off, gentlewomen. Everything you could ever wish to know about London, England, and Queen Elizabeth – God bless her. And, ah, forgive me, forgive me, but which of you is the lady and which the lady-in-waiting? You're both dressed very fine, you see, so I just–"

"I'm the lady-in-waiting," Sif said before Brunnhilde could even begin to think of a reply. She blinked in surprise.

"As you will, milady. Thank you." He nodded to Sif and offered Brunnhilde a short bow. "Your grace."

"We'll be down for that wine soon," Sif assured him and showed him out.

"Sif–" Brunnhilde began.

"I don't like Midgardians," she interrupted. "But the All-Father asked me to help you. You're the one with the knowledge, however tenuous, of why we're here. That means you're leading this mission and I'm subordinate to you. So, lady-in-waiting." She bobbed a curtsey so ironic it was almost an insult. "Shall I wash your feet?"

Brunnhilde couldn't help it: Sif's indignation sat poorly with her steel-strong sense of duty. She burst out laughing. The other goddess gave her a narrow-eyed glare that almost singed off the Valkyrie's eyebrows, but then a reluctant smile tugged at the corner of her mouth.

"All right, all right, you've made your point," she said, "and I'm grateful for your sacrifice in this matter." Brunnhilde took a breath; she well knew Sif's temper and reined in her mirth with savage precision. "Just… be nice, all right? We need information and that means we need friends."

"I'm always nice. Look." Sif smiled – or at least, she showed all her teeth in such a way that a prickle ran up Brunnhilde's spine. Brunnhilde let her head sag back on her neck and groaned up at the plastered ceiling.

Sif slapped her arm. "I will," she said, seriously now. "I won't let you down. We'll figure this out together."

"Thank you, Sif," Brunnhilde said quietly. Being on Midgard hadn't begun the way she'd expected, and it was only now she was able to relax that she could feel the fatigue pulling at her. And the nameless worry, too, sharper-edged here. Poisonous.

She stripped out of her cloak, armor and clothes and then dressed in a rich blue robe cinched with a silver belt from out of her pack. In deference to what appeared to be the fashion here, she plaited her hair and then twisted it up to sit on the back of her head.

Sif wore a vivid green gown. She also wore slender knives strapped to each thigh beneath her skirt, one attached to each forearm under her sleeves and a fifth, small and obvious and wickedly sharp, on the gold belt around her waist. She, too, tied back her hair.

Brunnhilde took Dragonfang – the sword was glamoured to be invisible unless she touched it and so no one would notice it hanging from her belt. Its familiar weight was a comfort to her. She strapped a dagger to her waist on the other side, just to match Sif and deter open hostility. Then she yawned and shook herself, blinking to clear her tired eyes.

"Ready?" Sif asked and she nodded. The raven-haired warrior gestured for her to lead the way. "Then let's see what passes for wine in this Realm and learn what we can from the thieving Peter. And if I find out those were pennies, not ha'pennies like he said..." The closing door cut off Sif's low-voiced threats.

•••

The wine was awful if you bought the ha'penny version, which did indeed cost what they determined, through careful observation, to be a ha'penny. The penny version wasn't much better, but a separate surveillance of the tavern's main room showed that they were the best-dressed people in here, and only the raggediest women looked to be supping ale, which it seemed they'd both much prefer and couldn't have.

Brunnhilde pushed away her second cup with a grimace and Sal glanced their way.

"Not to your liking, your grace? We've some proper fine stuff in the cellar."

"No, thank you. Peter has divested my lady of enough of her coin for one evening," Sif said quickly. Sal laughed and shrugged, then darted away to serve someone else.

Brunnhilde remained a little surprised with the grace with which Sif was accepting her subordinate role here, but she was grateful for it, too. And the evening had been useful so far. They'd played on being foreign nobility without actually saying where they were from, and they'd been regaled with tales of where to visit and where to avoid in the City of London.

The quarrel with King Philip of Spain had been dissected – at least in as much detail as Peter had, which wasn't much – and the ongoing religious battles laid out with far more zest. The Asgardians guessed that Peter, at least, was a zealot of this new division of their belief, the one their queen was the head of, though they didn't seem to worship her, which was confusing. Still, they couldn't imagine those who clung to the old ways being so incautious as to even raise the subject of religion for fear of being questioned about their own.

There'd been a moment of awkwardness when Peter had suddenly realized that if his guests were indeed from overseas, they too might hold to the old ways.

"Fear not. We neither cause nor seek trouble, by our words, thoughts, or deeds, but if my lady's coin isn't sufficient for you…" Sif had trailed off meaningfully, and that had been that.

"And, of course, there's the recent excitement at court. Her Majesty is building an extension to Whitehall Palace to house the Duke of Alencon, who's coming to court her," Peter said now as he poured rich, dark ale into a tankard and slid it across the bar to a customer.

Brunnhilde barely suppressed a yawn. They were sitting at the table closest to the bar so the tavern keep could continue with his stories, but fascinating as this was, it did nothing to help them answer the mystery that had brought them here. The Valkyrie's weariness was increasing by the hour.

"Do you think she'll marry Duke Francis?" Sal called over as she piled empty cups and tankards onto a large wooden tray, weaving skillfully through the crowd.

Peter hesitated, as if torn between honesty and loyalty. "Her Majesty will do what's right for England," he said at last, which wasn't an answer.

"Let's go for a walk," Sif said. "I don't think we'll get anything more of use from this pair and I'm keen to get a feel for the city. Other than the thoroughfares, the roads are all so narrow. I'd rather get used to them now so I know how best to fight in them when I have to."

"You think we're going to be fighting Midgardians?" Brunnhilde asked, surprised out of her growing torpor.

Sif arched an eyebrow and pushed away from the table. "You think the Midgardians are behind whatever's powerful enough to disturb the sleep of the leader of the Choosers of the Slain, all the way across Realms to Asgard?"

She had a point, the Valkyrie had to admit.

"Besides, I'll be disappointed if we don't," Sif added and winked. "That bout with you gave me a thirst for a decent scrap."

Brunnhilde feigned outrage as they pushed away from the table and waved their farewells to Peter and Sal. "I'll give you a decent scrap," she threatened, low-voiced, and Sif laughed.

"Stay away from Tunmil Street," Peter called as they reached the door. "The wrong sort of people go there. Mannered folk such as yourselves got no business round there, miladies. If you know what I mean?"

They didn't, but they waved their thanks for the advice. There were a lot of eyes watching as they exited into the early evening. Well dressed, foreign, and without a male servant or guard in attendance: the mystery surrounding them would only grow as time passed and the chances were high that someone might put two and two together and recognize them as the fighters from earlier that day.

It was likely they'd need to move inns more than once if they couldn't quickly discover the cause of the nightmares and what it meant for the Nine Realms. As far as Brunnhilde was concerned, that was the least of their worries. Wherever they ended up, they could handle themselves, it was the reputation they'd get by doing so that worried her. Humans had such strange opinions about who was "allowed" to be strong or defend themselves, not to mention how they did so.

The afternoon had advanced while they'd been inside and now the sun cast long, orange bands between the houses when they stepped into the small square. They paused to shade their eyes and take in their surroundings properly. It was pleasant not to be wearing armor concealed by a thick cloak, and they strolled without a destination in mind, their easy pace belied by how their eyes roved across streets and buildings, analyzing people and shops and markets. Looking for ambush points and the places where they wouldn't want to get surprised, discussing quietly how they'd fight their way free if they did, and smiling pleasantly the whole while. Brunnhilde wondered what the people passing them would think if they could overhear their conversation.

Sif kept checking in with her, but as the evening deepened and the roads narrowed and widened and narrowed again, shadows growing thick and clinging, Brunnhilde sensed no change to her or her surroundings. No burst of magic or pull of fear. No looming dread like that which gripped her during sleep. Try as she might, there was nothing wrong.

"Are you lost, ladies? Those are very fine gowns you're wearing for this part of the city. I think you're lost. I think you might be very, very far from home."

The voice came from the narrow, dark alley to their right and the feral grin that pulled at Sif's mouth when they heard it made the Valkyrie snort in amusement.

"Must you?" she asked softly.

"Oh, I must," the shield-maiden said cheerfully. "I really must." She turned to face the alleyway and put her hands to her chest. "Can you help us, sir?" she quavered and this time Brunnhilde had to bite her lip to keep from laughing.

"We're not here to cause trouble," she reminded Sif half-heartedly.

The warrior shot her an irate glare over her shoulder. "I'm not causing trouble," she said primly. "I'm stopping this fool from troubling anyone else he comes across. Ever."

The Valkyrie held up her hands. "Please, go ahead. Just keep the noise down, yes? Men's screams are so loud."

The man who'd spoken slunk out of the alley, followed by five others. They were ragged but intent and they moved well, fanning out across the street and one attempting to slide past to block their rear. Brunnhilde stepped casually into the center of the street, blocking him. The man hesitated, then jinked as if to run past her. The Valkyrie folded her arms and stared him down and he came to a confused halt.

"Now, my ladies, can I assist you to your destination?" the speaker continued as Brunnhilde and the fifth man continued to watch each other. He shifted his hand from where it hung by his side, the last of the sunlight glinting on a blade. In response, she turned slightly side-on and tapped the knife at her waist: best to leave Dragonfang glamoured unless she had no choice but to draw it. The man grinned, exposing crooked yellow teeth – he didn't expect she knew what to do with it other than cut fruit, presumably. Brunnhilde elected not to enlighten him.

"We know both where we are and where we're going," Sif said ahead of her.

The speaker chuckled. "No, I don't think you do know where you are," he contradicted with an air of regret. "You see, these are my streets, and the women who walk them are mine, too. The men who buy them pass their coin to me. The children who beg and steal from them give me half their cut. What will two such noble flowers as you give me, eh?"

Please, no. Don't do it. Please, Sif–

"A lesson you won't forget. A quick death. A slow one. The choice is yours."

Brunnhilde pressed her lips together. "Low profile," she murmured and saw Sif shrug.

"It's still low if they don't live to tell anyone."

The speaker broke into honking laughter and the shield-maiden took the opportunity of his distraction to glide forward and punch the heel of her hand up into his nose. Laughter became a squeal and a burst of blood from nose and mouth, an arcing backwards to land heavily on the cobbles with an explosive grunt.

Sif was squatting over his form before he'd managed to suck in a breath to bawl and she slapped her hand over his mouth. With his nose filled with blood, it cut off his ability to breathe, too. The other four men converged on her and Brunnhilde ran lightly forwards, pulling her knife. A man came in from her left and she side-kicked him low in the kidney, dropping him to wheeze on the ground. He'd be passing blood for a week and certainly wouldn't be getting back up to challenge her.

"Just passing through," she said calmly to the other three as Sif gently suffocated the ringleader. "No need to make a fuss." She glanced down. "Don't kill him, please."

The shield-maiden didn't move for a long moment, and then released the man's face. He sucked in a bubbling breath and began to cough as she stood up off him and faced the others. "Go away."

They grabbed their two downed colleagues and went.

Brunnhilde and Sif stared at each other. "Feel better?" the Valkyrie asked.

Sif sighed expansively and flung her arms out wide. "You know what? I really do."

"Then can we please go back to the inn and at least try and get some sleep?"

Sif's grin faded. "Of course. I'm sorry. How do you feel?" Brunnhilde shot her a disgusted glare and the shield-maiden held up her hands in placation. In silence – and in peace – they headed back to the inn.

"Are we even in the right place?" Brunnhilde muttered as they made their way back. They'd stopped at a small market and bought bread, cheese and dried fish, plus a stoppered jar of ale that tasted far better than the wine they'd had so far.

"Bifrost brought us out where we need to be," Sif said confidently. "We're just going to have to keep searching. It will all make sense after a good night's sleep." Brunnhilde shot her a sour look. "Ah. Well then, perhaps your dreams will show us what we need to do tomorrow?"

"If I even manage to sleep," the Valkyrie said, and then yawned. "Though I suppose if the dreams are clearer, that at least will be something. Odin's eye, but I'm tired."

"It's unlike you to be this despondent, Bright-Battle," Sif said, concern in her voice. She pulled them to a stop in the deep gloom of evening. A tall pole at the end of the road had a small fire burning at its top, casting a fitful orange light that only dimly reached them where they stood. Sif was little more than an outline in the dark, but her eyes glittered with worry and her mouth was a tight, thin line.

Brunnhilde made an effort to shake off her gloom. "Forgive me. I've no doubt we'll discover what we should be looking for come the morrow. For now, though, I'm to bed." She gestured at the inn just up ahead. "If you stay out, be discreet, lady. If possible, be unseen," she added. "After everything that's happened since we arrived, we really don't need to attract any more attention."

"Discreet I can do," Sif said confidently. Brunnhilde twitched but said nothing. If Sif of all people couldn't take care of herself, then Midgard was a far more dangerous place than she believed.

They reached the inn and went through the common room again. Sif headed for a table of merchants, insinuating herself into their company as if she'd known them for years. Her demure lady-in-waiting guise dropped like a handkerchief and something a little rougher, a little looser, entered her tone and posture.

Another disguise, and even better than the first.

The Valkyrie snorted as she took the stairs to their room, where she undressed and washed, and fell onto the straw mattress as if it was the finest down. She slept.

NINE

DESPERATE CHOICES

Brunnhilde woke screaming.

Before she could inhale to scream again, a cold blade was pressed to her throat, snatching her from the nightmare and into an entirely different one in the waking world. The Valkyrie grabbed the hand holding the blade, found the elbow joint, and pushed it viciously in the wrong direction. Her attacker grunted in pain. The bracelet on her wrist flared as she wished desperately for light, seizing on the magic in the stone and pushing it towards the slumbering coals in the grate.

Flames caught and flared, a jewel in the bracelet cracked and faded, and the skin on Brunnhilde's throat parted despite her best efforts. In the flickering glow, she and Sif stared wildly into each other's faces, so close they could have kissed.

"By the Norns!" Sif gasped, relaxing her knife hand despite the pain twisting her features. "What was that?" There were shouts of question and alarm from the rooms to either side. "Bad dreams!" she bellowed, making no effort to move her

124

mouth further from the Valkyrie's ear when she did so. Not that she had much choice, with her arm still locked and twisted the wrong way.

They stared at each other for another few seconds as the alarm became grumbled discontent and then faded into silence.

"You cut me?" Brunnhilde demanded, hoarse and still reeling from the dream. Almost – *almost* – she twisted harder, but then let go and flopped back into the pillow instead. It was sweaty beneath her neck. Her fingers went to her throat and came away smeared in blood. Not much, but still.

"What do you expect, you troll's ass?" Sif snapped, though she kept her voice lowered as she shook out her arm. "Screaming in the middle of the night as if you were being murdered in your bed!"

The Valkyrie gave her a very pointed look. "I almost was," she retorted and showed her blood to Sif, who scoffed.

"If I'd wanted you dead, you'd be dead," she tried, which Brunnhilde didn't believe for an instant. "You startled me," she added in an apologetic tone that wasn't quite an apology but probably the best she'd get. Sif made the knife vanish back... somewhere. Strapped to her forearm, the Valkyrie suspected. "I take it that's why you haven't been slee–" she started.

"Shut up," Brunnhilde said, jerking her hand up and almost smacking Sif in the face. The raven-haired warrior reared back, murder returning to the set of her mouth. "I... I remember. I could never remember before, but now I do," she added excitedly, shoving herself up to sitting and pushing Sif off the edge of the bed. And then everything she could now remember twisted that excitement into dread.

"What? What is it? By the Norns, just tell me!" Sif exclaimed when the Valkyrie stared sightlessly into the settling flames.

Brunnhilde jumped and met her eyes. "It's the Dark Elves," she whispered and then got up to throw a few sticks into the grate. She suddenly needed the light. "They're speaking of opening a path to a new world, a place of wonders and miracles. They're speaking to someone here, I think, trying to tempt them into opening this path. I can still hear the voice, the words. They speak so... sweetly." She shivered.

"That doesn't sound like them," Sif pointed out cautiously and Brunnhilde shrugged.

"Maybe that's why it's been so hard for me to identify what I was dreaming. Because I couldn't reconcile what I know of them, with the battles I've fought against them in the past, with what they've been saying. Promising. They promise such wonders," she added in a whisper laced with incredulity. Nausea writhed like eels in her stomach.

"But you said dread," the shield-maiden pointed out with that hard-headed practicality Brunnhilde often hated and now relished. She needed it, needed Sif's steadiness, the way she tracked a trail to its conclusion with the single-minded intensity of a starving wolf. "You said you wake up every time filled with dread and worry for the souls in Valhalla. It's why you're screaming. How can they be–" she made a face of disgust "–how can *Dark Elves* be sweet and yet make even such as you afraid? And what does a path to a beautiful world have to do with your worry for Valhalla? I take it this world of miracles they speak of is actually Svartalfheim? How is this path to open, anyway? And where, between their Realm and this one? Who's doing the opening?"

Brunnhilde held up her hand in a physical barrier to protect her from the torrent of words. "Enough, Sif. Please. I don't know, I don't have the answers to any of those questions. Not yet, anyway. I suspect if I sleep again, if that's even possible now, I might learn more. Maybe I'd remember better if I hadn't been fighting for my life the instant I opened my eyes," she finished acidly and then immediately regretted it. Fatigue and worry were making her dangerously short-tempered, and one of them needed to keep a cool head in this situation. Past experience indicated it was unlikely to be Sif.

But to her genuine surprise, the shield-maiden grimaced and held up her hands before the Valkyrie could apologize. "All right, I'm sorry, even though it was a natural reaction to being woken up by someone sounding like they were being murdered – bad choice of words, I know. But look, if you need to sleep, then perhaps I can help with that."

Brunnhilde arched an eyebrow and sagged back onto the bed. She put her face in her hands. "What are you going to do, fetch me a cup of warm milk?" she mumbled into her palms.

"Would it help?" Sif asked instead of responding to the sarcasm. Brunnhilde blinked and scrubbed her hands over her face and then the back of her neck, damp with sweat. She grimaced and pulled her plait over her shoulder to air it. The flames danced in the grate but couldn't give the lie to the fact it was the middle of the night. How long had she slept this time? Her body told her that however long it might be, it wasn't long enough.

"Actually, I thought you could use Frigga's bracelet to put a silencing spell on the room so that you don't disturb anyone else if the dreams are bad again. And I'll sit guard to keep you safe, so you can sleep without worry. Or, you know, nap and scream, at least."

The Valkyrie had to blink back the sting of tears that not even Sif's last jibe could stifle. "I... thank you, Sif," she said, her voice strangled. The shield-maiden waved away the thanks and wouldn't meet her eyes, embarrassed.

"Of course. I'm here to help, aren't I?" she grumbled.

"And by 'sit guard to keep me safe', you don't really mean put a blade to my neck again, do you?" Brunnhilde asked, striving to lighten the atmosphere.

Sif chuckled and shrugged. "That would depend on how loud you insist on snoring. I have little patience for these things, as I'm sure you know. Now go on, cast the spell and then lie down. Close your eyes, at least. I'll be here." Brunnhilde did as she was bid, sacrificing another jewel in the bracelet to the endeavor, and then stretched out on the bed once more. The idea of sleep was welcome, the idea of dreaming about Dark Elves less so, even though she knew that it was vital to the success of their mission. They had to learn more. *She* had to learn more.

"I'll always be here," Sif added under her breath. The Valkyrie heard it anyway and slipped into an exhausted, relieved sleep with a smile on her face.

By the time dawn leached through the shutters, Brunnhilde had shouted herself awake five more times and Sif had been forced to put her knives on the dresser out of reach after inadvertently cutting herself startling at the Valkyrie's sudden outburst.

Brunnhilde was weary down to her bones and every dream had only strengthened the voice in her head until she fancied she could hear it even while awake. Elvish was a beautiful language, with a music and lilt all its own. That of the Dark Elves was both different and not – its lyricism tended towards the darker tones and minor notes, a dirge rather than an aria. And yet in her dreams the tongue was beautiful and alluring, whispering of marvels and riches and power like nothing she'd ever known, all of which could be hers if only she'd chant along with the speaker.

Just say the words, speak them with me, speak them over and over. Concentrate, sweet Midgardian, don't you want to see Heaven?

I am of Asgard. I lead the Choosers of the Slain. I am Brunnhilde and my will is stronger than yours. You will not corrupt me.

It was a memory, not a conversation, and so there was no response. Still, she felt a little better for the defiance. As she'd done every time she'd woken, Brunnhilde swung her legs off the edge of the bed and clenched her fingers in her loosened hair, seeking to ground herself through the tug in her scalp. As Sif had done every time, she silently proffered a cup of water and cupped the Valkyrie by the back of her neck as she drank.

Brunnhilde's fatigue was like poison building in her veins, slowing her thoughts and reactions. If it did come to that fight Sif was so looking forward to, the Valkyrie knew she'd be more than a match for any Midgardian, but then their enemy wasn't Midgardians. They were Dark Elves, and they were fast and deadly and exquisitely skilled. Not only that, but they hated Asgardians and their greed and ambition were legendary. Whatever their plans were once the bridge was open, it wouldn't be good for Asgard.

"Haven't seen any weapons except our own," she grunted. "But we're talking iron on Midgard, aren't we? Steel?"

Sif looked up from washing her face, realization dawning. "That's right. Lots and lots of iron," she said soothingly. "Not that the elves are going to make it here, because you're going to find out who's casting the spell and stop them. I mean, there are probably some here already, for how else can they be casting the magic? But I can handle those, so there's nothing to worry about. All right? You don't need to worry."

The Valkyrie smarted at that. "No, that's not it," she said, straining for calm. "In the dreams, the voice calls me 'Midgardian'. That's who's working their magic for them."

"No Elves?" Sif asked, looking disappointed. She puffed out a sigh. "You're saying we need to find one guilty human among this whole city? I can't wait for you to tell me how we do that."

"Right now, I have no idea." Brunnhilde sighed and then yawned so wide her jaw cracked.

Sif swore and began strapping knives to her thighs and forearms. "Maybe that's what you'll learn while you sleep tonight?" she said with more hope than conviction.

Brunnhilde contemplated the possibility she might understand only a single aspect of the mystery per night of shrieking nightmare and could have wept. Instead, she gave herself a mental slap and then stood resolutely and began to dress. "We'll learn nothing at all if we stay in here all day. Put some clothes on and go and ask for breakfast, *lady in waiting*." Sif curled her lip and then executed a mockery of a curtsey that made the Valkyrie snort laughter. "You really don't ever stop, do you?" she asked fondly.

Sif shrugged and straightened, then strapped yet another blade to her body. Brunnhilde didn't like to think what would happen to her gown if she had to reach for that one. "What can I say, I'm the only funny one in Asgardia." She winked. "Ever seen the All-Father tell a joke?" she added pointedly.

That did make the Valkyrie laugh.

Sif smirked. "Besides, I like to keep you on your toes. Now, while I fetch my lady's meal, you sit there and try and work out how the elves are going about this magic of theirs. Try not to scream the place down while I'm gone."

She blew a kiss and slipped through the door before Brunnhilde could even begin to reply.

Lord John Dee sat in his library and stared at the wall. Fletcher, Francois, even Lady Jane and their beautiful boy Arthur had so far been unable to lift him from his gloom in the aftermath of his failure. Everyone had been here. Walsingham had been here, which was almost as bad as if Her Majesty herself had been in attendance. Witness to his failure.

His abject, babbling *nothing*. His perceived theatrics. He'd been convinced an angel would visit them and gift him with the reality of how to open the bridge to Heaven, to connect England with Paradise as was right and foretold. Hadn't Joseph of Arimathea himself come to England and brought the chalice from the Last Supper? England and Heaven had always been inextricably linked. Why else would England's king have discovered the true faith and shown it to his people?

And all John Dee had managed to do was take that faith, that truth, and fail in his task to call the angels and open the path. Fail in front of Walsingham. In front of *Bishop Aylmer*.

Oh, Father Michael had spoken of a strange woman appearing after the communion had failed, but Dee had seen nothing of the sort. As he was the one officiating the communion, any divine visitors would have shown themselves to him first. Besides, the poor man had somehow tripped over his cassock and knocked down three servants in his haste. His word couldn't be trusted.

The bishop had sent a note early that morning expressing false condolences on being found unworthy by the entity claiming to be an angel and positing that perhaps Dee was in fact being tempted by the devil.

Claiming to be an angel. *Tempted by the devil.* It was enough to make him scream. It was enough, in his secret heart of hearts, to make him wonder if Aylmer was right. Had he got it all wrong? Was the voice that of the devil, not an angel?

No. No! I refuse to believe that. The Church of England is my church. My God is the true God.

The man might as well have openly accused him of witchcraft or all of them of a collective lunacy caused by an overheating of the brain. Aylmer had gone on to advise that Dee refrain from attempting to repeat such a feat unless he first wished to take holy orders.

"Claiming to be an angel," he muttered, his voice rusty and disbelieving. It had been the only words to pass his lips all day.

What else could it have been? He'd felt that gathering power, felt the touch of a seraph's hand on the crown of his head. He was blessed, had been blessed. No one could doubt it. Not even the bishop of London.

And what did he have to show for it? No one had appeared. There had been no way forward when it came to it. He'd done all he could, put his heart and soul into that communion. Cried to the angels with every part of himself and his reward had been what? He'd lost everything, including his reputation, his standing at court, and his self-respect because *nothing had happened*.

Oh, the shew stone had glowed brighter than ever before and the power that gathered in the room had been undeniable, but still, for all that, nothing. Dee had been unable to complete the ritual and the angels, if they'd listened to him speak the seraphic tongue, had not deigned to reply.

When it became too much, when the power and the hurt from the stone grew unbearable, Dee had… given up. Dropped the stone with a gasp and broken the ritual, broken the building magic, the building *religion*. He had been found wanting, to Bishop Aylmer's obvious glee and Walsingham's thoughtful, silent regard.

He hadn't left the library since, spending hours poring over the notes he'd taken in the aftermath of each angelic communion to try and find where he'd gone wrong and why this communion had failed. Each repetition of the ritual had been stronger than the one before and had lasted longer. He'd read further through the book each time until he'd almost reached the end. Surely last night should have been it? Surely, he should have read the entire ritual and the angels should have appeared?

What had gone wrong? Where had he failed? *And in such company!*

Dee groaned long and loud and put his head down on the table, staring at the cherrywood box out of one bleary eye.

Dimly, he was aware that Jane was losing – or had lost – patience with him some time during the long, chilly night when she'd repeatedly exhorted him to come to bed, but the knowledge couldn't touch him. He'd been on the cusp of greatness, not just for himself but for all England, and it had been snatched away by his own failures.

It was too soon. I let my arrogance get the better of me. I should never have had an audience.

Walsingham would have reported his observation to the queen already, detailing Dee's failure. Bishop Aylmer could well be proclaiming Dee a witch from the pulpit even now. There might be soldiers on the way this very moment to arrest him and try him for witchcraft and what would happen to Jane and baby Arthur then? They'd be disgraced and tainted by his sins, cut off from their friends and contacts at court, ousted from their fine home and their names dragged through the mud until none would give them shelter.

And what would happen to the shew stone and the book? Would Aylmer proclaim them tools of the devil or would they find their way into Walsingham's hands, as so many secrets and important documents routinely did? Who would summon the angels and open the bridge to Paradise once Dee was dead and forgotten?

He needed to fix this. Somehow. He needed to conduct the ritual again – and again and again if that was what it took – until he'd mastered the power and learned the language and could open the bridge himself. And if he had only hours in which to do it, before Her Majesty's soldiers came to drag him to the Tower, then he'd best get on with it.

Dee returned to his papers and scrawled notes, looking for something, anything, that would assist him, something he might have overlooked that would allow him to focus and hold the ritual within him for long enough to open the bridge. There was nothing, of course. He'd memorized most of the notes, he'd read them so often. No, this was to come down to faith and strength, and this time Dee wouldn't be found wanting. He didn't need an audience; he didn't need outside validation. When the angels came to him, when the bridge to Heaven was open and England elevated as she should be, that would be reward enough. To do God's will was reward enough.

The maid knocked and came in, bobbed a curtsey at him, and set to cleaning out the hearth and laying kindling for a new fire. Dee drummed his fingers on the table while she fussed, barely reining in his impatience so he didn't snap at her, and even managed a reasonably sincere smile when she stopped at his elbow to clear away the previous night's supper things – the food was still there, the wine was not. She returned once more to collect the chamber pot and then the library was still and quiet and his again.

The fire was welcome after the long night he'd spent in here with the window broken and a cool draught insinuating its way into his bones.

"That doesn't matter," he reminded himself piously. "I offer up my suffering as penance and proof of my dedication. I will not leave this room until I have accomplished the angels' design for me."

Resolute and determined, he opened the lid of the box and removed the book, turning to the first page and laying his forefinger against it. He sucked in a deep breath, muttered another prayer, and picked up the stone.

Ten

Near Misses

Brunnhilde halted on the street so fast that Sif walked into her back.

"What's wrong?" the shield-maiden demanded, stepping to the Valkyrie's side and flexing her wrist in such a way that with a quick twist, a dagger would fall into her palm.

"Did you feel that?" Brunnhilde asked. They'd been wandering around London all morning, searching holy places, secluded places, haunting the mansions of the rich – as Sif pointed out, one thing about a rich person was usually that they wanted to be richer. If a Dark Elf seduced them with promises of wealth and fame, they might take it.

All to no avail. Worse, the roads here made no sense, hampering their admittedly vague plan. Every time they tried to head in a sensible direction, like west, within minutes the road would come to an end, or dogleg sharply, or split into three, or curve back on itself. *West* remained a distant dream unless they were prepared to leap across the roofs.

The Valkyrie had been sorely tempted when Sif suggested they do just that. Now, though, she closed her eyes and pressed her fingertips against her lids, not just to help her extend her senses but to try and stop their fatigue-induced burning. Sif had told her that she'd managed an hour of restful sleep in between the nightmares that plagued and then woke her. Each night it was less – what would this night bring?

Sif was silent now, boots scuffing the ground as she checked the road ahead and behind while Brunnhilde tried to feel what had stopped her. "There was … something," she said eventually, "but it's gone now. A whisper of something. It grew quickly – I could almost taste it – and then it stopped. Broke. Shattered."

"Elven magic?"

Brunnhilde chewed her bottom lip. "Dark but not. Familiar but strange, with an edge of… other about it."

"Dark but not? An edge of other?" Sif's voice was flat. She let out a breath so controlled it could barely be called a sigh, but which Brunnhilde knew was one anyway.

"I'm sorry I'm not being more helpful," she snapped, dropping her hand and rounding on the warrior, "but as the only one putting in any effort to sense this magic, you're just going to have to trust me."

There was long, dangerous silence and Brunnhilde reached for her friend's arm. "I'm sor–" she began.

Sif stepped backwards, out of reach, and glared. "You're very tired, and you're worried about Svartalfheim's intentions here and back on Asgard. I understand that," she said in a voice so cold it might have blown down a mountain on Jotunheim. "And for that reason alone I will not take offense at your tone or your implication of my lack of assistance. *However*. While you may be older and more powerful than I and enjoy the All-Father's respect and affection, do not mistake me for weak or for someone you can trample on easily. I am very much more than just my famous brother's little sister."

It was the Valkyrie's turn to glare, and angry words sat on the tip of her tongue that she swallowed with difficulty. She took a breath. "You are right, and I am sorry," she said formally. She meant it, too – mostly.

"I was entrusted with this mission alongside you, Bright-Battle," Siff added, softer now but still with that edge of steel. "I want to know what the elves are planning, and I want to help. But I'm not actually your lady-in-waiting and I'd appreciate it if you didn't treat me as such when we don't need to pretend otherwise. Nor am I your messenger or someone on whom you can vent your frustration – unless you want it reciprocated, that is?"

Brunnhilde winced at this reminder of their fierce former rivalry. "No. Of course not. What I said was unkind and untrue."

"Yes, it was." Sif hesitated, grimacing. "Though you're right: I felt nothing just then, no magic at all. But hasn't it occurred to you that the reason it calls to you and not me might be because it is powered by death? That is your province rather than mine. Or really any of the gods back on Asgard. If no one is looking for it, it might pass them by, especially if it only comes to them in dreams as it did you."

The Valkyrie stared at her, lips parted in shock. It hadn't occurred to her at all. She groaned and put her hand against her forehead. "If I wasn't so tired, I'd have seen that days ago," she muttered. "Though if it is death-driven, that just makes me even more concerned. Are people being killed to power this magic? I might not like the Dark Elves, but I don't like the idea of them being sacrificed to work this spell. And the sheer raw power that could be garnered by the taking of life... Odin's eye, I should have seen this!"

Sif chewed her lip. "Not necessarily," she said and Brunnhilde was surprised at the reassurance in her tone. She must really be worried to have let the Valkyrie's outburst go so quickly. "It wasn't until we came here that your dreams took on a shape and meaning you could recall. There was nothing to indicate why they plagued you before. But we now have definitive proof that out of the two of us, you're the only one who can sense it." The shield-maiden folded her arms. "Which is why, as much as I'd like to head out on my own and give us both some time away from each other, we need to stay together. Don't we? What good would I be on my own?" she added in a low mutter.

Brunnhilde winced. Sif's pride in her abilities was what drove her to prove her worth. It was the cornerstone of her sense of duty – and what often led to her reckless risk-taking. To feel useless here, in the Realm she had so little liking for, would make her more hot-tempered than usual.

And I'm not exactly the calm and controlled leader of the Choosers of the Slain, the Valkyrie reminded herself. There was a real possibility they'd end up at each other's throats as they had done for so long during their youth. She seized Sif's forearm in a tight grip. "There is *no one* I'd rather be in Midgard with," she said fiercely. "Your skills are unique and your abilities are remarkable and it is both an honor and a privilege to have you at my side."

Sif blinked, a little mollified. She nodded slightly.

"I think a division of labor is in order," she continued. "I'll do the magic-sensing…"

"Yes?" the raven-haired warrior asked, her mouth already curling into a smile.

"You break the heads of whoever's doing it."

Sif laughed and slipped her arm from Brunnhilde's grip. "Now that is a plan I can get behind. Which way?"

"South," the Valkyrie said. "Or south-ish, as far as these ridiculous roads will let us. The magic seemed to come from that direction."

"Good enough for me. Perhaps if we don't turn up anything today, we can search through the night?"

Brunnhilde snorted and they began to walk again. "Why not?" she said with an air of resignation. "It's not as if I'll be sleeping otherwise."

They'd gone barely a hundred yards before the road began curving to the west. The Asgardians sighed and cursed the humans who'd built this city. Together, they began looking for an alley or a crossroads to lead them back in the right direction. South.

Or at least south-ish.

William had rowed them back from Mortlake as fast as his youthful strength could carry them, and Hela had tracked the magical residue left by Bifrost to Clerkenwell, though by the time she'd reached it, there was no one there other than the usual humans milling like sheep.

Some careful questioning had led her to listen with growing contempt to the excited speculation about the fearsome warrior women who'd appeared to entertain the crowd, fighting for coin and showing off martial skills such as had never been seen before, apparently. The possibilities for the identities of the Asgardians sent by Odin were considerably fewer in light of that information, and the revelation that one of the women had black hair had confirmed, at least, the identity of Lady Sif. From there, it wasn't hard to guess who the other must be, and Hela had made discreet enquiries until she learned in which direction they'd headed.

"You should be careful if you see them again," she'd told the merchant who'd given her the information. "They're not what they appear."

The man had scoffed. "What are they then, spies for the Spanish?"

Hela had put her head on one side. "You said yourself several members of the court want to engage their services. What better way to get invited into the houses of the rich and influential than by appearing as simple entertainers?" She'd leaned closer. "What better way to get invited to court itself, to perform for the queen? Perhaps they're spies. Perhaps they're assassins."

The merchant had blanched and muttered his thanks before hurrying away. Hela knew that the rumor would fly through the market and the district, taking on shape and substance until, with luck, it would hinder the Asgardians' progress through the city and make them objects of suspicion wherever they went. If they didn't know about Dee and the elven stone yet, the rumors could buy Hela time to complete her examination of the stone and its magic before taking it back to Helheim.

And she needed that time, because not even a night's rest after an afternoon and evening of failing to locate the Asgardians had restored her magic. Either the stone itself or the ritual Dee had performed had stolen a good portion of it and she would risk nothing until she understood how and why. Until her strength returned, she would not risk visiting Mortlake again. The best she could do now was delay the Asgardians and replenish her power.

William had disappeared at dusk but returned this morning, still in his footman's finery and seemingly immune to her bad temper and her threats. If anything, his infatuation was only growing stronger. Three times so far today she'd felt the magic of the focal stone activate, edged with panic and determination. Dee's exhibition the previous day – specifically its failure – had clearly rattled him. If there was any truth to what she was feeling, then the man was desperate to make some sort of breakthrough.

Hela could feel the magic growing, the fishhook it had in her ribs pulling harder each time he performed the spell. Would the Valkyrie be feeling the same? Her particular sensitivity to the ending of life was surely the reason she'd been sent here: the stone was drawing on Dee's life force to fuel itself, she'd felt that clearly when she'd been in his presence. It would take his life before it was done, and that was likely the final step the spell needed to open the bridge – the sacrifice of a life to tear open the Realms.

But it had also seized on Hela's magic and stripped it from her. Magic fueled by her life essence. The stone fed on life until it was gone and then ate death. Only her power and abilities were a shield between the stone's appetite and Hela's precious life force. If the Valkyrie was even a hundredth as sensitive as Hela herself, it was likely she'd been called here by the death magic, too. She'd know the general direction in which she needed to go to find the stone. More worryingly the two Asgardians might have enough life force between them to sate the stone's appetite and render it dormant, allowing them to claim it for Odin.

Or maybe they'll unwittingly power the ritual and open the bridge. I dislike either outcome.

That was why Hela was haunting the southward road and had sent the boy to find the nearest warden. She stalked up and down a little more, the sun hot on her head and shoulders and her cloak thrown back to lessen the heat.

There was a crowd approaching, some sort of procession, perhaps. Hela scanned the faces. Was that–?

"My lady? I am Warden Mark Piper in charge of this district. I understand you have information for me."

Hela didn't reply, didn't even glance around, her gaze locked on two tall figures in the middle of the crowd. One fair; one dark.

"My lady? I got the warden for you like you asked," William said, brushing a fingertip against the back of her hand. She snatched it away, recoiling, and glared at him. He was blushing furiously but jerked his head at the armored man, who bowed slightly.

Hela glanced at him – tall and broad-shouldered, with well-fitting armor and a sword in a battered but serviceable sheath. A real fighting man, unlike the one who'd accosted her the first day she was here.

"You know of the Spanish spies afoot in the city?" she

asked. "Two women, foreign and pretty, pretending to be entertainers?"

"Well, my lady, that's the rumor. But rumors are like fleas, you see – no one's immune and we all love a good scratch."

Hela's lip curled. "I don't see," she said shortly and turned back to the crowd, went up onto her tip toes and then nodded decisively. "But that's them. The spies. There, you see? There, man!" She pointed. "So I suggest you go and arrest them at once."

"What?" Warden Piper stared at her as if she was quite mad, and then obligingly followed her pointing finger to the crowd, which had turned down a side street. "I don't see... two women, you say? That's hardly the sort of description I can use to make an arrest, my lady. I'd need more than that. I'd need evidence."

"Useless," Hela growled and shoved past him. "I'll settle this myself." She'd wanted a Midgardian to handle this so she didn't need to use any more magic, but clearly everyone here was incompetent. She hurried after the dispersing crowd – not a procession, after all, it seemed – when the warden caught hold of her arm, just briefly enough to stop her.

"Forgive me, my lady, but I can't have people causing a fuss in the streets. It wouldn't be proper for a gentlewoman such as yourself to be shouting like a fishwife."

"Shouting like a – do you have any idea who I am? Who they are and what they are capable of doing here? I'll do more than shout at them, you imbecile," Hela said and dragged her sword out of William's basket.

"My lady," Piper exclaimed. "I must insist you do no such thing. I will go and look for these women and – ah!"

The lad yelped too and then whooped as Hela cast her glamour to disappear from view and set off after the Asgardians.

"Idiots. Morons. I'd be better off dealing with trolls," Hela spat as she hurried after the dispersing crowd. Sif and the Valkyrie had been among them, she was sure of it: tall and cloaked, strands of dark hair blowing free from one hood and blonde from the other, and both walking with the predatory stalk of a born warrior. It had to be.

Despite her words to the warden, the goddess of Hel had no intention of revealing herself to the Asgardians. She didn't want a confrontation: she wanted them delayed. Hindered. Stopped from heading south. All he'd needed to do was arrest them; now, she'd have to do that herself.

Hela paused at the corner to make sure she was out of Warden Piper's view. Then, concentrating, she twisted her glamour into his likeness and stepped around the corner wearing his face and clothes. She was outside a theatre, the destination for the crowd, she presumed, though why the Asgardians would go to a performance – ah, no, there they were.

Holding the illusion tight against her skin, Hela marched towards them. How was it she'd been spoken to when she first arrived? "You there! You women! Turn and identify yourselves," she bellowed, her sheathed sword in hand.

The cloaked figures paused and then turned to face her. "Warden?" one asked, her tone high and wavering and somehow wrong.

Hela hesitated, suddenly wrong-footed. "Speak your names," she snarled and the pair pushed back their hoods to reveal … men. Confused, nervous men in gowns and wigs and far too many cosmetics, one dark and one fair. "What is this?" she demanded. "Who are... did Loki put you up to this?"

The men exchanged confused glances. "Who?" the other one asked. They were both very young, boys closer to William's age instead of men, with sweet unbroken voices and beardless chins at odds with their height and gangling limbs. What Hela had taken for a warrior's strut was instead a boy's attempt to control his body and seem older than his years. While wearing a dress.

"You..." she tried, and then trailed off.

A short, rotund man emerged from the theatre's entrance. "Where the devil have you been? And how many times must I tell you not to wear your costumes in the street between shows? We'll all end up in clink one of these days because of you! At least take off the wigs! One more episode like this and you'll both be replaced! Plenty of lads in London want to be actors, you know."

The pair glanced at Hela again, still uncertain, but it seemed they were more afraid of their employer than her – or the warden she appeared to be, at least. They turned and scampered into the theatre with their skirts bunched up and Hela was left standing staring at after them, nonplussed.

"Warden? Is aught amiss? I assure you, we've no pickpockets or street women among our number. We're all members of the guild and I've got a license to produce plays from his lordship the..."

Hela turned on her heel and stalked away.

"But why not?" she asked again.

William looked increasingly scandalized and it would have

been funny that Hela had finally found something to make the boy shut up if it wasn't so nonsensical. "Women can't act, Your Highness. They just can't. It would be obscene. It goes against nature and against God."

Hela whirled away and stood staring out across the river. They were back on its bank again – traversing its wide expanse was the easiest way to navigate London and all manner of people and goods were transported along its brown curving length every day. She breathed deeply, fists clenching and unclenching in the folds of her skirt.

"This Realm," she grated. Anger rolled like a corpse in the shallows. "This *backward, stupid Realm.*" She took a few more breaths while the boy hovered by her elbow, uncertain. "Very well. It wasn't them at the theatre. However, if they do need more money, they'll have to fight for a crowd again. When will there be more street entertainment?"

"Well, there's nearly always a few performers in the city, Your Highness," the boy hedged. "Look, just wait here a while, will you? I'll be back, I promise. Here," he added absently and shoved the basket's handle at her. Hela took it on reflex and William darted away before she could speak.

The goddess of Hel threw the basket to the ground, sword and armor clattering together under the covering of clothes. "I am going to *murder this entire city* if I don't get some answers," she said with the sort of icy calm that would have Eirik, her whole court and even Fenris the wolf tucking tail and cowering.

Fortunately for all of London, William was as good as his word and returned within half an hour. He was red-faced and panting, his hat askew and his doublet half undone. "God's teeth, but it's hot," he puffed and put his hands on his knees to get his breath back.

"Well?" Hela snapped.

William pushed upright. "All right, there's talk of the German Warrior Women fighting at the fair at Lincoln's Inn Fields this afternoon. Come on, it's only a few miles."

"Only a few... Absolutely not. I have had enough of traipsing through the filth like a common peasant. I will buy a horse and you can lead the way." She put her hands on her hips and stared around the river. "Now. Where can I buy a horse?"

By the time they'd walked south and found a horse market and Hela had selected and paid for a beautiful, glossy black mare, they were almost at the fair anyway. Still, she mounted up and rode the final distance, getting a feel for the animal and glad to be out of the stink and removed from the rest of the population. The combination of her clothes and the horse was enough that people automatically moved out of her way and watched her as she passed. A storm of murmurs followed at the mare's tail.

Besides, now she had the horse for the return journey to Mortlake, which improved her mood marginally. She'd seen the wide, flat-bottomed ferries operated by chains crisscrossing the river. She could lead the horse on, cross, remount and canter all the way to Dee, hopefully replenishing her magic as she did so. Then she'd finally unlock the secrets of the stone and take it and the book back to Eljudnir. She'd set Fenris to guard the stone and book while Hela herself luxuriated in a bath and scrubbed the stink of this Realm, this city and its people from her skin.

The fair itself was set on a wide green with brightly colored stalls and large trestle tables holding barrels of beers set at one end. The middle of the space was given over to entertainment, and crowds ringed around the various performers to watch, gamble, and jeer or cheer according to their preference. Hela had left the horse loose in the paddock at the far end of the fair, flipping a coin to the grooms to keep an eye on her. She'd contemplated telling the boy to stay, but the fair was crowded, and she had appearances to maintain.

The noise and bustle pressed against her skin and eardrums, distracting, almost overwhelming. It was probably for the best if the boy pushed through the crowd on her behalf. The alternative was Hela's loss of temper and the indiscriminate consequences of her death touch.

But oh, the temptation.

No. Conserve your magic, she reminded herself. She hated this: there had been only a handful of times in her long life where her powers had been limited – and limited her in turn. It did very little for her mood.

Hela waited in a small clear space between the edge of the stalls and the start of the crowd while William interrogated the vendors. There were at least three different pieces of music being played nearby, none of them in time or in tune with the others. Over that the shouts of merchants, the cheers of gamblers, and the applause of the crowd.

Still, her hearing was excellent. "The German Warrior Women fight today, don't they?" William was asking. "Are they here yet? I want to see. Big as King Henry himself was, I heard. Is that true? Where are they then?"

How much was genuine interest and how much playacting,

Hela didn't know, but she had to admit that the boy got results. He was back at her side within moments, grinning ear to ear under his crooked – again – hat. Her fingers itched to straighten it; she resisted the urge with an inner recoil of horror. This Realm was infecting her with its grubby brand of madness. The sooner she could see the Asgardians dealt with, the sooner she could return to Dee and finally Realm-jump home.

She wasn't going to glamour as a warden this time, oh no. Hela had a far better idea and one that would see her found completely innocent of what was going to happen.

"This way, my lady," William said, gesturing with the basket and taking her hand for an instant before jerking his own away as if he'd put it too near a fire. He blushed. "They're over there."

ELEVEN

A WRETCHED INSULT

"Why not, Bright-Battle?" Sif wheedled. "We've spent all day searching. Let's get something to eat, mingle with the crowd, and see what passes for entertainment here. We were rather too busy fighting last time to see what the others were up to."

"You think a human juggler is going to impress you?" Brunnhilde asked skeptically.

"Absolutely not," the warrior said promptly. "I want to see how bad they are so I can laugh at them, and I want a cup of ale if they don't have mead, and I want one of those meat pies I can smell. Come on, what's the worst that can happen? Besides, there's going to be so much gossip flying around a gathering like this. Who knows what we might learn that will aid us?"

"You think we should start asking who's casting elven magic in Midgard?" the Valkyrie asked sourly. Sif gave her an unimpressed look. She sighed and waved her on. "Fine. We'll go to the fair."

Sif did a little dance in place, an expression of glee so unlike her that it forced a reluctant smile onto Brunnhilde's face. "You're such a child," she said fondly.

The shield-maiden sucked in a breath. "You take that back," she said but she was still grinning. "Oh, come on. Food, beer, gossip, entertainment. If we don't learn anything after a few hours, we'll leave and start again, how about that?" She sobered. "I'm not treating this as a holiday, Bright-Battle. I haven't forgotten why we're here. But I do think it might do you some good to release some of this tension. At the very least, it can't hurt, can it?"

Brunnhilde supposed she couldn't argue with that, either. She waved Sif on ahead of her and they slipped through the throng milling about the sunny field. There was a paddock of loose, grazing horses and then various rings of cheering onlookers. Tiered wooden benches had been erected opposite a few, probably for the nobility to relax on while they watched the entertainments.

The Asgardians were dressed well enough that the man guarding the steps leading up to the benches bowed and stepped aside after they'd handed him a penny each – a price that made Brunnhilde blink, knowing what she did now about the expense of things here. But she couldn't deny her weariness and the chance to sit and watch some mindless fun for an hour might even be a good thing. She could let herself be occupied while her senses roamed ever-farther in search of the source of elven magic, elven lies.

They sat high enough that they could see over the heads of the crowd ringing the grassy space. Sif peered down and then slumped back immediately. "Jugglers," she groused and took an enormous bite of her pie, pastry crumbling to dot her bodice. "I could do better than that blindfolded with one hand tied behind my back."

"Maybe you should," Brunnhilde said absently. "Give them a show and earn us some more coin."

"I thought we were supposed to be inconspicuous?"

Brunnhilde eyed her sidelong and then gestured to their seats. "Practically invisible," she agreed blandly.

The shield-maiden snorted. "No one is going to recognize us as—"

"The German Warrior Women, last seen in Clerkenwell, will perform to entertain the crowd! Make way, make way."

Sif choked on her pie and Brunnhilde tensed, but no one was looking at them. In fact, all heads had turned to face to their right and a gap was opening up in the ring of onlookers, appreciative murmurs and excited chatter a rising tide all around them. Even the nobles scattered along the benches were straining forward, tracking the approaching cloaked figures.

"What—" Sif began in an outraged whisper. Brunnhilde clamped her hand on the warrior's and they both looked down as the pie crushed between their joined grip. "Ugh," Sif exclaimed and scraped the mess off her hand onto the bench next to her. She was about to complain when the figures stepped into the circle in front of them.

The Valkyrie passed her a handkerchief from her pack and then sat up straight, intent. "What is this?" she murmured and almost heard Sif roll her eyes.

"So you can ask it but I can't?" she complained, still wiping her hand, but there was no heat to her accusation. The warriors were stalking the ring in opposite directions, flinging up their arms to the crowd, demanding applause and cheers. When they passed each other, they lunged in lightly as if to begin combat; there were gasps and a few squeals from the audience, but then they kept marching.

"My lords, ladies and gentlemen, these two great warriors of fearsome reputation and worldwide renown are here for your entertainment. As a token of goodwill, gentles, a small show of English hospitality to two such terrifying killers while I tell you their history and origins, for such plays a part in their abilities."

The speaker stepped into the center of the circle and raised his arms: a small scatter of silver arced towards him from every side. He bowed gracefully and collected it.

"Born in the dark forests of Bavaria and raised by a legendary immortal warrior from the time of the Roman Empire, Greta and Hilda were taught only warfare from the time they could walk. Fed on a diet of raw meat and icy mountain water, they grew strong and fierce and mighty, full of courage and spirit. There may be some of you who were fortunate enough to see them perform in Clerkenwell, but here, today, they will give you a full demonstration of their talents. They–"

"This is horse–" Sif began.

"Quiet. I want to know what he says about us. And I want to see who's under those hoods."

"It's a wretched insult, Bright-Battle. Aren't you insulted? *I'm* insulted."

Brunnhilde shrugged. "Honestly? I'm a little flattered that we've been here one day and have made enough of an impression that people are impersonating us. That and the fact it helps us to stay anonymous."

"They're profiting from our reputation," the shield-maiden insisted and for a moment Brunnhilde thought she was going to go down there and confront the trio herself.

"If they're good enough, I'll toss them a penny myself," she said and felt something lighten in her chest at her friend's outraged squawk. "Now please be quiet, I want to know more about the immortal warrior who raised us. Have you ever eaten raw meat?" she added, just to get another squawk, despite her request for silence.

As stories went, it was entertainment in itself, as proven by the second shower of coins tossed onto the grass. And then it was time for the demonstration. The Valkyrie was just wondering whether they'd fight with their hoods on when the pair – tall and broad enough to pass for them under the shapeless material, she had to admit – tossed away the concealing cloaks. The first thing she noticed was the attempt at armor, which looked like it had been beaten out of large pewter dishes; the second was that they were men; the third was Sif's outrage quickly boiling over into anger.

Brunnhilde didn't know how anyone could mistake the pair for women, but they began moving before the cloaks had even drifted to the ground. Their eyes were heavily outlined in charcoal, their cheeks and lips were rouged and she supposed she should be grateful that at least they didn't have beards.

They wore wigs of what she was pretty sure was horsehair, one pale, one black, and the "Sif" in the ring tumbled backwards out of range with a comely enough series of backflips that it raised a cheer from the crowd.

The "Brunnhilde" followed and they came together in a

flash and clatter of swords that told her they were acrobats and possibly stage-fighters, but certainly no more.

"Well, they weren't taught to fight in the snowy forests of darkest Bavaria, wherever that is," the Valkyrie murmured even as the rest of the crowd was apparently convinced by their poor disguises. "They may also never father children if they, ah, don't loosen whatever's binding their ... parts in place. Surely they could have just worn looser trousers?"

Sif was rigid beside her, but she turned her head at that, so much tension in her frame her neck muscles almost creaked. "Do you think this is *funny?*" she hissed with such venom that the Valkyrie lost the last vestiges of her self-control and began to laugh, quietly into her sleeve at first, and then uncontrollably. Days of tension and weeks of sleepless nights combined to push her dangerously close to hysteria, and every time she looked at Sif, the shield-maiden's utter indignation sent her off into a fresh paroxysm of giggles.

"I'm sorry, I'm sorry," she gasped when it looked as if Sif was actually going to leave her there, possibly to shove her way into the ring and beat both impersonators to death with their own wigs. "It's just... how is anyone believing this? It's so obvious they're men!"

A young nobleman leaned over from the bench above at that. "Forgive me for overhearing, my ladies, but, well," he coughed delicately into his hand, "I fear if you were expecting the fairer sex to be here fighting, you have been duped indeed. Of course the pair yesterday were men. Why, it's beyond belief that someone of your delicate nature could indulge in such rough play as what's going on down there." He gave them a faintly pitying look. "Did you really expect women?" he asked again and made little effort to hide the smirk twisting his mouth.

Sif gave him a coolly appraising glance. "It doesn't matter what we believe," she said. "What matters is the people being hoodwinked and giving their hard-earned coin to a trio of liars and thieves." She folded her arms over her chest. "Besides, you can see from their footwork they haven't the first clue about real combat. They're standing far too close together for a start as if they don't have enough room to maneuver instead of all that space. That's what you do when you're fighting for show. For another thing, I'd bet every coin I have and the clothes on my back that those swords are blanks, without even an edge. Third–"

"Someone else doesn't buy the illusion," Brunnhilde said loudly, cutting Sif off before she really got going. The nobleman looked as if he'd been hit in the head with a pan anyway, his mouth hanging open in a speechless daze.

Sif swung back to view the so-called entertainment. A knot of onlookers was remonstrating angrily with the speaker of the little group, demanding the return of their coin, their voices strident. They were moving in concert, almost as if hypnotized or–

"They're under someone's control," the shield-maiden breathed. "Is it them? Dark Elves? I don't see any blueskins."

Brunnhilde was already casting out her senses for alien magic, sweeping the fair. More and more people were being caught up in the enchantment, the calls for the return of their money getting louder and more belligerent. The actors in the circle had come to a halt and were flinging their cloaks back on and pulling up the hoods, then bunching together and searching uneasily for a way out. One was scrubbing off his makeup: if he hoped to get out unnoticed he'd need to ditch more than that. He was wearing pewter armor, for Odin's sake.

The crowed wasn't turning violent – yet – but, as laughably outnumbered as they were, they'd be in real trouble if it did.

"Wait," Sif said suddenly, tensing. "I feel it. I feel… something." The Valkyrie turned to her in surprise and quested harder, but there was nothing. She felt nothing.

There was a shout of genuine anger and a scuffle on the grass. "We should get down there," Sif added, leaping to her feet and dragging Brunnhilde up by the arm. "They might need our help."

Distracted that Sif felt something she didn't, it took the Valkyrie a second to parse her meaning and then she nodded: indignation at being impersonated by someone as unskilled as those men was one thing, but the shield-maiden would never see people overwhelmed and attacked if she could do something to help.

They hurried down the steps of the tiered benches and began pushing their way into the crowd on the opposite side to the disturbance. Three score people were acting in concert now and the trio looked outright terrified. There was a flicker of something magical and illusory that tugged at Brunnhilde like a fishhook to her ribs. She halted and cast about, looking left and right and stretching out with her senses, but the connection broke and dissipated before she could get a grip on it.

The moment it did, the angry mob came to an uncertain, milling halt. The entertainers took their chance and bolted.

"I felt it too," she said, inexplicably relieved. "Just for a moment, but it disappeared before I could identify it."

All of Sif's unnerving attention snapped to the Valkyrie now there was no danger of a riot breaking out. "Why could I feel it this time but not before? And feel it before you did? Did whoever's doing this recognize us?" The shield-maiden's fingers twitched towards the knife in her sleeve. "Or was it a mistake that I sensed them? Is that why they stopped, to conceal themselves from our view? When it was just you sensing them–"

Brunnhilde grunted and cut her off. "No. Whoever they are, they're our enemies. They'd have turned that crowd on us if they'd known we were here. But just as they didn't see us, we haven't seen them." The Valkyrie turned in a circle and examined the dispersing crowd. Frustration clawed at her throat. "It didn't feel the same," she muttered. "That wasn't the magic I felt before. That was something else, something that you can sense."

"Which means I've been in contact with it before, been exposed to it, or attacked by it, before." She gave a short, humorless laugh. "That doesn't narrow it down as much as I'd hoped. Our troubles have just doubled. There's someone else on Midgard, isn't there?"

Brunnhilde rubbed her palms together, the rasp of sword calluses over skin a familiar comfort. "Yes," she said at last. "I think we're not the only ones called to by the Dark Elves' magic. But whether they're allied with Svartalfheim or seeking the magic's source as we are, I don't know."

Sif was quiet for a long time. "Well," she said eventually, with false brightness. "That's fun, isn't it? I do love a challenge, after all."

"Sif, please," Brunnhilde groaned. "Just for once, can you not?"

The shield-maiden raised her hands in surrender. "Apologies," she said soothingly. "So, let's be logical. Whoever did this, has to be here somewhere, close enough to see and manipulate the crowd, for whatever reason... oh no."

The Valkyrie's head snapped around. "What? Do you see them?"

"That was meant for us. Those actors, the so-called German Warrior Women, Greta and Hilda. They're us. Whoever was here was trying to get to us, only *we* were up there on the benches, not down here vulnerable to a crowd. Someone heard that *we'd* be fighting and set out to lay a trap for us. The sort of trap we'd be loath to fight our way out of because we'd be hurting civilians manipulated against their will."

It made a sick sort of sense. "So what was their plan?"

Sif shrugged. "I don't know how things work here, but I wouldn't be surprised if you can get arrested for being a woman and a warrior. I think it's one of their many sins. Maybe whoever planned this wants us out of the way so they can find the elven magic? Either way, if it had been us fighting down there, maybe if the crowd rushed us, we'd have hurt someone by accident. We'd definitely have been in trouble then and there's a decent number of official-looking men in armor hereabouts."

"So what do you want to do?" Brunnhilde asked as the implications of their predicament slid home like a dagger through flesh. "Slip away and hope we're not recognized?" Sif scowled and the Valkyrie managed a crooked smile. "Or go for a wander and see if they're still here so we can find out who it is and what they're doing."

"Now you're talking my language," Sif said and kicked ineffectually at her skirts. "Odin's eye, but I miss my trousers. And my armor. And my sword. And–"

"Yes, yes, let's get on," Brunnhilde interrupted, but inside she was brimming with worry. Something was wrong, its edges tickling her mind. She needed to know what it was. *She needed to.*

Hela had been too far away to see their faces when they uncloaked, but it had taken all of three seconds to realize the performers in the ring weren't the Valkyrie and the raven-haired shield-maiden.

She'd very nearly lost control of her temper and her magic, but instead she'd channeled both into an illusion and compulsion, one that spread from person to person via contact and as such cost her less to cast. It had been as much a warning to the Asgardians, wherever they were, as it was a reaction to this stupid Realm and its stupid people, but it had done little to make her feel better.

Now she rode the mare at a trot out of Lincoln's Inn Field with William running after her, red-faced, with the basket in one hand and the other clamping his permanently askew hat to his head.

She had a few more ideas to make the warriors' lives difficult. It was time to implement them all.

Hela turned the horse aside and dismounted when she reached a quiet street. She waited impatiently for the boy to catch up, then thrust the reins into his hand.

"You are to go home and then return to the inn near Mortlake tomorrow morning, early. If I am not there, you will wait for me. You will not leave, you will not move, you will not speak of me or my whereabouts. If you do any of these things, I shall wind your guts out on a stick and make you wear them for a hat. Am I clear?"

"Y- yes, my lady. Your Highness. Very clear."

She thanked the tailor for his idea of sewing a skirt and bodice together instead of making a full gown; she'd spent the previous evening unpicking the two and then tacking them back in place. Now, with a single hard jerk, she ripped the skirt free. William squeaked and turned his back, face flaming. Hela rolled her eyes and stepped out of the skirt, revealing her trousers and boots, greaves already strapped to her legs. She buckled on the rest of her armor and then dropped the skirt back in the basket. Lastly, she pulled out her sword.

"Turn around, little fool. Good. Now tell me, which is the fastest route to the house of Lord Walsingham?"

TWELVE

DESPAIR

Dusk was falling when Brunnhilde and Sif found a new inn, leery of returning to Peter's establishment after the events at the fair.

Their search for the Dark Elves' accomplice had proven fruitless, the fair so crowded that even when they'd split up to seek out the scent of magic, they hadn't been able to find it.

In the end, they'd given up and focused on the Elven magic again as being the bigger and more urgent threat. The more Brunnhilde reached for it, the more the voice she'd been hearing in her dreams reached back. It was disconcerting, whispering its lies in a silken tongue, inviting her to agree, to see its promises as a way to glory.

She ignored it as best she could, focusing instead on where it might lead her, but the magic was crafty and gave away nothing of itself. Whoever was manipulating it had apparently decided to rest for a while as there were no further bursts of power as the spell was activated. The Valkyrie was both grateful for it – it meant the ritual couldn't be completed – and dismayed, for she only had a definite idea of its location when the spell was active.

Now, however, they were footsore and despondent. Brunnhilde was both anticipating and dreading the coming night and the disrupted dreams and visions it would bring. She put up no protest when Sif insisted they stop at a brewery and buy a tall, cool pitcher of ale. Like Peter and Sal's inn, the new tavern keep had very firm ideas on what passed as an acceptable drink for "two such fine ladies as yourselves, gentlewomen, you grace my humble inn with your presence, here is my finest wine".

His finest wine was both poor and expensive and ordinarily Brunnhilde wouldn't have drunk it. Tonight, though, she lingered in the common room while Sif took the ale up to their room and then, on a whim, bought a bottle of the awful stuff and requested two cups. Sif returned quickly, alarm written across her features, and then frowned when she saw the Valkyrie sitting at a small table in a corner lit by what were probably the innkeeper's finest candles and candlesticks.

"I bought the so-called good stuff," she said when Sif approached. The shield-maiden arched a black eyebrow. "Maybe if I drink enough, I'll sleep tonight."

"What about the ale?"

"That's for after the wine runs out," she said darkly.

Sif winced. "Maybe you'll sleep," she conceded, "or maybe you'll be exhausted and hungover and short-tempered." When Brunnhilde just shrugged, the shield-maiden sighed, but she poured herself a cup and sat anyway. "This isn't like you, Bright-Battle," she said in a low voice that didn't carry to the next table, or to the barkeep, who was spending a suspiciously long time collecting cups and plates nearby, an ingratiating smile permanently plastered to his face.

"I know. I just ... we don't even know what we're looking for and now there's this second complication, this ally of Svartalfheim doing their best to delay us. And I know that sleeping will bring the dreams, and that that's probably a good thing. I'm just so tired, Sif. I'm so tired that I don't want the dreams." She laughed bitterly and drained her cup. "How's that for dereliction of duty?"

"Hey now," Sif said immediately. "Less of that. It's perfectly reasonable that you're finding this difficult and today's revelations have just added another layer of complexity to the whole mystery we're here to unravel. All this is falling on your shoulders, but think what we've learned so far. One: we know what the elves are planning and we can guess why – conquest. Two: we know that they're somewhere in the south of this city, and we're in the south, so it's only a matter of time before we find them. Shut up," she added at Brunnhilde's skeptical snort.

"Three: we know they have an accomplice, and that's something I can help with, because I can feel their magic. So I'll deal with them and you concentrate on finding the elves. Four..." she trailed off.

"Not much to go on, is there?" the Valkyrie said, topping up her cup again.

"No, no, wait. Four: each time you dream, you learn a bit more of what they want–"

"We know what they want."

"Shut *up*. You learn about the ritual itself. We have Frigga's bracelet, so maybe there's a way we can disrupt the spell they're casting." She looked doubtful even as she said it, eyeing the heavy gold bangle with its weight of jewels. Two already were cracked and dull and they'd need to use another tonight to muffle Brunnhilde's distress as she dreamed. It was unlikely to have enough power to disrupt a ritual that had called to her across the Realms.

"Perhaps," Brunnhilde conceded, instead of pointing out any of that because she didn't want to dampen Sif's enthusiasm any more than she already had. "I just worry that our plan seems to be that we wait around until I sense a burst of magic and then close in on its location as best we can. Each time that magic is activated, each time that spell or ritual is performed, the elves come a step closer to opening the bridge between here and Svartalfheim and despite all their promises, I really don't think they're going to arrive here carrying bouquets and gifts. Even with the Midgardians' profusion of iron, even with our aid, they won't stand against the Dark Elves' might and they need to, Sif. If Svartalfheim brings Midgard under its sway, they'll be able to attack Asgard from two points, with twice the warriors. They won't hesitate to use humans against us. They won't care how many lives are lost. They'll throw them at us without a thought, as if they're just meat for our swords to cleave.

"And the humans ... They won't stand against Svartalfheim because they don't know they're coming. They can't plan for an invasion they're ignorant of. And you've heard the talk – they speak of imminent war with Spain and what are they doing about it? Are they training soldiers? No!"

Sif was wide-eyed, her cup poised halfway to her mouth, arrested by Brunnhilde's outburst.

"Think about it," the Valkyrie continued after draining her cup again. "Say the bridge opens into London, what happens then? Midgardians start screaming and running, Dark Elves pour out and start cutting them down. Where do they form a defense? Who stands and fights?" She gestured at the crowded room. "Farmers, merchants, innkeepers, tavern girls. Where are the warriors, Sif? Where's the army? An iron frying pan might burn an elf, but it won't kill them. Only swords, spear heads and arrow tips can do that. And where are they? You think you and I together can hold the end of a bridge to another Realm?"

Sif took Brunnhilde's cup away. "That's enough," she said shortly. "You need to sleep."

"Weren't you listening?" the Valkyrie began, reaching for it.

Sif scooped it and the bottle out of her way. "You need to sleep so you can dream, Bright-Battle. You need to welcome the nightmares and learn from them. If I could do it for you, I would, but I can't. So you have to do this and do it tonight. We can't risk everything you just said coming to pass."

"Good evening, miladies. Anything I can help you with? We've still got a bite of supper left if you're hungry." The innkeep appeared at Sif's elbow like a ghost and Brunnhilde wondered how much he'd overheard. "Or some bread and cheese if you prefer, goes nice with that fine wine."

"No, thank you," Sif said quickly. "My lady's already eaten." The man nodded and didn't move, instead waggling his eyebrows conspiratorially. Sif was reaching for a ha'penny to encourage him on his way when Brunnhilde pushed back from the table and stood.

"This lady needs some fresh air," she snarled and marched to the door before either of them, not even Sif with her famous speed, could respond. She didn't stop until she was a few hundred yards from the inn on a wide thoroughfare, breathing deeply of air that was anything but fresh, redolent of horse dung and rotting vegetables. It didn't matter. Nothing mattered. Brunnhilde was *failing*. That was what mattered, but no matter how much she concentrated on their mission, the thought of sleeping brought unease. A whiff of fear.

She clenched a scarred fist and barely resisted the urge to punch it through the nearest wall... and keep punching until something broke – either the house or her temper.

"Devil worshiper!"

"Begone, succubus. We'll not have your sort around here, noble lady or not. God will still judge you – and your accursed husband!"

Brunnhilde spun to the outcry, her temper flaring with her. If they were speaking of her...

A horse-drawn carriage was stopped behind a wagon loaded high with barrels, and a small crowd of children and drunkards had surrounded it, heckling the slender figures within. A face looked out and the Valkyrie caught sight of a terrified young woman, pale and delicate.

"My husband has done nothing wrong," she said to Brunnhilde's surprise – she was braver than she appeared, especially surrounded with nowhere to go and only a maid and the coach driver to attend to her. "Her Majesty the queen examined both the book and the shew stone and found nothing untoward about them. They–"

"He's consorting with demons and you're one too if you say

otherwise," a teenage boy shouted, his voice cracking halfway through to the derision of his friends. The lad blushed and then picked up a broken piece of cobble. He had a point to prove now, a reputation to restore.

Brunnhilde caught his wrist as he pulled back his arm to throw it at the carriage. "What are you doing?" she demanded, making no effort to rein in her temper.

"Who're you?" the boy scoffed, but he couldn't free himself from her grip. "Get off me!"

A shrill scream interrupted them and the Valkyrie looked over to find a drunk had pulled open the carriage's door. Brunnhilde swept the lad's feet from under him and sent him careening into his friends, stepped into the gap he left and grabbed the man by the shoulder and the seat of his trousers and tossed him aside.

"Are you hurt, my lady?" Brunnhilde asked. The two women inside shook their heads. "Where is your destination?"

"H- home to Mortlake, south of London, to my lord husband John Dee. Who is not a necromancer!" she shouted past Brunnhilde and then quickly sat back in the carriage, her fingers knotted together.

"They are poor and uneducated, Lady Dee. Do not listen to their gossip," Brunnhilde said, leaning in to put her hand over the other woman's and give it a gentle squeeze. "It is a fine thing to see a beautiful lady who is so brave," she murmured.

She stared deep into the woman's eyes and then smiled and stepped back. Lady Dee brought one hand up to her throat, a faint blush staining her cheeks. "I'll see the wagon ahead of you is moved," Brunnhilde said smoothly.

She turned away, only for the man she'd ejected from the

carriage to make a clumsy, drunken swing at her. Brunnhilde leaned out of the way so that he spun in a circle and then kicked him in the backside and sent him stumbling into the crowd. "Get the wagon moving," she said.

"Or what?" yelled the boy she'd stopped from throwing the stone. He ducked out of sight when she looked over.

"Get the wagon moving."

Sullen, drunk and muttering, the crowd obeyed and Brunnhilde stood watching, her arms folded, as the carriage pulled away. Lady Dee looked back once, her fingers fluttering around her lips, and then she vanished back inside the carriage.

A presence arrived at the Valkyrie's shoulder. "Must you flirt with the humans?" Sif asked, low-voiced but smiling.

"Lady Dee of Mortlake," Brunnhilde said, ignoring the jibe. "Her husband has done something to rile the populace. Something magical." She looked at the shield-maiden with a raised eyebrow. "Fancy a trip to Mortlake in the morning? It's south of London, funnily enough."

Sif grinned. "I take it back. Flirt with whoever you like if you get results like that. Now all we need to do is get you through the night without being accidentally stabbed by a startled, beautiful, and entirely innocent shield-maiden." The warrior punched her arm and then gestured towards the vanishing carriage. "Maybe you'll have sweeter dreams this time."

Brunnhilde scowled but there was no heat in it, and she followed her laughing friend back into the inn. There, Sif retrieved the bottle of wine and the cups, and they retired to their room.

"Put the silencing spell on the room. Do you want to try for a full night's sleep or make an early start? We can set out a few hours before dawn if you'd like," Sif asked.

"Early, I think. I drew a little attention out there just now."

"And you call me reckless," Sif said.

"To be fair, you are," the Valkyrie said and then yawned, effectively ending the squabble. She changed back into her shirt, jacket, and trousers. If they were to be scurrying through the streets before dawn, best to do it comfortably. Her gown, cloak and armor went into her pack and then she stretched out on the bed, sighed from the tips of her toes, and closed her eyes.

Sleep came quickly. So did the nightmares.

Brunnhilde staggered on landing and her knee thumped down into the thatch of the roof. Immediately, a dog began barking inside the house, followed a few seconds later by a boy telling it to be quiet. Sif leapt up onto the roof to join her, her boots landing soundlessly in the thatch.

They'd left the tavern two hours before dawn and quickly taken to the roofs. Neither of them had any desire to meet the kind of people who haunted the roads through the night. Not again.

The Valkyrie hummed under her breath as she followed Sif across the roof and onto a another, a single long step to span the road below.

Sif stopped and spun to face her. "Will you be quiet?" she hissed.

Brunnhilde blinked. "What?"

"You're humming. You've been humming since we left the tavern. Are you trying to alert people to our presence?"

"I was not," she protested and then paused. "Was I?" The shield-maiden rolled her eyes. "Oh. My apologies. What was I humming?"

"I have no idea," Sif snapped, "but please stop."

Brunnhilde held up her hands, placating, and then gestured for Sif to continue. She took care to follow in the Asgardian's footsteps, trusting her to find the best way forward. Almost two weeks of practically no sleep and the Valkyrie could barely trust her eyes or her judgment. Thankfully, Sif would–

"You are doing it again," Sif growled, stopping and turning to grab Brunnhilde by the lapels of her jacket. "Why are you humming? *Why?*"

She wrenched herself free and wobbled on the uneven roof. "I'm not!" she protested, but this time panic bled in around the edges of her mind. Was she? "Hum it back to me," she demanded, checking the road below in both directions and then dropping down into it and beckoning. She dragged Sif into a patch of ebony shadow next to a wall. "Hum," she insisted.

Even in the dark, she could see the anger in Sif's eyes, but the warrior cleared her throat and softly hummed a melody back to her.

Brunnhilde jerked, her eyes going wide, and then she began to speak along with the melody. Words in Elvish, words sweet and terrible and a lie, an awful lie. Sif cut herself off but the Valkyrie kept chanting, the Elvish script dancing before her eyes in the darkness as if inscribed in fire.

She gathered her strength and fed it to the words and felt them come alive. She drew the words close and wrapped them around herself. She could see the bridge, shimmering, just out of reach. She stretched–

Sif slapped her across the face hard enough that her head snapped sideways and she cut the inside of her cheek against her teeth. Before she could even blink, the shield-maiden had her pressed against the wall with a knife sharp against the edge of her mouth. "What in Odin's name are you doing?" she hissed and there was death and threat both lacing through her voice like venom.

The words were still in her chest, begging to be spoken, but the blade crushing her lips was cold and steady and Brunnhilde knew Sif would use it. Instead of answering, she took a deep breath, kissing the edge of the knife, and then slowly let go of Sif's arm and shoulder, where she'd grabbed on instinct ready to throw her across the street. She pressed her fingertips into the rough stone wall against her back and wished desperately that the shield-maiden was another Valkyrie and they could communicate mind to mind without the need for words.

But no. Another Valkyrie, attuned to death, would likely be suffering as she was suffering. Instead of answering, the Valkyrie just blinked desperately and gritted her teeth, swallowing convulsively against the words burning their way up her throat. When Sif repeated her question, even more threatening, she tapped a fingernail against the blade silencing her.

The knife vanished and, as soon as it did, Brunnhilde slapped her hand over her mouth. Sif scowled and then sucked in a breath. "Are you... you're telling me you can't speak? Or that you can't–" Brunnhilde was already nodding "–control what you say? You want to keep speaking Elvish?"

No, I don't want to, but I can't stop it. But she couldn't tell her that. Brunnhilde nodded again, frantic. What was happening? The dreams... the dreams were in her waking mind now?

"Right. Ink, quill and parchment and somewhere to hide," the raven-haired warrior said in a no-nonsense tone. She searched around on the ground for a few moments and came back with a small, jagged-edged stone that she wiped ineffectually on her sleeve. She grimaced but didn't hesitate, holding it up to Brunnhilde's mouth. "Put this on your tongue. You won't be able to talk around it. Maybe it's your fatigue, or just the fact that you're closer to the source of the magic, but if it's insisting you speak the ritual, then we are very much running out of time. Lead the way. I presume you've got a better idea of our destination now?"

Brunnhilde did, actually. When the words had burst out of her, she'd felt the alien magic pulling, yearning, drawing her towards the southwest. She pointed, the stone cool and earthy in her mouth. She offered up a brief prayer to the All-Father that earth was the worst thing leaching from it onto her tongue and teeth and gums.

The Valkyrie hesitated, her eyes locked to Sif's. The shield-maiden gave her a crooked smile. "At least I'll get some peace and quiet now," she joked, but it couldn't cover the naked anxiety in her face. She patted her on the shoulder. "This is odd, and it can't be comfortable for you, but at least we're no longer just following the pretty lady you rescued last night. It seems like her husband really is dabbling in things he can't understand. But we'll find him and put an end to his ritual and make sure no path to Svartalfheim is opened. Won't we?"

Brunnhilde nodded – and tried very hard to believe it.

In her chest, Elvish incantations burned and bubbled and begged to be spoken.

THIRTEEN

FIRE

The flat-bottomed ferry didn't run until dawn, trapping them on the wrong side of the river as the night slowly faded. The delay ate at Brunnhilde and she stalked back and forth along the river's edge, her boots squelching in the mud. The river was a complication. Did they affect the disguise of noblewomen once more to cross or hope that this early in the morning, with their hoods drawn up and mist and smoke combining to haze the air, they might pass for men?

They spoke – well, Sif spoke – about stealing a boat and leaving a pile of silver in its place, but they couldn't guarantee the boat's owner would be the one to find the coins.

"You and your Asgardian honor," the shield-maiden had grumbled and Brunnhilde had just arched an eyebrow until Sif blushed a little. Her own honor was almost as unbending as the Valkyrie's. "There are worse things to do though, Bright-Battle," she'd said quietly in the end. "If it comes to it, with Midgard facing an elven army, it would be worth the risk."

Brunnhilde had hesitated, torn between duty and necessity, until Sif threw up her hands in despair. "Fine, let's just bloody swim it, then," she'd sighed and Brunnhilde had been about to agree, even though the thought of soaking her armor and weapons made her wince, when she startled a black cat invisible in the darkness at the edge of the water. It yowled and flashed yellow eyes at her and sped away. The Valkyrie leapt back on instinct, ripping out her blade and sucking in a great draught of air to prepare herself – and also the pebble she'd been holding in her mouth for the last few hours.

She collided with Sif even as the raven-haired warrior likewise vaulted into a ready position. The shield-maiden's blade had been restored to its proper place on her hip when they fled the inn and Brunnhilde was glad of it, for the stone was trapped in her throat, choking her and cutting off her ability to breathe. She forced her body to remain under her command until they'd realized there was no danger, and then she sheathed Dragonfang, grabbed Sif and shook her hard with one hand, the other pointing at her own throat.

"Odin's eye, the stone? Let go of me then, woman, and turn around." Sif pounded on the Valkyrie's back three times before the clang of fist on backplate told them it would accomplish nothing. Sif swore some more and began unbuckling Brunnhilde's armor while the Valkyrie twitched and fought every instinct telling her to convulse and claw at her throat.

The armor hung loose on one side and Sif returned to her earlier thumping, her fist heavy as a mountain as it landed between Brunnhilde's shoulder blades, four, five, six, *seven*, *eight* times and despite herself, the Valkyrie felt panic start to build. And then the ninth blow dislodged the stone and it flew from her throat and into her mouth, smacking hard against her teeth as it shot free and vanished into the dark.

Brunnhilde sucked in air, sweet as honey despite its edge of rot and sewage – and on the exhalation she began to chant. She slapped her hand across her mouth an instant before Sif did the same, the shield-maiden's own mouth a perfect O of surprise.

"Well," she said a little shakily and let go with extreme reluctance. Brunnhilde kept her own hand firmly in place and her teeth gritted. Still, her tongue and lips moved, the words scratching from her throat and mangled by her hand so that at least they weren't comprehensible. She prayed that was enough to deaden their power. "That was fast. One unobstructed breath is all it takes, is it? This is going to make things difficult."

More than you know, Brunnhilde thought as something caught beneath her ribs and began to tug, draining her strength more with each passing second. She wasn't giving it away this time, as she had been compelled to before; it was being taken from her against her will.

She gestured for parchment and charcoal, and by the hazy light of coming dawn – thank the Norns for an Asgardian's enhanced night-vision – she scrawled another message for Sif.

"'Something is weakening me,'" the shield-maiden read aloud. She gasped and looked up. "What, right now? Because of the spell?" Brunnhilde nodded. "But you only spoke a few words of it." This time she shrugged.

The shield-maiden put her left palm against Brunnhilde's brow and her right over her heart and closed her eyes. "I can feel it," she breathed and shuddered, grimacing. "Let me try…" The Valkyrie's ears popped as Sif clasped Brunnhilde's wrist and Frigga's bracelet between her palms and began to whisper, calling for protection. For a moment the pull on her strength dulled – and then the magic shattered in a burst of rainbow embers. Three jewels in the bracelet cracked and dulled.

The warrior cried out and stumbled back into the shallows. Brunnhilde leapt after her, steadying her. "Are you–" she began before the words twisted and rippled into Elvish and the theft of her strength jumped from a trickle to a flood. She jerked back from Sif as if bitten, sidestepping her and wading into the river. The words were flowing as smooth and fast as the inky water rising up her calves. She spread her arms and tilted her face up to the sky, the words pouring faster – and then Sif kicked her in the back of her knee.

Brunnhilde's leg buckled and she went down in the river and the shield-maiden grabbed her by the hair, slapped her other hand over her mouth, and then dunked her head underwater. The Valkyrie thrashed and struggled, but Sif's grip was relentless. She dropped her weight into her elbow, planted between Brunnhilde's shoulder blades, and pinned her in place. For a count of fifty. And then a hundred. A hundred and fifty.

The need to breathe was becoming unbearable. Brunnhilde found Sif's leg and tapped it three times. There was another moment of hesitation and then she was dragged up out of the water. She drew in a breath and the shield-maiden tensed, ready to force her back beneath the water again.

"Is it your strength being stolen or your abilities as a

Valkyrie? Is it your death perception?" she demanded, shaking Brunnhilde. "Blink once for strength, twice for duty."

Brunnhilde examined herself and then blinked – twice.

"Thunder and lightning," she swore. "All right. Pull in your power, Bright-Battle, pool it deep down inside, in your core. Hide it behind your duty and our mission and your–" she shook her by the hair "–your muscles. Shove it behind the bulk, yes? Make it as difficult as possible to access and maybe it will slow the theft at least. Do that now, please." She allowed Brunnhilde another breath. "Do it now or the next step is I gag you."

And back under the water she went. The Valkyrie didn't fight it this time. Instead, she gathered up the particular power that made her a Chooser of the Slain and all the other abilities gifted her by the Realm of Asgard and the All-Father's generosity. One by one she packed them deep inside her, small and golden and hidden, her senses retreating from the world until she felt small and exposed and cut off. Felt… human. Immediately, her lungs began burning, her diaphragm spasming as the urge to breathe grew overwhelming. She twitched, slapped at Sif's leg, and twitched again, before the warrior hauled her back into the air once more.

Brunnhilde coughed and breathed through her nose, Sif's hand still over her mouth, and then sat back on her heels in the river and turned inwards. The wanton theft of her strength, her life even, slowed down to a stream, then a trickle, then a dribble, and there it stayed. Not stopped, but not the deluge it had been before, either. She gave a tentative nod and then, even more tentatively, tapped Sif's wrist with her fingers. The shield-maiden removed her hand from her mouth.

They waited, taut with anticipation, for the words to burst from behind Brunnhilde's ribs again. They were still there – she could feel them – but in the same way that she was… smaller now, her senses dulled with her Asgardian perceptions tucked away, so too was the imperative to speak them. At least for now.

"It's," she began and Sif flinched again, then relaxed with a relieved huff, "it's better. Well, it's not, it's awful and I feel naked like this, but the compulsion to speak isn't so strong anymore." She took a breath, felt the ritual wrestle for control, and grunted, biting down on her sleeve and biceps instead. Bit hard enough to hurt and focused on the bright pain, categorized it as it dulled into an ache, focused all her senses on it.

When she had control again, she released the bite and then scraped her fingers across her scalp and over her face. She was so tired.

"And what you were sensing?" Sif asked, though she had to know the answer.

Brunnhilde shook her head. "By closing myself off, I've lost the ability to feel it. We were heading in that direction and I'm sure it's still there, but…"

"Say no more," Sif said quickly. "We've got a name and a destination, so there's no need to start experimenting. We're both already wet, so we may as well swim after all. Who knows, we might be at Mortlake when the sun rises?"

The Valkyrie nodded. "I'm still going to keep talking to a minimum," she said and was unsurprised when the shield-maiden grinned. She rolled her eyes but was strangely pleased by the warrior's obvious delight. It was normal, this teasing between them. It made her *feel* normal, despite the strangeness of cutting herself off from what made her who she was. "You'll have to lead now," she added. "My senses…"

Sif winced and patted her arm. "Of course. Leave it to me. You can still fight like this if we need to?" She held up her hands before Brunnhilde could bristle. "Of course you can, of course. Forget I asked. All right then, let's race. Last one to the other side buys breakfast."

"First one to the other side finds somewhere secluded where we can dry our clothes over a fire," the Valkyrie corrected. "Walking around dressed like this is bad enough, apparently, but it'll be even worse if we're soaked to the skin."

The shield-maiden pouted, but then pivoted and set off into the water with that confident, loping stride that ate up the ground and intimidated everyone who saw it. Brunnhilde shook her head: they really weren't being subtle anymore, were they? Although swimming the river in daylight would be even less subtle, she supposed. She followed Sif deeper into the water, the pack containing her gown and other supplies strapped across the back of her armor.

Together, they began to swim.

Hela's meeting with Francis Walsingham the day before had been enlightening, baffling, and frustrating. Initially, he'd mocked the idea that two women, even trained soldiers, could pose any threat to anyone, let alone Her Majesty Queen Elizabeth, who was wise and powerful and would see through any ruse attempted.

What he'd meant, of course, was that he expected to be the one to see through any such ruse, given that he was a man and the queen, despite being – apparently – chosen by God to rule England, was a mere woman. Hela had had to remind herself quite firmly that she was currently glamoured in the guise of a man to more easily convince Walsingham of the tale she was spinning and therefore it would be imprudent to twist his head off his neck and use it as a football.

Fortunately, word had already reached him of the strange entertainment in Clerkenwell and the ruckus at Lincoln's Inn's Fields and it hadn't taken too much more to convince him, via the judicial application of a little hypnotism, that the Asgardians, the German Warrior Women, were both real and a credible threat to the queen and her closest advisors. Did, perhaps, his lordship know whether any of those advisors might have recently acted in a way that could attract unwanted attention? It might be the assassins had more than one objective, with Her Majesty's death their ultimate goal but destabilizing her court an acceptable alternative.

She'd left Walsingham frantically dictating notes – and the Asgardians' descriptions, as provided by Hela – to a scribe so that copies could be made and circulated to all the wardens in London as well as the soldiers on duty at the queen's palaces and residences within the city.

The day's myriad frustrations had faded into insignificance as Hela rode her fine mare onto the ferry and then back to the inn a league from Mortlake.

Now a new day was dawning, the Valkyrie and the shield-maiden were being hunted across London and should cause her no further trouble, and Hela had an appointment with John Dee and the elven stone... not that he was aware of it. Her magic replenished, she would scoop up the artifacts, the man himself, and Realm-jump home. As long as the stone was inactive at the time, its drain on her power should be manageable for one of her strength and ability.

Hela rolled out of bed. She stretched, then called down for a bath, a large breakfast, and with instructions for the boy to see her horse saddled and bridled as soon as he arrived. He could then wait in the common room with a cup of milk and some bread.

Hela bathed and ate and dressed and then left the inn with William trailing eagerly at her heel and stuttering something about her appearance that sounded horrifyingly like *poetry*. She was about to cut him off when two tall figures stepped into the yard. Their clothes were wrinkled and damp, their armor was grubby and dull, and their hair was raggedy. They froze; Hela froze. The boy continued to the stable, stumbling over his words and blushing like a ripe apple before realizing he was talking to himself. He followed Hela's gaze and his mouth opened. She snapped her fingers and he stayed silent.

"You," the shield-maiden breathed, outrage and disbelief contorting her grimy features. "This is your doing? I knew I'd smelled the stink of this magic before, but hadn't realized it would be you. I didn't think even you would stoop this low, Goddess of Hel. Truly you have forgotten all the lessons and values of Asgard in your eternal quest for power." Sif's hand fell to her sword hilt.

The shield-maiden's words opened a floodgate on Hela's fury. One moment she was frozen in surprise, wondering how they'd managed to track her here, and the next she was incandescent with rage.

"Who are you to speak so to me?" she demanded, her voice ragged and barely recognizable. "Who do you think you are, you pathetic, mewling little goddess not worthy of the title? You are nothing but Odin's sword, Odin's dog. You should be *on your knees before me*, not prattling like some ignorant, over-indulged child."

Sif gasped in outrage and drew her blade. The Valkyrie twitched and slammed her hand down over the shield-maiden's, sliding the weapon back into its sheath. Despite her actions, she said nothing. A muscle flickered in her jaw as if swallowing words she was afraid to speak.

"You, at least, know to hold your tongue, Valkyrie. You should teach your companion the same, before someone cuts it out for her."

"Ah, my lady?" William ventured.

"My horse," she snapped. He flinched, bowed, and ran for the stables.

"I at least put others before myself," Sif was snarling, taking short, stiff-legged steps across the yard like a dog bristling for a fight. "I am dedicated to the All-Father's peace. All you want is power and more power, anything to fill the hole in your heart."

"*Enough!*" the Valkyrie roared and then immediately put both hands over her mouth.

"Hammer and lightning, Bright-Battle, I'm sorry. Are you all right?" Sif flashed Hela a look of pure hatred. "Now see what you've done on top of everything else?" she demanded, as if Hela had the first clue what nonsense she was babbling. "How could you ally with them? Why do you hate Asgard so much?" Her temper flared again, bright in the early morning, but Hela's was growing faster, a conflagration threatening to engulf them all.

She gathered her magic, ready to hurl them both back across the Realms to Asgard. The fishhook that had drawn her to Midgard in the first place tightened under her ribs with a sudden, painful yank. She attempted to sever it with an imperious gesture, only for it to hold her fast.

Hela gestured again, putting power into it this time – a bright burst of magic that was instantly whipped away from her. The words of the spell she'd heard Dee chant suddenly sparkled to life in her mind, demanding to be spoken. She dismissed them and tugged again at the link between herself and the elven stone. It was fixed tight, sucking at her magic as it had before.

How dare you? she thought viciously. *You want power, do you? Life? Then have theirs!*

Brunnhilde ran across the yard towards her, waving frantically. Sif was at her side, fury mixing with concern, and Hela gripped the fishhook beneath her ribs and thrust it towards the Asgardian warriors.

There was a tearing pain and then a wave of weakness washed over her – leaving the fishhook in place but stealing a huge amount of Hela's power again. Brunnhilde stumbled at the same time, but the Asgardians were little threat compared with the focal stone: it was capable of reaching much farther than Hela had realized.

Once more the words rose in her mind, begging, clawing, *commanding her* to speak them. They were harder to ignore this time, and the Valkyrie had staggered to a halt, her hand pressed against her breastbone in the same place where Hela's own fishhook sat. Her other palm was over her mouth.

You hear them too then, only your weakness makes you desperate to speak, doesn't it? You can't control yourself as I can. The stone's draining you dry, powering itself and the spell. Good. Then it doesn't need my strength.

Hela skipped to the side, putting distance between herself and the Asgardians once more. Again, she ripped at the hook, thrusting it towards the Valkyrie. It had already claimed her, it shouldn't need Hela. *It shouldn't need her.*

The hook stayed firmly in place.

"What have you done?" Sif was shouting. Again, she went to draw her sword and this time the Valkyrie was too distracted to stop her. "You murderous toad! I beg the All-Father that I be the one to bring you to justice this day!"

For possibly the first time in her life, Hela ignored an insult, too enraged by the Dark Elves' temerity in thinking to *steal her magic* to care about one upstart goddess who she'd kill later, at her leisure. She turned her back on the pair in furious contempt and raised her arms, flexing her magic and casting it – half again stolen by the shew stone – so the roof of the inn burst into flame.

Sif and the Valkyrie both shouted in alarm and then the latter began chanting Dark Elvish. Desperately, the shield-maiden put her hands over Brunnhilde's mouth, muffling the sounds and pleading with her to find her control.

From within the inn, shouts rose, confused and then afraid.

William arrived with her horse, agog and babbling questions. Hela mounted, paused an instant, and then dragged him up behind her. She kicked the mare into a trot and as they exited the yard, she cast a single glance back. As expected, the Asgardians' foolish obsession with justice and duty meant they both were fighting the flames and pulling panicked Midgardians from the smoky, burning depths of the inn. Neither had time to watch her leave.

Perfect. She wanted that stone and book. She wanted that power and the return of her own, outrageously stolen from her. And she wanted to rip apart Svartalfheim itself until she discovered who had had the audacity to interfere with the Goddess of Hel's own magic.

Teeth bared, she kicked the mare into a gallop down the road to Mortlake.

FOURTEEN

INCANTATIONS

The entire inn was lost to the flames and the Valkyrie was perversely grateful for the number of Midgardians and their possessions and animals in need of rescue. It was the only thing distracting her from the incessant, gnawing need to speak the spell and open the bridge to Svartalfheim.

The words churned uneasily in her chest as she emerged from the collapsing inn for what she knew would be the last time. She carried armfuls of clothes and pewter, a few precious silver ornaments. Behind her, Sif emerged from the smoke dragging a blanket on which were teetering four full barrels of beer. Perhaps with the money, beer, and some clothes they'd managed to save, the innkeeper and his family could try and start again.

Brunnhilde "accidentally" dropped several Asgardian silvers into one of the tankards she'd rescued before depositing it with the sad little pile of belongings that was all that remained.

She put her hands on her hips and surveyed the roaring conflagration, wiping absently at her smoke-stinging eyes. The yard was loud with awe and grief and hacking wet coughs: it had taken time for the Asgardians to find all the occupants and some of the bedchambers on the first floor had been well engulfed before they'd managed to reach them. Sif was already among the survivors, advising them to move down to the riverbank and put wet cloths on any burns. The air would be clearer down there, too, easier for tender lungs to inhale.

The innkeeper and his wife sat side by side on a mounting block in front of the stable – mercifully spared and all the animals taken out by stable hands – with their arms wrapped around each other as they watched their world burn.

Because of Hela.

The Goddess of Hel was long gone, fled back to her ally John Dee, no doubt, and while Brunnhilde was as keen to set out after her as Sif was, it had taken time to save what they could for the poor innocents caught up in the confrontation.

"At least our clothes are dry now," Sif said as she wandered over, a tired smile showing white teeth against her soot-streaked face. The Valkyrie barked a laugh and then nodded. She was tired: she was so fatigued she could fall asleep standing up. However, these people had been traumatized enough for one day, and their mysterious savior sleepwalking into a screaming rant in an unknown language was unlikely to improve matters.

"She's gone to Dee ahead of us, hasn't she?" the shield-maiden continued. Brunnhilde shrugged and then nodded. "I'll go and ask for directions. You … clean your face, at least."

This time the Valkyrie arched an eyebrow meaningfully. Sif swiped at her grimy face with her grimy hand and sighed. "We get the best jobs, don't we?" she said without much rancor, and walked away before the Valkyrie could work out how to respond to that only with facial expressions.

They were about ready to leave – a quick scrub in the river of their hands and faces had at least done something, but they needed somewhere secluded where they could bathe properly and change into their river-stained gowns. Whatever they did, Lord John Dee would likely take a single look at them and have them thrown off his estate as beggars. *Unless Lady Jane intervenes on my – our – behalf.*

Either way, they didn't have a choice, because no doubt Hela was already hurrying Dee to complete the ritual so she could welcome her allies from Svartalfheim. They were out of time.

The Asgardians accepted a cup of beer each from one of the barrels Sif had rescued, washing away smoke and char from their mouths and throats. They were saying their goodbyes when half a dozen horses clattered into the yard, the lead riders clad in serviceable chainmail and those behind wearing padded jerkins and helmets. Some sort of patrol.

"What's happened here?" the closest rider barked as he pulled up his horse. The rest clattered to a halt behind him, the animals tossing their heads and snorting at the proximity to fire. "By God, that's a mess. Anyone hurt?"

"No, warden, thanks to these ladies," the innkeeper said and Sif took an instinctive step closer to Brunnhilde as the newcomers all turned piercing gazes on them. "But we've lost almost all we owned. What'll we do come tax day?"

The warden ignored that question with an impatient flick of his head. "Just happened to be passing, did you, ladies, while wearing such… intriguing attire?" He swung down off his horse and his patrol followed. Their first mistake, Brunnhilde noted absently. If they wanted to get into a footrace with two Asgardian goddesses, they were going to be sorely humiliated.

Speak the words, Midgardian. Perform the ritual and the gestures, offer the sacraments and sacrifices. Open the bridge. Let us in.

Let us in.

She used the pretense of a cough to clap her hand over her mouth; with the other she tugged sharply on Sif's sleeve. The shield-maiden glanced over and then winced.

"Gentlemen," Sif said smoothly. "We're pleased to see you've finally arrived. We were loath to leave these fine people alone without adequate protection or someone to organize a roof over their heads until they can decide how to proceed." She paused as a soldier hissed in the warden's ear. "Is aught amiss, sir?"

"You're strangers to London," the warden said, his voice grating with tension and heavy with suspicion.

"Yes," Sif said, and no more. This time, Brunnhilde didn't lament her brevity. They instinctively knew that no woman of noble birth or means would bandy words with rough soldiers in front of a burning inn, no matter that the innkeeper had named them his saviors. The clink of Sif's fingernails against her sword's crossguard reminded the Valkyrie that they weren't currently pretending to be women of noble birth, dressed as they were in shirts and trousers with swords at their hips. No armor, although that could prove to a problem of its very own if things escalated.

Speak of glory, Midgardian. Speak of pathways opening and worlds meeting and wonders occurring.

Let us in.

Let us in!

"And yet you're not within the city limits. You're closer, in fact, to the small town of Mortlake."

From the way he said it, Brunnhilde knew she should be worried, but all she could think about was the voice in her head, the imperative to speak the words that would bring Realms together and glory to them both. It would be so easy just to speak, to sing, to chant the lines blazing like lightning across her mind's eye.

Sif said something, but the Valkyrie couldn't quite hear it over the whispering. As well as the scratchiness of inhaled smoke and sore lungs, there was the constant itchy wrongness of someone or something sucking away her strength like a leech on her skin. Although she'd reduced that theft to a dribble, it didn't seem to be stopping, and the weakness she already felt was alarming. A slow but relentless violation.

Brunnhilde blinked and focused. John Dee. Hela. Yes. They couldn't afford any more delays or they'd hand Hela the magic and the Realm of Midgard itself.

Hela, who had been insulted to her face by Sif and not retaliated. She should have broken Sif to pieces and Realm-jumped her to Asgardia to die a lingering, shameful death in front of Odin's throne. Instead, she'd cast fire on the inn. Something was very wrong with this whole situation.

Open the bridge to paradise, little human. Speak the words and lend us the strength and we will show you such wonders. Such wonders!

Let us in…

The Valkyrie stepped up to Sif's shoulder. The shield-maiden's hand clamped onto her wrist and squeezed – hard. "It seemed like a beautiful morning for a stroll along the river," she was saying. "These good people are lucky we were passing when sparks from the kitchen fire, I presume, exited the chimney and landed in the thatch. I wish you well and that these troubles are the last to befall you," she added to the innkeeper. "Fare you well, sirs," she said to the patrol and began to drag Brunnhilde towards the stable. They could squeeze past the wall and the closest horses and be out and away.

Brunnhilde went willingly. Movement made it easier to ignore the voice.

The soldier who'd been whispering to the warden waved a piece of grubby parchment. "It's them, sir," he said loudly. "No doubt about it. 'Tall and comely to look upon, one dark and one fair, dressed as men and armed for war. Apprehend upon the instant as foreign spies in the employ of King Philip of Spain, with designs upon Her Majesty the queen of England, Elizabeth the first of her name, at the behest of Sir Francis Walsingham–"

"Yes, yes, man, I know what it says," the warden snapped. He clicked his fingers and the patrol spread out, some turning their horses side on to better block the yard's exit. Sif and Brunnhilde halted.

"There is a problem, sirs?" Sif tried, but from her tone she knew it was over. Behind them, the innkeeper and his wife were loudly lauding their names and proclaiming them angels sent in their hour of need. "Are you ready?" she hissed.

"Hmm?" Brunnhilde said vaguely.

The warden snorted. "Angels? Witches, more like. Or demons. Look at them! Wenches dressed as men belong in gaol, where they can't corrupt decent women or hurt themselves or anyone else with those weapons." He turned to the innkeeper's wife. "You shouting about how they're kind and decent folk? Best be careful you're not tainted with witchcraft yourself."

The gathered group shrank back together, muttering prayers and protestations of innocence.

Why not speak the words, human? Why not chant the beautiful, pretty words of power that summon us? Don't you want to meet your heavenly lords?

Speak and you will see us. Welcome us. Join us.

Let us in.

Brunnhilde pressed her lips together in a firm, disapproving line, breathing in short bursts through her nose. The closest soldier recoiled, but better these men expect a fight than they got a million blue-skinned, white-haired, murderous Dark Elves descending on their Realm.

"I assure you, sirs, we are neither witches nor demons, just simple women," Sif said, still edging them forwards.

"Gaol, Warden? Surely we'd all be better off if they were burnt at the stake," another member of the patrol complained. There was a rustle of low-voiced agreement.

"I think we've been delayed here long enough," Sif continued, making intense eye contact with Brunnhilde and emphasizing the word "delayed".

The Valkyrie gasped and then bit her tongue savagely. Of course that had been Hela's plan with the fire. The patrol's arrival purposely searching for them indicated the goddess of Hel had been busy setting obstacles in their way. Again, there was something strange about that, but Brunnhilde couldn't hold the thought long enough to examine it.

"And I think you're going nowhere but with us," the warden said firmly and the whole patrol drew their swords. The still-burning inn shone gold and orange in the steel blades, dancing and flickering, and someone screamed.

Sif let go of Brunnhilde's wrist and they separated on instinct, space to move and run and fight if they needed it. The raven-haired warrior faced them square on and lifted her chin.

"Gentlemen, attend if you please," she said, and while her tone was pleasant, it carried the whipcrack of command within its silkiness. The men clad only in padded jackets straightened automatically at her tone, used to obeying it, while those in chainmail scowled as the one with the parchment stuffed it into the waist of his trousers and gave them a wordless growl of threat.

Brunnhilde's fingers skated over Dragonfang's hilt and the sword shimmered into view. Too late, the gasps of surprise told her she'd made a mistake.

"We are traveling entertainers of German origin," Sif tried but the warden was pointing an accusing finger.

"Witch!"

"–*traveling entertainers*," Sif repeated, louder, even as she paced sideways. "We astonish and awe our audiences with our martial skills. We are traveling through England seeking new audiences to enthrall. Can you kindly tell us the way to an inn that might have a room to rent?" She looked behind her. "And isn't currently on fire?"

Brunnhilde was impressed. Sif gave no indication of the seething indignation the Valkyrie knew she must be feeling at being called… well, any of the things they'd been called so far. She knew Sif was feeling it, because she shared the warrior's affront and was seized with a strong and compelling desire to show these arrogant, ignorant fools exactly who they were and what they could do. As welcome as this adrenaline-fueled return of her senses was, she knew that now was not the time for violence.

It was a pity no one had told the soldiers that. The six-strong patrol split into three, two retreating to guard the yard exit and a pair heading for each Asgardian. "Bind them. They will be taken to the Tower," said the warden. "They'll answer to Lord Walsingham himself."

Sif gave it one last shot. "Gentlemen? I believe I asked you a question," she barked and there was less silk and more steel in her tone this time. The patrol noted it, too, but instead of responding the way an Asgardian warrior would – with obedience and alacrity – they seemed astonished and outraged at being addressed in such a manner.

Speak the words. Speak the words, human. Speak and free us, let us in, let us join you and you will know paradise.

Speak the words. Let us in. Speak the words. Let us in. Let us in. Let us in let us in let us in let us in!

Brunnhilde shook her head hard, her breath catching in her throat as the compulsion grew in strength yet again.

"Odin's eye," Sif swore.

Marvel: Legends of Asgard

"Now listen," Brunnhilde began – or tried to. What actually came out of her mouth was Dark Elvish, a stream, torrent, a flood of words faster and faster as the spell that had been building all morning – or even long before that – took control of her tongue and demanded to be spoken before she could stop it.

And it was all the warden's fault. Even as she chanted, Brunnhilde moved towards him, Dragonfang sliding from its sheath with a deadly rasp. He would pay. They'd all pay. Blood and death and the bridge's opening. Blood and death and the Dark Elves' dominion!

"Valkyrie, no!" Sif yelled. She kicked the nearest soldier in his chest so hard his breastplate dented and he flew across the courtyard to thump into the stable wall with a dull clang. The shield-maiden ran at Brunnhilde and tackled her away from the warden in the instant before she cleaved him in two. Despite the fear in his face at her incomprehensible chanting, he slashed wildly at her and managed to clang his sword tip against Sif's backplate as she wrestled Brunnhilde away. Any thoughts he'd had of taking her to this so-called tower were clearly lost to him: he was attacking to kill.

Arrows whined around their ears. One sparked off Brunnhilde's pauldron, ricocheted, and cut open her ear as it spun away. The pain restored a little of her clarity and then Sif grabbed her by the elbow.

"Jump." She vaulted the pair of them on to the nearest roof. The inn's roof. The burning roof. The thatch gave way and the shield-maiden skipped onto a burning beam, dragging Brunnhilde with her. Brunnhilde, who was struggling to pull her arm out of Sif's grip so that she might make the appropriate gestures to accompany the ritual.

Her death perception was active and growing, changing, and then being torn free, speeding away across the landscape to Lord Dee and Hela and their Dark Elf allies. Spooling out of her like the thread of her life in the hands of a Norn, measuring where it should be cut.

Her free hand curled into the first shape and drew it across the sky, her fingers weaving elegantly through the coiling smoke – smoke that responded, sluggishly, to her movements. As if enamored of her, it curled around her wrist and wove between her fingers and the palm of her hand. Almost she could feel it. Almost. Brunnhilde paused, mesmerized, and then the beam collapsed and dropped them both into the burning building.

Screams of shock and astonishment became shrieks of alarm as they disappeared from view into the choking, roiling smoke and billowing orange flame. The heat was incredible, stealing the air from the Valkyrie's lungs as she wheezed on impact with the ground. She rolled to her knees, the next lines begging to be spoken, but the fall and the heat and the lack of oxygen combined to trap her voice in her chest. She coughed and broke from the trance.

The Valkyrie looked around in surprise. "Why are we back in here?" she croaked and then coughed some more. "Is someone trapped?" She began searching through the flame-lit darkness and Sif grabbed her elbow, her fingers digging into the pressure point hard enough to drive a spike of pain and numbness all the way down to her thumb. Brunnhilde cried out and recoiled.

"What?" she snarled.

"Don't you remember any of that?" the shield-maiden demanded, gesturing furiously towards the outside.

"Can we get out of here before you start interrogating me?"

"No! Because there's a patrol of six soldiers looking for us and you were halfway through the bloody Dark Elven ritual instead of helping me find a way of escape that wasn't, I don't know–" her gesture this time nearly smacked the Valkyrie in the face "–us roasting alive!"

She let go and Brunnhilde backed away, uncomprehending. She remembered none of it. All she knew was that the words were burning in her chest – or maybe that was just the smoke.

You were doing so well, little human. You were so close. We … were so very close to you. Could you not feel it? Do you not want that? Speak it again, Midgardian, and we will show you such wonders.

Speak it again.

Let us in.

"Stop it!" Brunnhilde screamed, both hands pressed to her head. "Stop it, stop it, *stop it!*"

The shield-maiden called her name, but the Valkyrie whirled away into the smoke and fire, plunging deeper into the inferno. Not so much heedless of the heat as hoping it might somehow put a stop to the voice and its incessant, seductive whispering. A small and distant part of her knew that that ending would require the ending of her life; the maddened, exhausted and frightened part of her decided it was a trade worth making. To protect Midgard and give Sif a chance at solving this, Sif who wasn't affected by the voice, who wasn't plagued by it, and who knew the name of Lord John Dee and could bring him to the All-Father's justice.

Burning thatch fell on her head and shoulders as she pushed deeper into the inn, the roof beams above her groaning and screaming as the long-dried sap within boiled and looked for a way out. Something shifted, grated, and then settled again and the Valkyrie came to a stop beneath it.

"I'm sorry, All-Father," she said – or tried to. In an act of cowardice that would shame her if she lived beyond this moment – which she did not intend to – Brunnhilde put her hands over her ears so she might not hear the words she spoke.

There was a great shifting above her, shivering through the very air and ground until it vibrated in her boots and ribs, and then the rest of the roof came down.

Something that might have been a groan and might have been a curse scraped its way out of a throat as raw as if it had been flayed.

"There's a knife poised just above your mouth and if the first words you speak aren't Asgardian, it's going to pierce your tongue and then I'm going to tie it to your ear." The cold practicality in the voice told Brunnhilde it wasn't a joke. "It is going to hurt. It is going to bleed. And you are going to let me do it. Why? Because we have three choices here, Bright-Battle. I kill you. I gag you in a way you can't escape. Or you regain control of yourself. Now, what's it going to be?"

The air was clear and although her skin was tight and scorched with heat, the Valkyrie didn't have the maddening, burrowing, impossible-to-ignore agony of deep burns to her body. Which was a surprise. Very close by, she could hear the gentle lap of water, smell wet mud, and feel a cool breeze on her over-hot skin. Something above her shifted and a shadow fell over her face, sudden enough that she blinked open her eyes and flinched. Above her, outlined in bright sunshine so that her face was cast entirely into shadow, Sif waited. She held a piece of cord in one hand and a knife in the other.

Don't listen to her, small one. Chosen one. Blessed one. Listen to me. The words are beautiful and the path is so close now. We are so close. Let us in, my bright, brave human. Let us in.

"It still thinks it's talking to a Midgardian."

Sif leaned back very slowly. "Go on."

Brunnhilde packed her Valkyrior abilities tight and small and close inside her – what little she had left – and she clenched her fists and recited the first verse of one of her favorite ballads in her head until the voice had receded a little. "It keeps calling me human or Midgardian. Telling me how well I'm doing. Telling me how close they are, how close the bridge is to being ready. Telling me to speak the words again."

The shield-maiden let out a long, slow breath and sheathed her knife. She put a slipknot in the cord and then looped it three times around her vambrace where it was a very obvious reminder. "I wouldn't have really," she began.

Brunnhilde slashed a hand through the air. "Yes, you would have. And I need to know you would have. And I need to know that you will. If the time comes." She seized the warrior. "Tell me you will. Tell me what you'll do. I need to hear it."

Sif licked her lips and then let her face go cold and distant again. Slowly and precisely, she repeated her earlier threat, imbuing the words with so much promise that the Valkyrie shuddered at it.

"Good," she said hoarsely. "And pray Odin neither of us forgets it."

"You were so far gone that the smoke was like a cloak around you," the shield-maiden said suddenly, and there was both awe and revulsion in her face. "I could barely see you, and then I thought, well, if I can't see you, Midgardians won't be able to, either. So I stole inside your cloak of shadows and jumped us over the wall and away on the other side, then looped us all the way back around a league or so distant from the inn. The smoke vanished but you were still … gone. Babbling for some of it, but when I pinned your hands together it seemed to break the trance. Once you couldn't make the gestures it was as if it … left you."

The Valkyrie sat up, drained of magic and almost of will, only Odin's trust and Thor's respect and affection and this beautiful, reckless, and fickle-hearted shield-maiden's concern holding her together. She could feel the bruises her friend's fingers had dug into her wrists as she'd dragged her over roofs and across fields. She didn't comment, and not only because she didn't dare risk speech.

Instead, she knelt in the mud at the water's edge as the river lapped and gurgled gently, thick with silt and stink. Though that might just have been her. She sucked in air through flared nostrils and tried not to scream her frustration and her grief – grief for her loss of control, her loss of self, her loss of self-*respect* – in case it became something else.

Sif trod a slow, wide circle around her, muttering to the sky and casting worried glances first at Brunnhilde and then along the banks towards the distant, twisting pillar of smoke. Who knew whether the patrol and the warden were still looking for them, or whether they were presumed lost in the fire? Bits and pieces were coming back to her. Brunnhilde suddenly remembered Sif jumping them both up on to the roof. That would be hard to explain if anyone recognized them as the self-proclaimed German Warrior Women who'd saved the patrons and owners of the inn.

Sif came to a sudden halt, her hands on her hips. "All right, at least tell me that you got a good fix on the location this time. All that mystic chanting and posturing must have told you something, right? Is it still Mortlake?"

It was more practical than Brunnhilde had hoped she'd be, and she snorted and nodded, pointing further upriver. "Not too far," she croaked tentatively and then immediately held her breath, hands hovering ready to slap over her mouth. It appeared her fatigue and the shocking lack of strength and power she had – her death perception was as thin as a spiderweb – meant that she was useless, at least for now. *That's a surprising relief.*

"At least we fled in the right direction, then," the shield-maiden said sourly and then thumped her fist on the outside of her thigh. "Fled! Us! From the likes of them!" and she was off again, stalking and complaining despite the scratchiness of her voice as the sun climbed ever higher into the sky.

Brunnhilde shifted until she was sitting cross-legged and could rest her elbows on her knees and her mouth against her palms. She stared wearily across the river, her gaze idly following the boats skimming its surface. Most were heading downriver and out to sea. Fishing boats. Others, smaller, were being rowed hard against the current. The Valkyrie blinked slowly, her eyes stinging and her weariness creeping up to lay itself around her neck and chest like a great warm cat. She blinked again, even slower, Sif's words fading into a muted buzzing. The next time she blinked, she kept them closed, resting her eyes.

Just for a moment.

FIFTEEN
WHITEHALL PALACE

Mortlake. Just the village's name made Hela clench her teeth. She'd half a mind to burn the place to the ground. Never had she loathed a place or its people so intensely. She'd rather treat with Odin's mewling whelp Thor than stalk the streets of that grubby little village again. And yet here she was, riding towards it.

Still, Hela was grateful to be riding.

She hadn't realized until they'd slowed to a canter just how much magic it had taken to set the roof alight. Well, just how much magic she'd had to expend while the majority of it was stolen from her. Stolen!

She'd pointed the horse in the right direction and then dove inwards to examine her powers and the fishhook link to the focal stone. Had it had formed that day in Hel when she'd first tasted the whiff of magic, or in Dee's library as she waited to reveal herself? Either way, she couldn't currently divest herself of it, and neither could she use her abilities without sacrificing a portion of them to the stone. Every time she thought she was ready to seize it and Realm-jump home, another complication arose. It was maddening.

The stone was linked to Dee as well, though in his case it was his life force being drained, more rapidly with repetition of the spell. There was a third link, stronger than the others, to the Valkyrie. Very strong, in fact. That made Hela feel considerably better.

Lastly, there was a link, faint but growing, with the stone's twin in Svartalfheim. Detectable for the first time, it gave Hela another insight into how this magic worked. And how she'd make it work for herself.

She'd believed that everything would be fine as long as the stone wasn't activated by Dee's reading of the book. Now, she knew better. Her most important task now was severing the link between herself and the stone so she could Realm-jump with it and the book. As things stood, to jump now might drain her magic, or perhaps open the bridge itself. Neither outcome was desirable, especially not if Hela was in the way of an army of Dark Elves set on taking Midgard.

She couldn't use magic in the crystal's presence, and she couldn't – wouldn't – leave Midgard without it. For now, at least, she was trapped here.

The revelation soured her mood further and by the time the horse turned into the village of Mortlake, she was seething. Her best option now was to remove Dee, the stone, and the book from Mortlake and conceal them somewhere until she'd learned what she needed to. And keeping Dee separate from the crystal should prevent him from activating it and any further subsequent theft of her power. Hela couldn't use her magic in the stone's presence, but she was more than a match physically for any Midgardian. No one would be able to stop her.

Decision made, she let the horse slow to a meandering walk and told the boy to scramble down. His arms had been wrapped tightly around her waist for the whole journey and she'd had more than enough of his infatuated proximity.

William landed on the road with a thump and looked up, a complaint half-spoken. He took in her expression and snapped his mouth shut, taking the horse's leading rein and setting off with his shoulders hunched.

It was almost noon when the village came into view around a bend, the big, brick-built house sitting back from the river like a crouching spider.

"My lady? Are we to see the magician again? Can I meet him this time? I've never met a real magician."

Hela turned a withering glare in his direction. "You've met me," she pointed out.

William was silent as he rubbed the mare's whiskery nose. "Yeah, but you're a god, said so yourself. Queen of Hell, you told me. You're not normal like his lordship's normal. You're... different."

"And don't you forget it or I'll make you wear your intestines as garters," she said absently. The boy laughed and Hela was struck by his utter refusal to believe her threats. She wondered when she'd stopped being offended by his lack of fear, and then wondered when he'd stopped being afraid of her. Perhaps he never truly had been.

They walked towards the house in silence, Hela sulking at the fact she couldn't even scare a lad in this rotten, backward

Realm. The memory of the fear and awe on the faces of her subjects in Helheim and Niffleheim did little to soothe her when taken alongside the stone's rampant theft of her magic. Oh, the price those Dark Elves would pay for this.

"Can I then? Meet the magician?"

Despite her hauteur, Hela gave a stiff nod. The boy whooped and she immediately regretted her decision. "Only because you're my servant and I wouldn't be here alone," she pointed out. "So don't embarrass me. What will I do if you embarrass me?"

William bowed and grinned. "Guts for garters, my lady, I know." He paused. "So, uh, what should I do?"

Hela rolled her eyes. "Knock on the door, little fool."

William grinned, looped the mare's reins over a handy rose bush and hurried down the path to rap on the heavy oaken door.

A servant opened it and then blinked at the boy and past him to Hela. He dropped into a low bow. "May I help you, my lady?"

"I'm here to meet Lord Dee, the queen's magician," Hela said. "It's about the book and the crystal and I'm in a hurry."

The servant's eyes widened. "The, the what?" he stammered, but it was clear he knew what she meant. "I'm afraid my lord is engaged at present."

Hela tapped her foot on the flagstones. "Then I will wait inside for him and take some luncheon while I'm at it," she said, and swept past the servant into the entrance hall. William followed, silent as a shadow and his eyes gleaming with delight in the gloom. "You, boy, mind your manners," she snapped and he gave her another cocksure grin.

"Well?" she asked as the servant spun about to follow her, or possibly shoo her back out like some errant chicken. "Will you send for him or must I wait like a common serving girl in the entryway upon his pleasure? Where is he, anyway?"

"My lady, I, that is, might I have the honor of your name?"

"Lady Hel…ga, of Niffleheim."

"Ah, of course," he said as if it meant something to him. "And your association with my Lord Dee?"

"I'm here about the book and the stone, I've already told you. It's a matter of magic and faith," she added with utter confidence. "This way, isn't it?" Hela led the servant to the library where they'd all gathered for Dee's aborted summoning of the angels.

"Ah, of course, of course," he said, bewildered that she should know her way about the house. "Please, allow me, my lady. I shall see about refreshments and inform his lordship immediately. He is… I'm afraid he's been closeted with his studies all morning and expects to be away to London soon. He may not have the time to meet with you if the queen has need of him."

Hela sniffed and put her nose in the air. "As I said, I'll take luncheon while I wait. But be sure that you do inform him on the instant and impress upon him the importance of our meeting. I expect him to make time for me and I don't have all day. The sooner he sees me, the better for all concerned."

The servant was completely flustered as he led Hela into the library. The heavy curtain was tied back against the wall and the dining table and chairs had been removed. There were no traces of what had passed there a few days previously. There was also no cherrywood box on the small desk in the corner.

"God above," William breathed as he made a tour of the shelves. "That's a first printing of *Jocasta*," he said, pointing at a book. The servant and Hela both blinked, confused. "I've never even read it, let alone seen it performed by competent actors."

"You know *Jocasta*?" the man asked.

"'And so forgetting laws of nature's love, no sooner had this painful womb brought forth, his eldest son to this desired light, but straight he charged a trusty man of his, to bear the child into a desert wood, and leave it there for tigers to devour'," the lad recited absently, running reverent fingers over the book's spine. "Always gave me the shivers, that bit did."

Hela turned an icy glare on the servant. "You think I would employ idiots?" she demanded.

The man bowed, lower this time, and stuttered out an apology before slipping from the library. Servants always recognized power. As expected, this one bowed to her even though he didn't know who she was. Well, except for Lady Helga of Niffleheim.

"*The Tragedy of Gorboduc!*" William exclaimed, sliding a second leather-bound book off the shelf. He sat cross-legged on the floor and was immediately lost in its pages. Hela stared and then shook her head, dismissing the strangeness. Perhaps she'd underestimated the Midgardians. Some of them, at least. She paced the library, extending the merest tendrils of magic in an effort to locate whatever hidden place Dee had found to conceal the book and the elven stone. So far, she'd only sensed the ritual itself, but she hoped proximity to the stone – and a stone holding so much of her own power –

would be visible to her senses. And yet... nothing. Perhaps that theft had done more than weaken her. Perhaps the stone had used her magic to glamour itself. *Or perhaps it isn't here at all.*

William was oblivious, lost in his reading. He lingered over the book, his face hidden by a fall of mud-brown hair and the red hat that, yet again, sat crooked on his head.

"What's taking so long?" Hela muttered when she'd given up on trying to find the energy signature of the shew stone.

The boy wrinkled his nose. "I 'spect his lordship is making his escape to a more secluded part of the house and that servant'll come in any minute to tell you to come back tomorrow."

Hela stopped pacing. "What?"

William looked up. "You didn't really think Lord Dee would see you on a whim, did you? That's not how it works, my lady. You're a stranger. Nobody knows you or if you're important." He held up his hands. "Except me. I know, Your Highness. I know who you are. But you won't get to see his lordship, I'd bet this fine leatherbound folio on it. The servant already said he expects him to be off to London soon. Standard excuse, I imagine, when strangers come calling. But don't worry, he'll still offer you lunch to make up for it."

"He wouldn't dare," Hela snarled, indignation thick enough to choke her. "*Does he not know who I am?*"

"Afraid not, Your Highness. No one knows who you are. You're in a fine fancy gown and I'm pretending to be your servant, but you're still a stranger. Lord Dee's a nobleman and the queen's own magician. I doubt he's got time for strange ladies, no matter how fine they look."

She was genuinely nonplussed. "Get up," she snapped and crossed to the door and wrenched it open. The servant was on the other side, one hand poised to knock and the other holding a heavily laden tray. He recoiled, the tray wobbling, and steadied it with both hands. Behind him stood a young woman with a tentative smile.

"Where is Dee?" Hela demanded before either of them could speak.

"My lord husband has been called to court by the queen," the woman said. "We are sorry your journey has been wasted, but I should be delighted if you'd join me for lunch and we can arrange a more suitable time for you to return."

Anger was a low vibration trembling all through Hela's form and the urge to death touch them both was almost overwhelming. Behind her, William coughed a laugh and then appeared at her elbow with the basket and an innocent expression.

"Where *exactly* has he gone?" she demanded in a low growl. The servant flinched. Lady Dee merely narrowed her eyes.

"Whitehall Palace," she said smoothly. "My lady, perhaps you…"

Hela pushed past them and left, breathing steadily so as not to give in to temptation and set the house ablaze. She'd used enough magic doing that earlier today. Her mare was still waiting patiently by the rose bush and cropping at the grass and herbs bordering the path. She unlooped the reins and mounted, then hauled William up behind her again. The servant stood in the doorway looking aghast. Lady Dee watched from a window, a thoughtful frown creasing her brow.

"What?" she snapped, and the servant dropped into a low bow, averting his gaze. "What?" she asked again, this time to the boy as she turned the horse and kicked it into a walk.

"Ah, well, fine ladies usually ride side-saddle and, of course, don't have their servants up on the horse with them," he mumbled and then clutched at her waist as she pushed the mare into a trot.

"This Realm is ridiculous," Hela declared. "You deserve to be conquered by the elves. If I didn't need the stone, I'd let it happen and applaud."

"My lady?" William asked, muffled, his face pressed to her back.

Hela sighed. "Never mind."

Once they reached the road to the ferry, Hela had made William dismount and lead her horse as he had before, carrying the basket containing her armor and sword. Now, as they neared the palace, the queen of Hel found herself drawn to it in a way she couldn't explain. At first, she thought it was familiarity, after all she'd probably passed the palace more than once on her journeys to Mortlake. Then she wondered whether it was just the knowledge that the queen of England lived there. Was she feeling some sort of kinship with a Midgardian? Hideous. Impossible. Or perhaps Dee really was here and had the stone with him?

Eventually, though, she understood what she was feeling: there was another strand of Svartalf magic linking to the palace itself. It had a different feel, more grounded, earthier, than the link to the stone itself, wherever that was. This was where the bridge would open – straight into Whitehall

Palace. It was clever, she had to admit. Take the queen and the city would fall on the instant. Take London, and you had England. And from what she'd gathered from local gossip, though it might well be hyperbole, if the elves took control of England, they had power over quite a large part of this world.

So much power from the simple capture of one woman.

Intriguing. It gave Hela much to think on.

For now, though, the presence of a second anchor point to this Realm suggested that there might be another way to get what she wanted without risking any more drain on her magic. If Dee's focal stone powered the bridge, then there must be a corresponding item here in the palace to open it. If she could claim this artifact, she could return home and then alter it so that it responded to her magic, not that of Svartalfheim. Then she need only place it where she wanted it – Asgardia, for instance – and open a bridge herself. Hela's powers were vast enough she wouldn't need a focal stone. Just the anchor point itself.

Yes, this was a far better solution.

First, though, she had to find it.

Of course, just when she'd decided this Realm had no security to speak of, there were armed soldiers everywhere. Here, in the very place where she didn't need scrutiny, she was already being watched. She was surprised that Queen Elizabeth was residing within this warren of buildings, none particularly more regal than the next. Which one belonged to her? How was one supposed to be impressed when there was a literal building site on the grounds?

That was the banqueting hall where the duke of Alencon

would be entertained as he and the queen negotiated a marriage alliance. William had told her that much.

As he led her mare around the edge of the foundations, Hela became abruptly aware of something else: the building site itself was the source of the power she could feel.

Something about the foundations – maybe something buried there – was establishing a link with Svartalfheim. Hela stood up in her stirrups and stared at the earthworks and piled timber and stone, the partially built walls and the masons poring over designs while others oversaw the digging out of the footings.

"May I help you, your grace?"

Hela hummed a negative and kept looking. If she could just get down there…

"Your grace? No one's permitted any closer, my lady. I must ask you to turn back." This time Hela blinked and tore her gaze from the holes and trenches that, try as she might, meant nothing to her. They were just holes and trenches. She needed to inspect the site as soon as possible. She needed to be *in it*. Magic drifted from it like smoke. How could no one sense it? This was where calamity would strike for them, where the bridge would open. Only it wouldn't have angels treading upon it, but blue-skinned demons bent on destruction.

Hela didn't care about that, except inasmuch as she claimed the magic and the bridge as hers by right of conquest. She would–

"Excuse me, your grace? Are you quite well? Can you hear me?"

Two soldiers stood across the road leading to the building site, in full armor and with pikes crossed before her horse.

Real soldiers, not like the warden and his bullies she'd come across so far. She sat back in the saddle, rearranged the folds of her cloak to show off the silver thread in her dress and the heavy gold torc at her neck, and then stared down at them impassively.

"This is Her Highness Princess Helga of Niffleheim, on diplomatic business regarding the duke of Alencon's arrival. She has an appointment."

Hela raised her chin an inch and waited for one of the soldiers to call William a liar. They didn't. The lad was a natural born storyteller – or was going to have a spectacular career as a confidence trickster. Still, a princess? On the one hand, it was a demotion that put her lower than Elizabeth, which may or may not have been intentional. She didn't have an entourage or even a guard, after all, which any self-respecting monarch would be surrounded by. On the other, she was a goddess so far above England's queen that it was laughable and as such she was above such petty point-scoring.

Mostly.

The soldiers scrambled to bow and move out of her way. "Welcome to London, Your Highness. Are your trunks and servants following on?"

"We have already secured Her Highness's lodgings," William said airily and stuck his nose in the air as he sauntered past, leading her horse. Hela wasn't sure whether to laugh or kick him in the head. She settled for maintaining her poise until they were well past the gawking soldiers.

"Where now, my lady?" the boy asked, dropping the act as soon as they were out of sight. "Are we going to see Lord Dee? I hear Walsingham's got an office here somewhere."

"That's quite enough familiarity for now," she said with a snap. "I want to get closer to that building site. I want to see what's going on."

William smirked. "I thought so, the way you were staring at it. That's why I said you were here on the duke's business. That's the hall being built to entertain him, so that way you can–"

"Yes, thank you. I followed your logic," she sniped and again got only a grin in return. "So, I need permission from Walsingham?" Her lip curled at the thought of begging for a favor from anyone, but the spymaster was exceedingly clever, and she'd be wise to tread carefully. Her earlier meeting with the man, even glamoured as she was, had gifted her with a grudging respect for him.

"Couldn't say. You'd have to start with someone's secretary and work your way up to a meeting with a noble, at least, is my guess. But, you know, I'm not from London, Your Highness. But I'll do as you say, whatever you say, Your Highness. Just name it."

"Mercenary little beggar," she murmured.

William blushed, as his face was so wont to do. "I crave no other tribute at thy hands but love, fair looks, and true obedience." He recited the words as if they were a poem, or lines from a holy book. His eyes shone.

Hela snorted. "As long as you know who it is who owes the obedience," she said.

William's face lit up as if she'd offered him a boon and he bowed low. "My life to serve, O Aphrodite," he said fervently.

Hela ran her tongue across her teeth. "Yes," she said eventually. "It is." She gestured imperiously. "Well. Find a stable so that someone can take care of the horse. And then find me one of these secretaries."

"As you say, my lady," William began and Hela gave in to the temptation to boot him in the ear. "Ow!"

"Am I not a princess? I'll thank you to address me correctly from now on or I shall find myself another servant. One with better manners and better connections at court."

The lad gave her a mutinous glare and then evidently thought better of complaining. He adjusted his hat, rubbed at his ear, and then took up the leading rein again with an expression of long-suffering dignity hilariously out of place on one so fresh-faced. Hela absolutely refused to be charmed by it.

Sixteen

Broken Magic

They were filthy and smoke-stained. Brunnhilde was stumbling with exhaustion as they hurried through the fields towards Mortlake. The patrol who'd confronted them at the inn had trotted past towards the town, staring ahead and to either side in an open search pattern that had Sif dragging the Valkyrie into a muddy ditch.

An hour later they trotted back again, this time more slowly. Brunnhilde didn't see them then, either, and again the shield-maiden had to take charge of hiding them. This time behind a thick hedgerow bordering the road.

"We're not going to make it very far at this rate, Bright-Battle," Sif said. "They've probably roused the village to be on the lookout for us. We're going to have to find somewhere that we can bathe and change our clothes or we're going to be recognized the second we set foot in Mortlake. Any ideas?"

"Duck pond," she said and pointed. Just those two words

were almost enough to trigger a torrent of Dark Elvish. Brunnhilde held her breath and squeezed her eyes closed, fighting for control. She could see the words in her mind's eye, written like whorls of fire, and every second she didn't speak them they burned her deeper. It wasn't just compulsion now, it hurt not to comply. For a human, she expected it would quickly become unbearable. Perhaps that was why Lord Dee was seemingly so intent on casting his great new magic. Not only had he been seduced by Hela, but he was physically unable to prevent himself speaking the words of the ritual.

Fortunately, the raven-haired warrior was adapting well to Brunnhilde's monosyllabic responses. "Oh, well spotted, and with the patrol gone, there's a chance it will remain unvisited long enough for us to get clean. We'll build a fire, too, and let our clothes dry while we scrub ourselves and the rest of our gear." Sif grinned suddenly. "Skinny-dipping on Midgard was definitely not something I thought would happen during this mission. It's a nice day, it might even be fun."

"Hela."

The smile dropped from the shield-maiden's face. "I haven't forgotten, Valkyrie. I'm just trying to give you something else to think about." She slapped Brunnhilde's arm. "Best to keep weapons near to hand even when we're in up to our necks, though."

The Valkyrie nodded vigorously and turned deeper into the field, heading for the sparkling pond at its center.

She hadn't gone more than fifty strides when Sif tapped a fingernail against her backplate with a dull clang. "You're humming," she said with a note of warning in her voice. "Bite it back if you can, my friend. A quick bath and a change of clothes and we can hurry on our way to Mortlake and put a stop to whatever his lordship and the queen of Hel are up to. No need for you to add to the predicament, is there? Wait, don't answer that. Just walk a bit faster, yes?"

Brunnhilde did as she was told, propelled not just by the anxiety in her friend's voice but by irritation and the slow-growing pain in her chest and throat as the Elvish demanded to be spoken. She wasn't going to lose control again, no matter what.

At the edge of the pond, Brunnhilde threw off her cloak and pack and tugged off her boots. Her sword belt and armor followed in short order and then she simply threw herself headlong into the water. No point changing out of the clothes first: they needed to be washed, too.

Sif stood on the bank with an affronted glare. "So I'm gathering the firewood, making the fire, checking we're unobserved, and all the rest of it, am I?" she complained, but didn't seem too put out.

The water was cold enough to make her gasp, but Brunnhilde didn't care. She dived deep, searching for the bottom, and hooked her fingers around a large stone to keep her anchored in place. Soot and sweat leached slowly from her skin and she relished the imperative to hold her breath, stronger even than that spell's demand she speak its words.

She scraped her free hand through her hair and across her scalp, lifting dirt, ash and tiny pieces of thatch that had fallen from the inn roof as it burnt. The dim water darkened as the char drifted from her skin, clothes, and hair and, eventually, she let go of the stone and floated back to the surface.

Brunnhilde felt more peaceful than she had since their

arrival. And then she opened her eyes and found Sif defending herself against four members of the watch patrol from the inn.

The shield-maiden had her back to the pond and was grim and silent as she deflected swords and a halberd from cleaving her flesh. Her own sword was still sheathed – she was blocking, not fighting back.

The Valkyrie swam silently to the edge of the pond and found her sword right next to her. Sif must have kicked it over as she engaged the four. Four? Weren't there six?

"There she is!"

She spun in the water and found the other two running around the edge of the pond towards her. Snatching up her sword, she kicked off the bottom and leapt straight up – over Sif's head and the heads of the men crowding her – to land far from the approaching pair of soldiers. She cracked the nearest man on the helmet so hard with the pommel of her sword that she dented it and he collapsed without a sound. The sheathed weapon came down on another's shoulder, driving him to his knees with a howl of pain. She kicked the third in the back so hard he flew past Sif and into the pond. The fourth, the shield-maiden dealt with in similar fashion, catching his arm and spinning him up and over and into the water back-first.

The Asgardians faced the final two soldiers, exchanged a single glance, and drew their blades at the same time. The men turned tail and ran back to their horses, but Brunnhilde had had enough. She sprinted after them and then past them and caught one in each hand, her fingers closing around their throats and lifting them off the ground entirely. Then she smashed their heads together with a dull clang of metal and carried them back to their comrades.

Sif had fished out the two in the water and they made use of the patrol's own shackles to tie them all to each other. Finally, the shield-maiden looked up. "Took your time down there, didn't you? Feeling better?" she asked sourly.

Brunnhilde blew water off the tip of her nose and shrugged. "Didn't need me," she said and gestured.

Sif drew herself up proudly. "Of course I didn't," she said. "But this does somewhat make a mockery of the plan to bathe and rest here."

The Valkyrie sidestepped away from the pond and gave Sif an elaborate bow, gesturing her towards the water. The warrior snorted a laugh but was already unbuckling her sword belt and stamping on the heel of one boot to drag her foot clear. She didn't undress, either, and while she was busy scrubbing the stink of smoke from her hair and clothes, Brunnhilde gathered fuel for a small fire and lit it. Then she approached the two soldiers who'd been dunked in the pond. She grabbed their cloaks and dragged them up over their heads and then tied the ends together so they couldn't see out.

Nothing to do with modesty: she didn't want them seeing the cut and color of their gowns and knowing what their new disguise would look like.

"Are you going to kill us?" one asked, muffled by the weight of soaking wool swathing his head.

Brunnhilde thought about answering him. Despite everything, she didn't want them to be unnecessarily afraid, even though that would work to their advantage. But the Elvish was less a burn and more a wildfire in her chest and she daren't do anything that might let it out. She remained silent and felt vaguely disgusted with herself when the soldiers' breaths became ragged with apprehension.

She concentrated on stripping out of her wet clothes and into the damp, wrinkled gown, and then wringing out her trousers and shirt and draping them over her pack as close to the fire as she could get them without catching light. The gown's embroidery was ruined and stained from being folded up in her pack as they'd swum the great river hours before. It needed laundering and pressing.

Sif finally emerged from the pond and swapped her clothes, too, casting a curious glance at the six-strong patrol. Unconscious or blindfolded, they were no threat.

"We look awful," she announced as she attempted in vain to smooth the creases out of her skirt. "This is ridiculous. We need clean clothes in order to go into a shop and buy clean clothes." She looked at the patrol again and then pointed. "We could take theirs," she mouthed.

It was tempting, but then being dressed in trousers seemed to cause enough trouble as it was. Brunnhilde shook her head. Sif sighed and sat down next to her, close enough that she could whisper without the Midgardians overhearing.

"So we steal clothes – and leave silver behind, I know, I know – or we go to this Lord Dee dressed as beggars and maybe even pretend we are. Which do you prefer?"

Neither. I want–

To speak the words. Speak our words, Midgardian. Speak of magic and pathways and worlds colliding. Speak of visitors from afar, glorious and terrible and beautiful. Speak the words of power and we will return that power to you. Let us in.

Let us in.

Let us in!

Brunnhilde shoved her booted foot into the fire and held it there until that was the only pain she could feel. The stink of scorched leather wafted around them. She was panting, her lips moving, breath becoming whisper becoming word–

The Valkyrie stuffed the meat at the base of her thumb into her mouth and bit down savagely. Not for the pain, this time – that no longer seemed to work. Just to physically prevent herself from speaking. She stood and beckoned. The shield-maiden gathered up their packs and followed, confused but willing to go along. She indicated the patrol. Brunnhilde shook her head. The horses? Another shake.

Brunnhilde had a plan – she just needed to find a few seconds when she wasn't compelled to speak Elvish in which to relay it.

Mortlake was pretty, even if they were not. The Valkyrie had managed to crush the voice down again, but she knew it was temporary, and either her control was slipping as she grew more tired and anxious, or it was gaining in strength. Because they were approaching the source of the spell? She didn't know the answer to that, either.

It had given her just enough time to relay her idea to Sif, though, who'd taken it and embellished it as Brunnhilde retreated once more into silence. It was a risk, of course, because they couldn't be sure what the patrol had told the town's inhabitants. Still, the townsfolk were no true threat and neither, in theory, was John Dee. It was Hela and any Dark Elves who might be in Midgard that they needed to worry about.

After their slow progress through the fields and then their sojourn at the duck pond, it was late afternoon by the time they made their way into Mortlake. There were people on the streets and they attracted the attention of almost all of them very quickly. Brunnhilde tensed and then did her best to hunch and limp, as Sif had ordered. The shield-maiden herself was supporting the Valkyrie's elbow and helping her along. Their clothes, fine but ruined, and their muddy faces and lank hair proclaimed them victims of a disaster.

"My ladies! God above, what has happened to you? May I be of assistance? I am Father Michael of this parish's church. Please, please, let me aid you."

Brunnhilde stared at him in blank silence, barely having to fake it: she was beyond tired and the spell's voice was a constant whisper in her head, making it almost impossible to concentrate on anything else.

"... fire a few miles up the road. The inn we were staying at is destroyed and we've lost everything," Sif was saying. "My lady was trapped in the flames. I fear she's suffered a terrible shock. We'd heard of Lord Dee's generosity. I hoped he might lend us his aid or the wisdom of his medical knowledge." The shield-maiden leant in close to the man and dropped her voice: Brunnhilde didn't hear any more.

"His lordship's away to London, I believe, my ladies," the man said wretchedly. "But please come to my church and I will do all I can to soothe you both. As soon as he returns, I will escort you there myself."

Sif's performance of weepy gratitude was fit for the finest stages in Asgardia and in other circumstances would have had Brunnhilde in fits of laughter. Now, she followed numbly.

There was another stone in her mouth to keep her silent and all she could think was that Dee was away and the house was empty. Couldn't they simply break in and destroy anything they found that was powering the spell?

Is he with Hela? What might they be doing in London? Is that where the magic is now? Should I be in London to enact the–no, no, to put a stop to the… – to perform the ritual.

Speak the words, Midgardian.

No. Please.

Come, my loyal follower. Speak the words that will link our worlds and bring you glory such as you've never seen.

Let us in, human.

Let us in!

The Valkyrie stumbled, wincing and putting her hand to her head. Her lips parted as she prepared to spit out the stone and Sif reached over and swiftly pushed her jaw shut. "She's been speaking wild words, Father," she said earnestly. "We really must see his lordship."

"I fear you've been misinformed, my ladies," Michael said. "Lord Dee is a great man, but he's no physician. To my knowledge, he's never so much as lanced a boil or bled a man to balance his humors."

Brunnhilde took one look at Sif's face and began to giggle, snorting so as not to choke on this stone as she had on the last.

"But he is a magician?" the shield-maiden insisted as the priest led them into a side door of his church, doing her best to ignore Brunnhilde's unladylike hilarity. They entered a small office, richly appointed. He gestured them onto a wooden pew softened with cushions.

"Well, yes, in a manner of speaking," Michael said. "Though of course magic itself is dangerous. Astronomy, I believe, is his area of–"

"What happened at that inn was an evil spell," Sif interrupted and the priest dropped the pitcher he'd just picked up. It smashed on the flagstones, shards of pottery flying and a great splash of water drenching everything.

Brunnhilde looked at the edge of her skirt, filthy already with water, mud, smoke and now wet again, and laughed some more. It was edged with a seductive sort of hysteria.

So close, little human. We are so close to you now. Speak the spell, say the words and open the path and we can be together forever. Let. Us. In.

"Evil spell?" Michael squeaked and grabbed at the cross hanging from around his neck. "My ladies, please, where are your crosses or medallions? Have you… were they stolen? Were you robbed by witches or devils as well as subject to their fiery torment?"

"We believe so, Father, yes. That is why we must see his lordship. I fear that my lady is under some curse and I'm sure his knowledge of magic is enough to recognize and remove such a terrible thing."

"You have no idea," the Valkyrie managed, the words mangled by the stone in her mouth.

Father Michael was rummaging frantically on a shelf. He hastened back across the room and thrust a rude wooden cross on a leather cord at each of them. "Put these on immediately and join me in prayer. Put them on and bow your heads!"

The Asgardians did so, and Father Michael began a stream

of loud, desperate prayers for intervention, his hands clasped together as he knelt on wet flagstones facing away from them. Sif and Brunnhilde exchanged questioning looks: they needed to get to Dee's house, whether the man himself was there or not.

Silently, Sif stood and crept to the high, narrow window looking out over the church grounds. She turned back to face Brunnhilde after the merest glance. "I can see the mansion from here," she breathed, so quietly that Father Michael wouldn't hear it over his own loud-voiced prayers. "I can keep an eye on it. It's you who's apparently cursed after all. You're the one he's interested in, so keep his attention however you can. Maybe I can sneak over there."

Brunnhilde was too tired and too plagued by the dark and seductive voice in her head to argue. Her plan had been to plead being victims of the fire instead of trying to appear as clean and regal noble ladies. Garner Lord Dee's sympathy and use that as an invite into his house. But if he wasn't even there, then Sif breaking in might be the best they could hope for. As for keeping Father Michael's attention, perhaps a quick burst of Elvish or a show of her abilities – her Valkyrior glamour, maybe – would entertain him. Another laugh gripped her, and she realized she needed to do no such thing – fear and fatigue combined to make her seem mad enough.

She should probably be angry about that. The Valkyrie's eyes fluttered closed and she leaned her head back against the wall behind the pew. Slowly, the tension drained from her gut and shoulders, where she'd been holding herself tight against the ever-growing burning of the words. It took all of

Brunnhilde's vaunted self-control to keep the stone upon her tongue and the words within her chest, unspoken if not unfelt. But that control wouldn't last forever.

The house across the village green from the church was glowing as if it, too, was on fire. A beacon in her mind incandescently bright. The same brightness, the same burning, as the words scrawling themselves across her mind's eye. House and spell called to each other and Brunnhilde was trapped in the middle, being slowly torn apart because she refused to give in.

Father Michael appeared determined to run through every prayer he'd ever been taught, and possibly many he was making up as he went, in his desire to spare the Valkyrie from any taint of witchcraft and free her from the so-called curse. Would he think he was drawing forth the devil if she lost her battle against the words, or was it more likely he'd think her the witch or devil at the heart of it all?

"Excuse me, Father, but I believe Lord Dee has returned. We shall trouble you no further." The shield-maiden's voice was polite but brooked no argument.

The priest's prayer stuttered to a halt and he turned a wounded gaze upon her. "I assure you, my lady, that I am invoking God's grace upon you and your companion. Lord Dee is a great man, but he is not a man of the cloth. I believe you are better off remaining here and immersing yourself in prayer and repentance."

Sif paused in the act of hauling Brunnhilde to her feet. "Repentance? Repentance for what? We have done nothing wrong. We are the victims here, priest."

Brunnhilde winced at the warning note in her friend's

voice. It was the sound of Lady Sif coming perilously close to the end of her patience. Father Michael, of course, remained oblivious.

"I just meant that if it was magic that cursed you in the first place, relying upon it to lift that curse is folly. What if instead he doubles the curse's potency? You are clearly both ladies of fine standing, but I cannot imagine such learning formed a part of your education. In this, I pray you allow me to guide you. I am beseeching God for His intervention on your behalf and if you are truly innocent, I have no doubt He will give it. Until then—"

The raven-haired warrior dragged Brunnhilde to her feet harder than necessary and then grabbed their packs from the floor. "I thank you for your prayers, Father, but if you are convinced of our guilt then I do not believe those prayers will be answered, for you do not speak from a clear heart. As such, we will take our chances with the magician... who has returned home," she added for the Valkyrie's benefit.

Brunnhilde felt a great rush of relief. It was nearly over.

Michael seemed genuinely nonplussed at their precipitous departure, standing amid the broken pieces of pottery and gaping after them like a landed fish. An exhausted, manic laugh bubbled up in Brunnhilde's chest at his expression and she pushed Sif between the shoulder blades, hurrying her along before the tatters of her will finally gave way.

They burst out of the church and strode across the village green towards the mansion fronting the river. Once more, they were the subject of all attention, even if their sojourn in the church seemed to have blunted the edge of the villagers' suspicion. The Valkyrie no longer cared. The spell was in touching distance. An end to this waking nightmare, this awful, seductive loss of control.

Speak the words.

She was going to find the source of the magic and she was going to put a stop to it. And no one, not even Hela or all her legions of warriors from Helheim, was going to stop her.

Seventeen

Revelations

Lord Dee's house was an impressive building of red brick and small, leaded windows set back in an herb garden with an approach lined by rose bushes.

That's it, that's it, just a little closer. Come to me and speak my words, come to me and pour your power into me and open the pathway between our worlds. Let us in, little Midgardian. Let us in.

The Valkyrie didn't pause for niceties. She reached the heavy oak door and pounded upon it, and Sif just managed to slide between her and it before the door opened. A man stood there, scowling and then surprised. He bowed hastily, straightened and took in their appearance. A little of the scowl returned to his face.

"My lady must see his lordship immediately," Sif said quickly. "We have been caught up in the most terrible fire a few miles down the road – perhaps you saw the smoke earlier? We've lost all our possessions and, worse, there has been talk that the fire was set deliberately. Set with magic. Everyone knows your lord is the wisest man in England when it comes to esoteric matters. We consider ourselves most fortunate that if this evil had to befall us, it would do so close to his lordship's residence. Please, may we see him?"

All through the torrent of words, Sif had been edging softly closer. With the final request, she stepped fully into the entrance hall, the servant ducking back out of her way. Brunnhilde followed, almost vibrating with the force of the Dark Elvish inside her. It was here, it was so close, she could almost smell it, almost reach out and touch it–

Yes, touch it, touch the stone. Touch us and we will come to you, show you marvels beyond your ability to comprehend. You just have to do this one final thing and we shall be with you, human. We shall be with all of you.

Touch the stone, speak the words.

Let us in!

Brunnhilde staggered and put her hand up against the wall. The servant yelped in alarm and steadied her, calling over his shoulder for help. A maid appeared at the other end of the corridor. "Tell his lordship he's needed in the sitting room, Maisie."

"He's only just now returned," the woman tried.

"It's an emergency, lass! This way, your grace," he added, but the Valkyrie saw which room the girl vanished into. Saw, too, the burst of magic – invisible to mortal eyes – that swept from the room as the door opened. She pointed a shaking finger.

"This way," the servant tried again, gesturing along a different hallway, but he was leery of touching her with any strength and she easily shrugged him off. The man flapped his hands and darted around her, but Brunnhilde made her labored way to the room with the half-open door.

"Thank you for all your help so far, my good man. May I know your name?" Sif said earnestly.

"Fletcher, my lady," he said wretchedly, "but really, no one should disturb–"

"I'm afraid the shock my lady suffered has been too much for her. I don't think she will listen to reason." Sif pivoted smoothly between Brunnhilde and Fletcher. "Thank you again, Fletcher. We shall remember you in our prayers." She turned away and followed the Valkyrie into a small, book-lined library.

For Brunnhilde, the rest of the world dropped away. A man that she supposed to be Lord John Dee was sitting hunched over a table upon which stood a stack of ink-splotched paper, a book, and a beautiful, spherical crystal. It drew her gaze. It drew all of her attention as if it was the north and she a lodestone.

John Dee was not staring at the stone – he was berating Maisie. The serving girl was backed up against a far wall to evade his anger, but it found a new focus when the Asgardians swept in.

"Lord Dee," Sif began and gestured. "Off you go, Maisie, there's a good girl. Lord Dee, my name is Lady Sif and this is Lady Brunnhilde. We are–"

Brunnhilde spat out the pebble and took a deep breath, the spell ricocheting around in her mind like a bird trapped in a building. The stone bounced on the rug next to Sif's foot, and the shield-maiden spun and clapped her hand over the Valkyrie's mouth. "*Absolutely not,*" she snarled with so much vehemence – so much banked violence – that the Elvish actually stopped on its way out of her mouth.

Brunnhilde was vibrating with the need to speak, but there was the implacability of approaching death in Sif's expression – and the Valkyrie knew it wasn't an idle threat. With intense effort, she dragged her gaze from the crystal to the man. Dee was tall and slender with a long white beard. And Dee was failing. Brunnhilde could see it in him as easily as if he was a warrior dying on a battlefield. The spell that wanted her power was taking his, too – his life force. A few more weeks and it would kill him.

"Lord Dee," Sif said without moving, "my companion here is touched with magic. She has felt your working of it and it has called us across many, many leagues to be here. But sometimes it takes her wildly. We are hoping to learn what it is you do here so that she might be less affected by it. Or that you might somehow cure her of her affliction."

Whatever the man had been expecting, it was clearly not that. His gaze snapped to the objects on the desk and Brunnhilde managed to extend one finger from among her clenched fists and point at it.

"Impossible," Dee said softly. "It is impossible you could know anything about this or the angels. You are not from London? Not even from England unless I miss my guess."

"No, my lord. As I said, we have traveled far to seek an end to these fits that overcome her. She learned your name in a dream, my lord," Sif added. "She has learned many things in dreams these past nights."

Dee leant forward, something sparking in his expression. "You know of this stone?" he demanded.

Brunnhilde twitched and Sif reluctantly took her hand from the Valkyrie's mouth. Brunnhilde clamped down on the theft of her strength, her abilities as a Chooser of the Slain, and focused. Hard. "It speaks to me." Her voice was a harsh rasp, as if she'd been roaring orders on a battlefield for the last day.

"What does it say?" he breathed.

Sif cut in quickly. "We, ah, we do not understand the language," she said apologetically. "My friend says it is otherworldly?" She made it into a question and hooked Dee, who sucked in a breath and the end of his mustache, which he began to chew furiously.

"Of course you would not understand it," he said loftily after a moment to consider, or perhaps to decide how much to lie. "It has taken me many weeks of study to make what little progress I have accomplished so far. And I am a learned man," he added, his words so close to what Father Michael had said that Sif twitched in renewed outrage. "Do you care for a demonstration?"

Brunnhilde stumbled backwards, her hands up to ward off any words. "No," she gasped. "I hear it enough in my dreams."

Dee went very still. "The voice? That is impossible. And you cannot understand it anyway, you've said so yourself." He seemed determined to reassure himself on some point and the Valkyrie got the feeling he was jealous of his knowledge and loath to share it. That was fine by her: she knew she wouldn't be able to withstand listening to him chant the elven spell, no matter how badly he mangled the language.

"Can you tell us where you found the items, my lord?" Sif asked, stepping towards the table.

"No further!" Dee snapped and then hurried to the door.

"Fetch me Francois, and tell him to bring his blade," he said to whoever was outside – Fletcher, probably.

"A blade?" Sif said, feigning alarm. "My lord, we are no threat to you. Brunnhilde is suffering under this... this spell or delusion or sickness. We seek only to bring an end to what ails her."

"Is that so?" the old man asked with a shrewd glitter to his eye. "My possession of this ancient book and the shew stone is known only to a few high-ranking members of Her Majesty's court. You are not members of that court, and yet you know of it."

"My lord, all of London knows you attempted a great magic recently. They are calling you a witch and a devil worshiper," the shield-maiden said placidly. "Your lady wife, too. Brunnhilde rendered her some assistance yesterday when her carriage was accosted. Did she not tell you?"

Dee slumped. "Jane? These foul lies are aimed at her, too?" He held up a hand for silence and they waited awkwardly until a soldier entered the room, the jingle of his chainmail preceding him. He took up station beside the desk and if he had any qualms about it being two women he was facing, he let nothing show on his face.

"Well, now that everything is in order and we are sufficiently cowed," Sif said, sarcasm dripping from her tone, "please explain the objects, my lord. How do you know the language contained in the book? Who gave the items to you? Was there anything... unusual about their appearance?"

Dee was tight-lipped and mutinous, whether jealous of his knowledge or afraid of further rumors spreading if he spoke. Brunnhilde stepped forward. She was the one hearing voices: may as well confirm her reputation for madness and spare Sif. "The book does not promise what you think it does," she said with an effort as the elven voice in her head shrieked at her to be silent. She winced and spoke on. "The people we think are behind this would be tall and lithe, with white or silver hair and skin a pale blue. They would speak your tongue with thick accents and wear armor made from lacquered wood. They–"

"I'm sorry, did you say *blue skin*?" Dee's eyes crinkled and he coughed a laugh. "Oh, my dear, you really are quite unwell, aren't you?"

He seemed delighted by the fact and leaned back in his chair, steepling his fingers in front of his face and looking along his nose at them, suddenly at ease.

"No, my ladies, we have not met with elves or faeries lately," he said indulgently, failing to notice how they both flinched. "I fear you have read too many fanciful tales. These are sacred items sent to England from Heaven and through them, I speak with a seraph. The Archangel Uriel. They tell me of the glory that awaits England and through Her Majesty, Queen Elizabeth, all of Earth. I am to open a bridge to Paradise, you see, and with an army of angels marching at our side, the English will conquer the world and bring it to civilization. In a few years' time, England will rule over a vast empire stretching to every corner of Earth. We will recruit the finest soldiers from all our new domains, and together with the angels, we will go to war."

"Go to war, my lord?" Brunnhilde managed, a croak in her voice. "Against Asgard?" she demanded, for surely that was Hela's purpose.

"Asgard? Never heard of it. No," he continued with a beatific smile. "The angels will lead us, and we will lead the world, in a war against the devil himself."

The poor ladies looked alarmed, as well they might at such talk of war, especially after suffering a terrible event as they had. Dee tried to moderate his tone, but it was impossible that this bedraggled creature could know anything of his shew stone and a communion with the angels.

Blue-skinned warriors? He snorted. "My dears, you are welcome to avail yourselves of my hospitality. Indeed, we have been quite busy today, by all accounts. But it is our Christian duty and so we offer it gladly. I will have baths drawn for you and my good wife will prepare fresh clothes for your comfort while these are laundered. Afterwards…"

"The voice you hear, is it in your dreams or just when you speak the spell?" the fair-haired lady asked. "I hear it in my dreams. I hear it awake. I can hear it right now and I promise you, my lord, it does not say what you believe it does."

"Nonsense," he said affably, but there was a snap in his tone. "I have heard you out and offered you my home to rest in. That is more than enough, don't you think? If not for your fine manner and garments, despite their current state, I should think you–" he cut himself off before saying *harlots or thieves* "–to have nefarious purposes here. Francois, please escort them to one of the guest rooms and have Maisie draw them baths and then inform Lady Dee to attend upon me."

He stood and stepped forward, Francois at his side, so that they might herd the ladies out of the library and restore its peace. Before he'd been summoned to Whitehall, he'd been close to deciphering another word of the angelic language. He was eager to return to his studies.

"A path between worlds," Lady Brunnhilde said, refusing to be moved.

Dee halted so fast he rocked on his heels. "What did you say?" He raised a hand to still Francois, who faded to the side, giving them some space. He looked back over his shoulder at the desk and his writings. "Impossible. You could not have read that from here. How do you know those words?"

Up close, Lady Brunnhilde was red-eyed from the fire and drawn with fatigue, trembling from head to foot as if suffering with an ague. Dee wondered if she was, if this was some strange illness, but her words...

"I dream them at night. I hear them in the day. You say the path will open to Heaven and let out hordes of angels to fight the devil? What if it's the other way around? What if you're opening a path to Hell?"

The lord recoiled and clutched at the cross hanging around his neck. "How dare you accuse me of such," he gasped. "I am a good son of the Church, Her Majesty's most loyal subject. I am a scientist, an astronomer–"

"A magician," the dark-haired lady pointed out.

Dee sputtered. "I consort with no devils or demons," he said, outraged. "Perhaps you are the demons, in fact. Demons or succubi sent to tempt me. No, I will hear no more of your nonsense. You are welcome to rest here as I said, for we are pious Christians and know our duty, but you are forbidden this room and my presence. Francois, see to it."

The man moved forward with his hand on his sword hilt, though other than that he was courteous enough. The Lady

Sif sidestepped him, faster than Dee could blink, and was at the table before he could turn.

"No!" he shouted, alarmed, but it was too late: the woman had scooped up the shew stone and the book. She staggered as if shot, crying out in pain, and dropped the precious items to the carpet.

"Bright-Battle? Bright-Battle, I can't. I don't have the strength. Take them and Realm-jump home. I'll be fine!" She gasped the nonsensical words as if they meant something and then grabbed Dee and Francois both. The lord cried out at the immense strength of her grip: how was such a thing possible? Francois was wriggling, trying to twist free, but then Lady Brunnhilde advanced on the sacred objects, fear and desire vying for supremacy in her expression. "Sif?"

"Yes! Take them and go!" the other woman shouted. Ordered.

"*Don't touch them,*" Dee bellowed with as much strength as he could muster. "They don't belong to—"

She picked up the stone. There was a flash of light so bright that the black-haired woman – witch? – staggered backwards, dragging her captives with her and then releasing them while they were all still blinded. "Valkyrie?" she yelled, but the other woman didn't respond. "Valkyrie, where are you?"

Someone shoved him and Dee fell against Francois. The two men went down in a tangle, blinking furiously. A heavy thump. Breaking glass. A slamming door. Dee scrambled away from his guard and in the general direction of his desk – he hoped. He alternated rubbing his eyes with patting frantically at the carpet until his vision returned, spotted with after-images.

The women were gone.

"The shew stone! The book, Francois!"

"Here, my lord. They're both here." Francois hesitated and then picked up the cherrywood box from the desk and used the tip of his sword to poke the stone and the book inside it, before snapping shut the lid and thrusting it into Dee's hands.

"Take it and Lady Dee and the boy and get yourselves to the church, my lord," Francois hissed urgently. "I'll deal with these witches."

Dee stumbled to the door. His dear Jane had their son in her arms and was flying down the stairs towards them, recklessly fast and in danger of tripping over her skirts.

"My love?" she shrieked. "What is happening?"

He wished he knew; instead, he grabbed her free hand and hurried her toward the open front door. Where were the witches? What had happened?

"My lord? My lord Dee?" a voice called from outside and Francois growled and leapt between them and the opening. To everyone's relief, it was Father Michael who appeared. "My lord, I had the most extraordinary visitors not long ago. They insisted upon coming here. I wonder whether you met them?"

Dee abandoned Jane, pushed past Francois, and grabbed Father Michael by the front of his cassock. "You saw them too? The women, witches, angels? Tell me you saw them too!" he demanded, shaking the priest. "Good God, Father. Good God and all his angels, but *what is going on?*"

"You know, of course, that King Phillip has spies throughout Europe? And you've heard of the two women lately arrived in London? I have followed them here. They arrived a day or two ahead of me and I have lost sight of them. An oversight, but foul weather delayed my ship."

Hela sipped from the goblet and met Lord Walsingham's cool stare with one of her own. "I found one of your wardens as soon as I landed and asked him to inform you of the spies. I trust that he did so? Warden Piper, I believe?"

Walsingham's cheek twitched. Hela sighed. "My lord, it would be much easier to have this conversation if you would grace me with an answer. I understand that you have the queen to protect. Well, my priority is his grace the duke of Alencon. I have been sent on ahead to ensure that all is proceeding as it should be and that proper security is in place for his arrival. There are those who would seek to strike at both England's and France's monarchies by striking at my lord."

"You seem remarkably well informed for a wo–"

"Diplomat? Princess? Yes. I am." Hela took the coolness of Walsingham's stare and returned it, tenfold. Colder than a frost giant's cradle. The man cleared his throat and dipped his chin, just enough to indicate he understood and accepted her rebuke. "As I said, if it please you, I will need access to the new wing of the palace Her Majesty is having built for my lord's comfort and entertainment. He is most particular about his surroundings and ensuring that all is complementary and to his taste." She leaned forward, conspiratorial. "I would hate for Her Majesty to be embarrassed if, for example, she were to order tapestries featuring hunting scenes."

Walsingham's black, beetling eyebrows shot up his forehead as if racing each other. "Hunting scenes? We have it on good authority that the duc d'Alencon enjoys the hunt."

Hela nodded, improvising as she went, using all the

information she'd gathered on this accursed Realm at her disposal. "Indeed he does. But this is a marriage negotiation. He feels that depictions of marital harmony and devotion to the Church would be more appropriate."

Hela spoke with the calm assurance of a born diplomat and saw Walsingham's mouth tighten a fraction. She suppressed a smile. No doubt someone's tapestry order was about to be revisited. She wondered, idly, whether the spymaster would seek confirmation of her story. Not that it mattered: from what she understood of the geography in this part of Midgard, it would take weeks for word to reach him and she'd be long gone by then.

Besides, why shouldn't she have some fun considering what she'd been through and the words she was about to speak? Hela took a fortifying sip of wine and then plastered a smile over her condescension. "Why else do you think he asked a woman to come here? I have a shrewd mind, my lord Walsingham, and while I can and will ensure the duke's safety and security while he is in England, I can also approve of any gentler touches that Her Majesty may wish to make to his quarters. What he likes and dislikes, so that each may make the most favorable impression on the other."

Walsingham sat back and pursed his lips, sighing long through his nose. "You are most persuasive, Lady Helga. You will, of course, acquiesce to both an armed guard and a female companion for your security and comfort?"

Hela inclined her head. "But of course, my lord. I traveled here under straitened circumstances. It shall be a genuine pleasure to relax in female company for a short while. It has been far too long since I have felt entirely at my ease."

"Your dedication to your lord is admirable," Walsingham said, "and yet I have never before heard your name. It is not French, I believe?"

"You will not have heard of me, Lord Walsingham. While you are Her Majesty's greatest intelligence gatherer, we in Europe still maintain a few of our secrets." She grinned suddenly, so brightly that Walsingham startled and then couldn't resist smiling back. Perfect. "As for my name and history, I am from a tiny kingdom in the far north, where it is bitterly cold for much of the year. I am the last surviving member of my line and my enemies were closing in around me. I was forced to give up my throne and throw myself on the mercy of others. His grace the duke was magnanimous enough to take me in and, given my history of, shall we say, creative thinking to stay alive as long as I did, he gave me an occupation suited to my talents."

Walsingham breathed out a long, fascinated breath. "Remarkable," he said softly. "Most remarkable. Her Majesty the queen would find you a delight."

Hela ducked her head in demure acknowledgment. "And I would be in awe of meeting her. To have done what I could not, to maintain her throne against all the men who would steal it from her. Well, she is a wonder of the age. The foremost woman in the world. A true queen."

Walsingham sat forward and topped up her goblet with more wine. "Allow me to speak with her," he said decisively. "Not only would you be a valuable source of information about his grace, but I think there's something about you–" his voice took on a musing tone and Hela pushed down a spike of unease "–something she will find absolutely fascinating."

The queen of Hel breathed out. "And I her, my lord. That I can guarantee. For now, though, a woman's work is never done. If I might beg leave to retire? There is much to oversee."

And if I have to bandy such vacuous words much longer, I may well accidentally tear your head from your shoulders and use it as a puppet to speak to your bloody queen.

She breathed out again, straining for calm.

She still had much to learn here. Whatever was in that building site, its power was immense but… diffuse. Not focused. It wasn't trying to steal her magic, though that could well change if she cast any.

She smiled through gritted teeth as Walsingham stood and ushered her to the door. She still couldn't risk using magic, not until she knew more.

What are you having built here, my elven enemies, that will draw the bridge into being?

And how can I seize it for my own?

EIGHTEEN
TWO QUEENS

"Your Majesty, as discussed earlier, may I present to you Her Highness Princess Helga of Niffleheim, the envoy of his grace the duc d'Alencon. Her Highness is here to ensure the duke's safety and comfort during your marriage negotiations."

Hela dropped into a low curtsy at the foot of the dais. Queen Elizabeth was a woman wearing entirely too much white makeup and the sheer amount of brocade on her gown meant that she probably couldn't feel her lower extremities, but nevertheless she exuded power.

She hadn't managed to access the building site yet, despite Walsingham's promises, and the companion and guard assigned to her were clearly both reporting back to him on her and William. The lad had taken to court life as if born to the nobility, swapping tales with the other footmen, but always watching her, his dark eyes begging her to notice him.

Hela put him from her mind and straightened to give the queen an assessing look. She received exactly the same in return and dipped her chin in acknowledgment. This was a woman well used to navigating male-dominated waters. Hela could respect that.

"Princess Helga? The name is unfamiliar, but Walsingham tells me you are from a small kingdom that is likewise unknown to us. It is a blessed day when our knowledge can be expanded. But how does one such as yourself end up working for my dear duke?" Hela knew that the spymaster would have told Elizabeth that tale as well. Was she hoping to find inconsistencies or was this a powerplay to belittle Hela in front of the rest of her court? Hela was not used to biting her tongue, but for the sake of her mission she did her best.

"I am much humbled to be in your presence, Your Majesty, especially when I have had the misfortune to be unable to cling to my throne as you have to yours. When I found myself without a crown or a friend in the world, I had no choice but to travel south and ended up in France where his grace the duke was Christian enough to shelter me and offer me a means of repaying his generosity. He is a great man, Your Majesty. You are most fortunate in your choice of suitors."

Elizabeth smiled, but it was the sort of smile someone gave when biting into a rotten apple. Everyone knew this was no more than a political match. One that was highly unlikely to produce an heir given the queen's apparent age. The situation with Spain must be dire indeed for her to be considering marriage at this time in her life. Hela couldn't imagine she wanted or needed a husband and on that, they were of one mind.

"And what is it you wish to do while you are here, Your Highness?" Elizabeth asked.

Hela took a breath and squared her shoulders, raising her gaze to pin Elizabeth in her throne. Charm and confidence had worked on Walsingham and they would work again. "I will need access to the building site to ensure that there will be no dangers or hidden passageways that might inconvenience his grace. I will also need full oversight of all planned decorations and furnishings, but my prime duty here is my lord's security. To that end—"

The laughter began at the rear of the court and quickly spread until it washed against Hela's back like an incoming tide.

"Only the French would be stupid enough to send a woman on a diplomatic foreign mission," someone muttered.

"Do they take us for fools? What can she hope to achieve? She's probably trying to secure herself a rich husband." Hela turned to face the audience and glared the nearest of them into submission. She reminded herself that she was too close to achieving her goal to be goaded and clung to that by her fingernails. "I assure you ..." she began.

"Or she's fleeing a scandal. Child on the way, is it, and no father to claim it?"

Hela's patience withered. "You would speak of women as if we are the weaker sex when your own ruler is a woman? You would not only think such wild and untrue thoughts, but you voice them openly in her presence? Who are you to question the queen's abilities and, if you would not dare question hers, how dare you do so mine? Men? You are nothing but cowards with no conception of power or duty."

The voices this time were not raised in amusement but in outrage.

A richly dressed man of middle years whose belly strained against his velvet doublet stepped forward, his florid jowls wobbling with indignation. "Listen here, my lady. You may fancy yourself descended of royalty, but you are nothing more than the hireling of a grasping French pig who thinks to bed himself into wealth."

Walsingham gestured and soldiers leapt from their stations to surround the man.

"How dare you," Elizabeth muttered, fingers clenched on the arms of her throne. "How dare you speak so. Throw him in the Tower until he cools down and then he and I shall have a talk about loyalty, diplomacy, and appropriate conduct before one's monarch."

She turned a flinty stare upon Hela as the unfortunate noble was escorted away. "As for you, princess, you are a guest in my court and an envoy for my proposed husband. I advise you to conduct yourself with decorum and womanly restraint. Uttering threats like a common peasant? Impugning the courage of my court? I had expected better, my lady. Much better."

Hela ascended the first step of the dais, her temper burning in the fires of her dying patience. "And I had expected better of you, my queen. You allow these men to insult you as if they could have any idea what it is like to be you. You pretend to be a weak and feeble woman when you are one of the most powerful rulers in this world. You dishonor yourself and you dishonor your sex. How dare that man speak? How dare *you* remain silent? Where is your outrage? If they will not give you respect, then you must take it, not sit in impotent silence like–"

"Seize her!" Elizabeth shouted and a soldier grabbed Hela roughly by the arm, wrenching her around to face him.

Hela punched him in the face.

"Now you respond?" she demanded of Elizabeth. "Now you show your ire, to me? When I am the one defending you?" The soldier grabbed her again, this time trying to twist her arm up her back.

"Get your hands off me, you filthy human. Don't you know who I am? I am so far above you, and above your mockery of a monarch there. *I am the queen of Hel and you will let go of me right now!*"

He gaped as the court erupted into chaos. All the frustrations and mishaps and petty misogyny of the last days bubbled up in Hela and then boiled over and she welcomed their heat. Grabbing his face, Hela channeled her death touch into the hapless soldier.

Instantly, the focal stone in Mortlake activated and began dragging at her power. Hela growled and shoved even more magic into her hand, the stone's theft only driving her fury. The soldier began to scream and convulse, the skin of his face blackening and falling away.

The screams took on a shriller tone and a dozen more soldiers leapt at her despite what she was doing to their comrade. With a shriek of pure rage, Hela gave in to both her frustration and her savage joy. For the first time in her long life, her death touch was not lethal – the stone was siphoning away her magic almost as fast as she could conjure it – but it was still enough to injure. And injure she did, grabbing soldier after soldier by whatever naked skin she could get her hand to. Almost exclusively, that meant their faces.

She was distantly aware of Elizabeth being hurried away as the court emptied of flailing, panicking nobility and then a crossbow bolt punched through Hela's sleeve and then her arm, the narrow head passing cleanly through her flesh and out the other side.

She roared and ripped it free, fully intending on murdering everyone here in whatever creative ways she could manage, but her magic refused to heal the wound. It was almost entirely depleted, and her great strength with it.

There were at least a dozen hands on her, dragging her arms behind her now and shackling them as the last of her magic ran out. Pain ripped through her arm and shoulder. "You have no idea who I am," she snarled, weakness taking her knees from beneath her. She sagged in their grip and then, with a monumental effort of will, forced herself upright again. "Let me go and you'll never see me again. I want only the magic that is emanating from here. Give me that and you can all live. No harm will come to your–" her lip curled "– *queen.*"

Someone thrust a sack over her head. Hela writhed and struggled, but the decimation of her magic was overwhelming her like a tidal wave. Even so, the soldiers weren't strong enough to overcome her entirely, and even if they stuck their swords in her, they would find her hard to kill. For now, though, she didn't quite have the energy to break the chains binding her.

"Take her to the Tower and put fifty guards on her. No one is to enter her dungeon. No one is to touch her or allow themselves to be touched by her. She will be tried for a witch. Get her out of here and send for a physician for the wounded."

Walsingham's voice was wintry cold and had no give in it. There would be no parley with him and, weaker than she would ever admit, Hela put up little resistance as she was dragged out of the palace and shackled into some sort of cart.

They rattled away. In the darkness of the sack, Hela allowed herself a moment of bitter regret. A moment, but no more. She'd been impetuous, but her stature and position demanded it. She could still win this. If she was to be tried as a witch, surely they would want someone learned in the arcane arts to interrogate her. Someone trusted by the queen. A magician, even.

Despite her predicament, Hela smiled.

"... hilde? Bright-Battle, can you hear me? Groan if you can hear me."

Brunnhilde groaned.

"Odin's eye, at last. I was this close to contacting Heimdall to open Bifrost and march an army down here. And not one with the intention of going to war against the devil." There was a pause while the Valkyrie lay still, not daring to open her eyes or move or speak. "Unless you count that Norn-cursed idiot John Dee as the devil, anyway. Or Hela," Sif muttered, as Brunnhilde had known she would. "And where was she while we were being thrown across libraries, anyway? Wasn't she supposed to have been there? What mischief was she up to this time?"

"For Frigga's sake, Sif, shut up," the Valkyrie groaned. "Am I intact? Still got my limbs? I can't quite feel them."

There was a silence part-offended, part-amused. "Open your eyes and find out, O laziest of Valkyrior."

She did so, with more trepidation than she cared to admit. She blinked. "Where in Odin's name are we?"

"A field," the shield-maiden said sourly, though that was evident.

Brunnhilde's memory returned, and she sat up too fast and then reeled as dizziness hit her. "The stone and the book. Did I get them?" She began flailing about the grass surrounding them. "Where are they?"

"What do you think blew us across the library? It certainly wasn't John Dee. We didn't … they're still there. At his house."

Brunnhilde flopped back, every bone creaking, every muscle screaming. "I feel like I've battled a dragon singlehanded and lost," she muttered. "My strength is gone, or nearly all of it, anyway. My death perception. Everything that makes me a Valkyrie. That one single touch of the stone ripped it almost whole from me. You?"

"I … not everything," Sif said, frowning. She looked almost offended that she still had strength left. "I could touch the stone, but it made me dizzy and sick, stole my senses."

"We should be grateful you retained some strength and ability," Brunnhilde said firmly. "It'll be you fighting Hela if it comes to it."

The shield-maiden gaped. "Me fighting… And I should be grateful for this?" she asked slowly.

"As I recall, you threatened to drag her back to Asgardia in chains," the Valkyrie pointed out helpfully.

Sif paled. "Norns preserve me," she said quietly and was lost in horrified contemplation for a long moment. "Mortlake's a mile that way," she managed eventually. "When the stone knocked you out, it glowed so brightly with your magic that I couldn't physically get near enough to touch it. It threw up some sort of protective barrier I couldn't breach, so I tossed you over my shoulder and ran. I've got our packs, too."

"And you have a plan?" the Valkyrie asked, mainly because Sif looked shifty now.

"I can't glamour, so we'll have to spy on Dee's house and wait until he leaves or it gets dark, then we break in and I steal the artifacts. Like I said, it made me dizzy, but I'm pretty sure I can touch them for long enough to put them in my pack. Then I summon my brother's attention, he opens Bifrost, and we're gone. Without the stone, they can't open the bridge. We rest in Asgardia, pick up reinforcements – my preference is the God of Thunder – and then come back here to make sure anything that needs finishing gets finished. Including Hela."

"You want two goddesses of Asgard, dedicated to justice and truth, to rob a misguided old man?"

Sif leaned forward and glared. "You want me, your most loyal and entertaining companion–" Brunnhilde snorted softly "–to get withered into dust by the queen of Hel? After what happened earlier, surely Dee knows he's in too deep. He'll be grateful to lose the objects."

Brunnhilde put her arm over her face. She could sleep here for a week, a month. With the voice missing from her head, she might even sleep in truth, restfully. The luxury of it was almost enough to make her weep. "There's no compulsion," she said suddenly, sitting up again. "I can speak."

Sif rolled her eyes. "Wondered how long it would take you to notice that. But that might not be a good thing."

"No," Brunnhilde said softly. "It means the stone might have enough power to open the bridge."

"That's why we need to move fast. If Dee doesn't leave, maybe you can, ah, distract him?" The shield-maiden held up her hands. "If you've a better plan, I'm listening."

The Valkyrie didn't have a better plan. "How are our clothes? The other ones, I mean," she added, lifting her arm far enough to examine her stained sleeve.

"Crumpled, damp, smelling of pond water. But mostly clean."

"Delightful. All right, let's commit a burglary." Sif grinned.

"You're excited by this, aren't you?" Brunnhilde demanded, but without much heat. She was too tired for outrage.

The warrior pressed her lips together. "The great Bright-Battle, favored by Odin, leader of the Choosers of the Slain, advocating theft from Midgardians? Of course I'm loving it." The shield-maiden dragged the packs closer and began pulling out their other clothes. "We've still got the silver, except for what you left at the inn," she added, slanting a glance in the Valkyrie's direction. "That was well done, by the way. We can leave some for Lord Dee too, so it won't really be theft, will it? Just an exchange of goods for coin. Without permission."

Brunnhilde winced, her honor and sense of duty at war with each other. Duty won, and not least because of the catastrophe that would befall Midgard if the stone and book remained in this Realm.

"We should leave Asgardian coin," Sif added as she struggled out of her gown. "That way when Hela confronts Dee, she'll know it was us. She won't punish him then, will she?"

Brunnhilde swallowed hard. "We can pray not," she said slowly. There was nothing more to say after that.

The house at Mortlake was, unsurprisingly perhaps, busy with activity when they returned. A small crowd had gathered and there were five horses stamping and tossing their heads in front of the building.

The Asgardians exchanged doubtful looks. "Are they leaving?" Sif asked quietly. "That could make things easier for us. If we ambush them on the road away from the village, we can be in and out in seconds and no one gets hurt. They won't even realize it's us."

The idea made Brunnhilde uncomfortable, but she couldn't deny that it favored them. Perhaps things were finally going their way. The short walk back to Mortlake had sapped her remaining strength and her death perception, when she'd reached for it, was little more than a faint glow where once it had been a steady flame. What would the stone take once her abilities were gone? What would Brunnhilde *be* once they were gone?

John Dee emerged from his front door, shrugging into a doublet. Lady Jane followed, trying to drape a lush velvet half-cloak over his shoulders as he fiddled with his buttons. Beside them was a trio of urgent men, all dressed in armor.

From this angle, the Asgardians couldn't see their faces or hear what they said even with their exquisite senses, but the alarm in Dee's expression was unmistakable.

"A witch?" he demanded, with the air of someone repeating something yet again and coming no closer to believing it this time around. "Is Her Majesty safe? Unharmed? Jane, enough.

Back to the church with you until this is over," he added. "I won't have you and our son's immortal souls imperiled by these creatures. Francois, put the cherrywood box in my study and guard it well."

A groom brought a fine bay horse around. Dee swung himself into the saddle with spry ease for a man of his age and length of beard.

The soldiers mounted too and then they trotted towards the Asgardians' hiding place. "Lord Walsingham said to fetch you, my lord," they heard. "They say she burned men's faces off when they tried to restrain her. It's some devilry. His grace Bishop Aylmer has been summoned, too."

"A bishop and a magician," Dee said. "A dire circumstance indeed. Let us hasten, then." He kicked his horse into a canter.

Brunnhilde and Sif stared at each other. "Aren't we the witches?" the shield-maiden asked, confused. "I thought… wait. Thunder and lightning, Bright-Battle, Hela wasn't here. And she didn't turn up after you blew yourself across the room, either. She must have felt that. Even I felt it, and I'm not attuned to it the way you are."

"So, for reasons unknown, Hela visited the queen of England and attacked her," Brunnhilde said. "I mean, it does seem like the sort of thing she'd do. And if she's now a prisoner, that must mean the stone has weakened her, too."

"We won't get a better chance than this. Dee and Hela are both gone, Lady Jane's heading back to the church. This is perfect."

Brunnhilde pushed herself onto her feet. "You get the stone and the book. I'm going after Dee. He seems to be the only person on Midgard who can touch them without pain or penalty. Who knows what Hela will convince him to do if left alone with him?"

Sif grimaced. "You're going to need to glamour and then follow on foot... fast. Do you have the strength?"

Brunnhilde bit back an angry retort. Sif wasn't mocking her. "It's going to hurt," she allowed. "But I can do it. You be quick, safe, and unseen. And don't forget to leave the silver. And don't take them out of the box."

"I won't. I'll see you back at the duck pond."

"I'll find you," the Valkyrie promised.

"Odin guide you, my friend. Be wary of Hela."

Brunnhilde nodded, summoned up a little of her remaining strength, and glamoured herself. This time, the stone *twitched* but no more, already glutted on what it had stolen from her earlier that day. She took a deep breath, settled her armor and Dragonfang more comfortably, and began to sprint.

Nineteen

Prisoner

The cell was as dingy and uncomfortable as she had expected and they'd left the shackles on, a long chain dangling between her wrists that gave her freedom of movement. She assumed they were purely decorative or to serve as a reminder of her status, because it would be far too easy to loop the chain around someone's neck and pull it tight. Although in her case, at least, no one was prepared to get close enough to her for that.

The wound in her arm had been washed and roughly bound, but it throbbed in time with her heartbeat, a distracting burning hurt that wasn't healing. It shortened her temper even further.

The door was thick, heavy oak with a small, barred grille two thirds of the way up through which soldiers watched her and whispered to each other in nervous undertones. Hela sat on the low, hard cot pushed against the far wall and watched them back. Despite the toll taken on her magical reserves and her predicament, she was serene. She knew that Lord John Dee had been sent for and all she needed to do was convince him to let her go.

Despite visiting his house, she'd only met his servant and Lady Dee, so she had no fear of being recognized. Her biggest concern was what Odin's virtuous helpers were up to.

She'd felt the enormous blast of magic earlier, and unless she missed her guess, she'd say that one or both of them had made physical contact with the stone, for the speed and intensity with which the magic and power had built and radiated outwards, sending an echo through the building site upriver from Hela's location, had been far greater than when she herself had cast magic in its presence.

Whichever of them had touched it would have had her abilities, and possibly even some of her life force, stolen. She'd be no threat for the next day or so while she recovered. Hela smirked at the thought, smug that she hadn't touched the stone herself. It did mean, though, that the focal stone must be nearly fully powered and the bridge about ready to open.

She was aware of a faint voice in the back of her mind, scratching around like a mouse in the thatch. It alternated between begging and commanding her to speak the words of the ritual. It had grown markedly in strength since she'd burned through so much magic in Elizabeth's presence, but Hela was a goddess of vast and unknowable power. No one could command her as no one would survive such an expression of arrogance. Still, it was an irritant, especially here in the quiet of her cell with nothing to distract her. If not for the fact she wanted the stone and the magic for herself, she'd speak the words just to see the bridge open and

Midgard fall. It would be the perfect time for her to launch her own attack on Svartalfheim, too, with all their warriors here.

Hela indulged the fantasy for a while, imagining the battles here in London and the elves encountering the hated iron of weapons and armor while legions of her warriors took the cities and fields of Svartalfheim.

Soon, she promised herself. For now, she had a better way to make use of her time. Hela touched the torc at her throat and closed her eyes, seeking Eirik. The connection was difficult to establish and weak when she did as she battled her drained abilities, and she felt her seneschal's alarm at the wavering of their communion.

"My queen! What has happened? I have not heard from you in more than a day."

"I have been... inconvenienced, but there is no need for alarm," she lied automatically. "Though upon my return I will have my vengeance on Svartalfheim. And Midgard, too, if I am disrespected once more." Eirik grunted his surprise but said nothing. He knew better than to ask for details. If Hela wanted him to know, she'd tell him. She did not – at least not yet. "How are Helheim and Niffleheim? My palace?"

"All are peaceful and secure, my queen. Eljudnir remains under Fenris's baleful eye and my own. Your subjects are content and there are no threats at your borders. Do you wish me to send warriors to Svartalfheim now? Do you need our presence at... your location?" She could sense his curiosity and appreciated his restraint.

"No to both." She paused and searched inside herself, the levels of her power and magic, the reserves of her great strength. Not enough. Not quite. "My business may keep me in Midgard a day or two longer," she admitted reluctantly.

She felt the return of Eirik's surprise, this time that she was in the human Realm: he knew Hela didn't normally treat with humans or prize their souls highly.

"I will be back in touch later," she said, not wanting to admit how taxing she found even this small communication. "Guard my Realms well, seneschal. Fenris and I will both know if you do not."

"As my queen commands," Eirik responded.

Hela cut the communication and slumped back against the wall, abruptly exhausted. She ground her teeth and then gave in and relaxed onto the cot, wrapping her luxurious cloak around her and turning her back to the door and the watching soldiers. The Dark Elves, the humans, and those two Asgardian busybodies would all pay for this – and pay dearly.

Hela was awakened less than an hour later by the grating of a key in the lock. She stretched and sat up as the door swung open and Lord Dee and a man she vaguely remembered from the night of the ritual in Mortlake stepped inside with a visibly shaking guard between them and her. Hela smiled and rose gracefully to her feet.

"My lords, how may I be of assistance?"

The man who wasn't the soldier or John Dee stepped forward and brandished an ornate gold cross in her face. Hela arched an eyebrow. "Very pretty, decent craftsmanship. Is it a gift?" She reached out and snatched the cross from him before he could pull it back and the soldier squeaked and lunged at her with his sword. Hela pinned him in place with an icy glare.

"Do not threaten me unless you are very prepared for the consequences," she said pleasantly. She broke eye contact and made a show of examining the cross again, turning it over in her hands and weighing it thoughtfully. It was clearly some sort of test and she presumed from the covert glances the man and Lord Dee exchanged that she had passed it. She held it out. "I have enough trinkets at home."

The man – the bishop, Hela suddenly recalled – spluttered but took the cross back and held it close as if he thought she would change her mind and snatch it again.

"I am informed that you attacked members of the court today and attempted to end Her Majesty's life," John Dee said. Hela admired the fact he didn't phrase it as a question.

She retreated to the cot and sat back down upon it. "Untrue. I may have lost my temper somewhat," she admitted, "but your queen was never in any danger from me. Indeed, I may be the only one who can save her from what is coming."

"The duke of Alencon?" the bishop asked sarcastically. "Isn't that the lie you told in order to gain entrance to the royal presence?"

"When I fooled your queen's spymaster, you mean?" she asked with a smile. They'd already decided her guilt – not that she was denying her actions when the whole court had witnessed them – so there was little point in playing coy.

"We know you are not a foreign royal," Dee added, as if she should be impressed at his powers of deduction.

Hela put her head on one side and tutted. "That is where you are wrong. I told the entire court who I am; could that piece of information have not been forwarded to you in preparation for this interrogation? I am the queen of Hel."

She was unsurprised when both men scoffed at her assertion. "Does something amuse you, my lords?"

Instead of answering her, the bishop turned to John Dee and lowered his voice, as if that would help him. "She can bear the touch of the cross, so she isn't a demon or devil. Ward your mind and body, my lord. She may be a succubus, a witch, or one of the fae. Who and what she is, whether simply deluded or extremely clever or employing the infernal arts, I leave to you to decipher. I'll have no more dealings with her." He looked over to Hela and scowled. "I suggest you stop speaking such nonsense and cooperate with his lordship while you still can. The queen has yet to decide your fate, despite my strong advice to her already, so I suggest–"

Hela stood and the three men shrank back a step. "I have more power, more warriors and more magic than your queen has ever even dared to dream of. I do not accept her authority over me."

The bishop drew himself up to his full height and stared down the length of his nose at her. "Then I suggest you make your peace with God, for upon my return to court, I shall exhort her to have you executed for treason."

"How very Christian of you," Hela said, and the man gasped and reeled back a step in outrage.

"Your grace, wait," Dee tried, but the man swept out of the cell without a backward glance. Hela folded her arms across her chest but, to her surprise, Dee didn't follow him. "You may leave," he said instead to the soldier. "Lock the door and I will call you if I have need of you."

The guard obeyed with alacrity, almost leaping back out into the corridor and dragging the heavy door closed with a dull boom. They waited in silence while the key skittered and scraped against the lock before turning and then the soldier's shadow faded from the grille in the door.

Hela put her head on one side. "What is it you think you're going to do with me alone in here?" she asked.

Dee had the nerve to look offended. "Your virtue is quite safe with me, my lady, you may be at peace about that. Would you care to take a seat?" he continued, gesturing at the cot behind her.

Hela stood her ground. "No, I'd rather just get this over with. It's becoming tiresome." She paused and then smiled. "Why don't you tell me about your shew stone, as you call it, and the book written in the language of another Realm?"

The man stumbled backwards as if she had slapped him, the color draining from his face. "You really are a witch," he breathed. "Was it your sisters who invaded my home this morning?"

Hela scoffed. "I can assure you, my lord Dee, that Brunnhilde and Sif are my sworn enemies. They are part of the reason why I am here, in fact. They are demons sent to stop me in my quest."

This time, Dee looked skeptical. He crossed his arms beneath his beard and chewed one end of his mustache as he watched her. "You proclaim yourself to be the queen of Hell and yet you say they are demons sent to stop you, not aid you? And you know their names, indicating a relationship with them."

"I know your name, John. Does that make us allies?" She laughed at his recoil.

"No. Your story makes no sense, my lady, and I am afraid I

am running out of patience, and you are running out of time. Bishop Aylmer will recommend your execution. If you wish to avoid it, you must give me something."

"My story, as you call it, will make perfect sense if you allow me to finish telling it," Hela snapped. "I am not the queen of Hel by choice, but rather was condemned to such by the Father of All simply because he feared my strength. He has decided that your world should be punished for its hubris and so has sent the stone and book to you. He tells you that the bridge will open a path to the angels when in fact it will lead to a dark and vicious Realm full of bloodthirsty and uncivilized warriors intent on conquering your world. Every word of this is true," she added with self-righteous conviction. *Mostly.*

"The Father fears my abilities and condemned me to the cold and isolation of Hel rather than reward me as I deserve. However, if you free me and take me to the building site at Whitehall Palace, I will have a better understanding of his plan. I will retrieve what I need hidden there, and then accompany you back to your home where you will give me the stone and the book. I will remove them from this world, thus keeping it safe, and all humanity can rest in God's grace. When he sees your humility, his wrath will be cooled. You can thank me in your prayers."

Dee spat out his mustache and had the temerity to laugh. "My lady, I'm afraid that is the most ridiculous story I've ever heard in my life. Were it not indecent, I would recommend you for a career on the stage but as it is, it seems there is no more I can do for you. If you will not tell me how you injured those soldiers, then I cannot in good conscience beg the queen for leniency for you."

"Midgardians," Hela muttered under her breath and began to gather her magic. Her earlier nap had restored a little of her strength and she'd need it to mesmerize him and then cast the illusion that she was still in this cell.

Tension began to charge and then crackle in the air as if a lightning storm gathered overhead. Dee could feel it too; his eyes grew wide with alarm. "What are you doing?" he began before there was a pop and a shimmer in the air – not Hela's doing, not her magic but not elven, either – and the Valkyrie appeared at the man's side.

Dee screamed.

She was tall and beautiful and terrible, blonde hair cascading down her back and her armor gleaming in the high, slanting light from the barred window above the cot.

From outside the cell came shouts of alarm and running feet and then a face pressed against the grille. "Who? What? How did you get in there?" the soldier gasped and fumbled at the lock. The hinges squealed as the soldier opened the door and then froze in place. Brunnhilde waved him away and he fled, vanishing along the corridor.

"Believe nothing this person says," Brunnhilde said loudly, with a snap of command in her tone. "Her tongue is made of lies. She wants the stone for herself and she will let this world burn if it means she will get it."

"How dare you," Hela began, stepping forward. The Valkyrie had the audacity to draw her sword and Hela came to a halt.

"You," Dee whispered hoarsely. "You appear out of nowhere, outlined in light and clad in divine armor. You command Her Majesty's own troops without effort, as if born to it. It is… tell me it is you with whom I've been communicating this whole time." The Valkyrie didn't even nod before a beatific smile crossed Dee's face and he fell to his knees before her. "O holy seraph, you bless me with your mighty presence. Forgive all the sins I have committed thus far. Forgive me for listening to this devil's lies, O mighty Uriel."

"No," Hela snarled and took a step forward, ignoring the sword and gathering her magic again, this time to strike and rend and kill. "No, he is mine! You shall not have him, nor the magic, nor the stone. He is *mine!*"

Brunnhilde raised her sword. "Stay behind me, my lord. The queen of Hel is dangerous indeed." She met Hela's eyes as she said it, and the goddess saw both the truth and the respect reflected there. She also saw the legendary Dragonfang in the Valkyrie's hand and how its point was unwavering in its aim at her heart. "You have come here for greedy, immoral purposes, Your Majesty. You have come here to exploit these people. You do not care what happens to them or the Dark Elves once the war begins, do you? Not as long as you get what you want."

Hela stepped up close so that the tip of the sword was pressing against her bodice. Daring Brunnhilde to thrust it home and knowing she wouldn't. "I am the queen of Hel," she snarled in the Valkyrie's face. "Who are you to think to raise a blade against me? To raise even so much as your voice?"

"I am sent by the All-Father to ensure this Realm remains at peace," the Valkyrie replied evenly, the sword steady in her hand. Still, there was sweat glistening along her hairline at the enormity of what she was doing – who she was threatening. "To uphold that, I will do whatever I must."

"Will you, indeed?" Hela murmured. "I should like to see you try. I suggest you remove yourself from my presence and allow me to continue my work."

Their eyes locked and the air crackled between them. "I'm afraid I cannot allow that, Your Majesty. You are putting lives in danger by collaborating with Svartalfheim. Lord Dee," she added without looking away, "you will take me to this new construction site of which Hela spoke. I must see what is happening there."

"I will, angel. It will be my honor to attend upon you."

Brunnhilde twitched, distaste at the deception clear for a moment, and then she stepped back, Dragonfang breaking contact with Hela's chest. "Then let us go now."

Brunnhilde had a very bad feeling about everything she'd just done. Had she really held her sword to the ruler of Helheim? Hela was correct: who was she to dare to behave in such a manner? She had every right to go to war against Asgard for the insult, if not to simply hunt Brunnhilde down and destroy her – lovingly, slowly, over weeks.

But before that, if Elizabeth did order her execution, Hela would slaughter any who came for her. Whatever restraint she'd shown in the court – if maiming instead of killing could be thought of as restraint – would vanish if anyone was determined to do her harm.

But why didn't she kill anyone? Why allow herself to be captured, allow me to threaten her? And now she's letting us leave?

The Valkyrie came to an abrupt halt. *Hela's lost her magic, the same as I've lost my strength. It must be.*

At her side, Dee stilled, his eyes going wide and panicked.

"There is… no!" he stuttered and lunged out of the cell, heedless of Brunnhilde's shout.

There was a burst of power from the direction of Mortlake and Brunnhilde knew it was Sif in Dee's house. The elven stone was fighting back.

The queen of Hel smiled and lifted one eyebrow. "What could be happening?" she murmured. The Valkyrie bared her teeth but then Dee vanished along the corridor.

"Wait. Tell me what you know," Brunnhilde commanded, and the man halted, torn between running off and obeying the angel.

"Someone's stolen it! The shew stone, the book. Someone has stolen my, I mean your, sacred items, angel. The items that will open the bridge to Paradise as you have commanded me. We must go, immediately. I must have them back. *I must!*"

Hela snorted a laugh. "I think your precious angel knows who that someone is, don't you?" she asked. Before she could say any more, Brunnhilde left the cell and slammed the door, turning the key the soldier had left in the lock and then pocketing it. "Why don't you tell him who's got his precious stone now, Valkyrie?" the goddess called after her.

Brunnhilde was tempted for a moment to embrace a little of Sif's recklessness and invite the queen of Hel to break out of the cell if she wanted Dee to know anything but she bit it back with savage discipline.

"Lord Dee, please slow down," she called ahead to where the old man was clattering down the stone stairs. The soldiers gathered at the end of the corridor leading to Hela's cell were close to panic and drew back as one at catching sight of Brunnhilde, muttering prayers and putting hands on sword hilts.

She tossed the cell key to the nearest. "Keep an eye on her, but don't get too close," she said and strode past as if it was entirely normal for her to have appeared in the cell the way she had. She'd had no choice but to reveal herself when it seemed that Dee was falling under Hela's sway, disproving another of their theories – that she'd recruited him into her service after allying with Svartalfheim.

Brunnhilde knew even less now than when she'd first started being plagued with dreams. Could it be that Hela had responded to the stone's summons in a similar way? Could it be that she wasn't allied with the Dark Elves after all, and that Dee really had no idea what he was involved with? His attunement with the stone was undeniable if he could sense that Sif had taken possession of it, but that didn't mean he was a willing ally of either Hel or Svartalfheim.

The man burst out of the Tower, startling soldiers on patrol, and hurried for the stables and his horse. Brunnhilde groaned. "My lord, you need to procure me a mount," she said. She had no wish to run with her enchanted speed behind his horse all the way to their destination. It had been hard enough keeping up with him on the way here.

"Yes, yes, whatever we need, but we must hurry." He didn't even look at her, obsessed with his connection with the focal stone and its location. It was obvious to the Valkyrie now, too. The stone was active, though she couldn't tell if it was drawing Sif's strength as it had done hers and, she was now convinced, Hela herself.

She could feel it and it was moving. Moving fast. Moving closer. *Sif, my friend. What are you doing? I was supposed to come to you.*

The bad feeling she'd had when confronting Hela became worse. Something was very wrong. Sif had been able to touch the artifacts without losing all her strength, even though they disoriented her. It was Brunnhilde's death perception – her Valkyrior abilities – the stone had stolen first, just as it had stolen the Goddess of Death's magic. It was death and all that was associated with it that the stone wanted. Sif didn't have that, and so its attack on her had been lesser. Lesser, but not nothing, and so she'd planned on scooping the box into her pack and carrying it at arm's length. Instead, both Sif and the stone were hurrying closer to London.

Dee was mumbling under his breath, mangling the elven language but speaking fragments of the ritual and all of a sudden the voice in Brunnhilde's head began to whisper again.

We are so close to you. Speak the words of the ritual, work the magic that powers the spell that opens the path for us. We are so close. Let us in!

"Where is the building site?" she asked loudly, cutting off both the voice in her head and Dee's whispered chant. "Where?"

"Whitehall Palace, that way. But the crystal–"

"Between us and Mortlake?" Brunnhilde interrupted and he nodded wretchedly. "Then that's where she's going. Somehow, she knows about the power of that place. Perhaps the stone told her."

They reached the stables and Dee demanded his horse and a spare for his guest. The grooms hesitated, but he was well known and a member of the queen's own court. They brought out a dappled grey and the Valkyrie swung up into the saddle without hesitation.

The pair clattered out of the courtyard, turned their horses' heads towards the river and kicked them into a canter. She had no idea what to expect, and the skin on the back of her neck prickled as they left the Tower's shadow. As if Hela was watching from her cell window. Tracing their path. Biding her time.

TWENTY

WARRIOR OF ASGARD

Whitehall Palace was enormous, a vast collection of buildings rather than a single structure as she'd been expecting. A small city within the city, even.

It was bathed in afternoon sunshine when Dee and Brunnhilde pulled their foaming mounts to a halt on the outskirts. The Valkyrie threw herself out of the saddle and helped him to dismount. The old man was almost as pale as his beard from the pace they'd ridden, but that hadn't been why he stopped: the stone was here. They could both feel it and the roaring imperative in Brunnhilde's head was regaining control of her voice and mind. The urge to speak the spell grew with every stride, but so did her worry for Lady Sif.

They abandoned their horses to grooms, ignored their polite questions about when they needed the animals back, and began striding into the complex of buildings.

Brunnhilde caught up with Dee and grabbed him by the arm. "My lord, I beg you to be careful. While I sense no evil intent from the person who has taken possession of the stone–" she still couldn't afford to admit that she and Sif were working together and risk losing the trust he had in her, even if it was based on an assumption she had neglected to correct "–but that does not mean that there won't be danger. That woman you spoke to in the Tower is powerful indeed. I will do what I can to protect you from her, but I must know whether you are working with her."

Dee tugged ineffectually at her grip, mumbling Elvish again, and she forced him into stillness and repeated her question. "No, no," he said absently, "I don't know her. She didn't sell me the crystal. Nor her witches from this morning."

Brunnhilde blinked. She'd thought, at first, that the nature of her manifestation in the cell meant that Dee just hadn't looked too closely at her out of respect or fear. Now she was confronting the possibility that changing her attire and loosening her hair had somehow convinced him she was an entirely different person.

She gave him another sidelong glance even as she reminded herself this was a good thing, and then shouts echoed from deep among the buildings. The Valkyrie tensed, clutching at Dragonfang's hilt so that the sheathed blade shimmered into view. People rounded a corner at speed and raced towards them, raced past them, glancing fearfully back over their shoulders and paying the pair absolutely no attention. They were dusty, heavyset men wearing thick leather aprons and tool belts hung with hammers and chisels. The masons from the building site?

"What's happening?" she tried but no one would answer her. "Stay close but don't get in my way," she ordered, and Lord Dee nodded convulsively.

"As you command, archangel Uriel." The Valkyrie grunted, focusing on the direction from which the masons had come. "That is your name, is it not? You are the archangel of wisdom. You are–"

"Quiet now, my lord. There is magic and danger both ahead of us." The man subsided and she was pleased to note that he didn't start speaking Elvish again, even though the urge to do so was growing in her with every passing second.

Brunnhilde gritted her teeth. It wasn't just her proximity to the stone – pulsing in her awareness like a great beacon, a heart beating incandescent power through its chambers – power it had stolen from her, from Hela, and possibly from Sif. It was also this place. It was whatever the masons had been building here, whatever was being carved into the foundations of this banqueting hall. She understood Hela's preoccupation with it now.

She grabbed a handful of Dee's velvet sleeve and towed him along in her wake, faster and faster until they were both running in time with the stone's rhythmic pulsing of power and yearning as it called to her, summoned her. *I'm here to stop this*, she reminded herself.

We are so close, gathered just on the other side of the bridge, the veil, between worlds. A host of wondrous beings, an army of glory and power. Just speak the words, speak the words, little human, speak them and let us in.

Let! Us! In!

Behind her, John Dee jerked and slowed. Brunnhilde hesitated, torn between sprinting forwards and staying by his side. She looked back and he was chanting, no longer mangling the elven language, no longer broken fragments of the spell or out of order phrases. Without understanding what he was saying, or why, or how, he began to craft the ritual, drawing shapes in the air. His eyes were blank, as if staring into another world, an inner vista populated with angels. Only these angels had blue skin and white hair and were going to tear this city down around his ears if they made it here.

"Stop! My Lord Dee, you must stop speaking! *Stop!*" She hurled Asgardian power and authority into her voice. Dee tore his arm from her grip, leaving her with only a scrap of velvet sleeve, and then shoved her in the chest with a force that was entirely beyond his frail human form. Brunnhilde's feet left the ground and she flew backwards several yards before crashing to the flagstones in a hideous screech of armor on stone.

By the time the world had stopped spinning and she'd regained her feet, the old man had vanished around the corner. "Odin's eye," she swore and leapt forward in pursuit. She darted between the buildings and across a wide expanse of courtyard, past a walled garden smelling of herbs, and found the building site so recently vacated by the masons.

Found Lord John Dee, blank-eyed and chanting in the foundations and the deep carved ritual space that had been laid into it.

Found Lady Sif, similarly blank-eyed. Passing the stone and the book to Dee – by hand! – and then drawing her sword and taking up position beside him. Her movement wooden and controlled by another.

"No," Brunnhilde breathed, and then bit the inside of her cheek savagely until she tasted blood. She swallowed the coppery mouthful and the elven words that demanded to be spoken, blinking away tears at the suddenness of the pain.

When she could focus again, Sif had turned to face her, a terrible emptiness stealing life and expression from her features. She had settled into a defensive stance and raised her sword. To Brunnhilde. *Against* Brunnhilde.

"No," the Valkyrie repeated and to that, finally, Sif's blankness receded. In its place, a slow, cruel smile twisted her face, and she raised her free hand and beckoned.

Hela had waited patiently in her cell as the magic built far off in Whitehall. This time, the elven stone did not sniff out and steal her power and she was free to observe it from a distance.

As suspected, it was some form of death magic, either powered through willing sacrifice or possibly ritualistic murder. In the light of this, it made sense that the magic had called to both herself and the Valkyrie, attuned as they were to the ending of life.

The whispered suggestion of a ritual had returned, and she ignored the imperative to join in as she had done before. This time, though, instead of dismissing the words from her conscious mind, she concentrated on them and the gentle flickers in the muscles of her hands and arms that suggested summoning and binding and opening ceremonies to be performed.

This way, even though she was nowhere near the site of the ritual itself, she learned the shape and feel of it. It would be vital knowledge for when she took the stone, the book, and all the artifacts here on Midgard and modulated them to answer to her magic and open to a location of her choosing.

Now the spell was reaching its conclusion and Hela was keen to see what happened next. Sure in the knowledge that the elven stone no longer wanted or needed her power, the goddess made her move. She snapped the shackles off her wrists, tearing through the iron like it was paper.

Then, she created an illusion of herself to appear in the corridor outside the cell. There were shrieks of alarm at her sudden appearance and the clatter of footsteps as at least one soldier took to their heels, whether in fear or to find reinforcements, Hela neither knew nor cared. There was still one soldier out there and that was all she needed.

The illusion prowled down the corridor towards him. "Unlock the cell door and step back," it said, "and you will neither be hurt nor killed. Do not test my patience: quickly, now."

Hela's real form pressed against the wall next to the cell door and she waited for the scrape of the master key in the lock. As soon as it came, she jerked open the door from inside, dispelling the illusion and stepped through into the corridor, yanking the soldier inside.

"Thank you for your assistance. I shall not forget it. Now, I suggest you think up some plausible excuse to explain to your queen why you're in the cell and I'm… not." She bared her teeth and swung the door shut between them.

The soldier looked strangely happy to be in the cell and Hela gave him a wave before sauntering down the corridor and stairs. Now that the focal stone was not drawing her magic in that endless little dribble, her strength was returning quickly. She emerged from the Tower and cast a glamour over herself that blurred her features and made her appear unremarkable, easily forgettable, and then walked casually out of the Tower's grounds and onto the riverbank.

Hela took a breath of fresh air and dispelled the illusion as soon as she was out of sight of the Tower guards. She still needed to marshal her reserves of magic.

"My lady! Your Highness, over here!" Hela blinked and turned towards the voice. It was William. He ran to her side and seized her hands, kissing her knuckles. "I knew you'd escape somehow, my goddess," he said breathlessly. "You are truly a marvel, a muse, a magician beyond compare. I wonder that you are not some dream sent to torment me with your beauty." Hela clucked her tongue in pretend disapproval and removed her hand from his. "I knew they wouldn't be able to hold you for long, Your Highness."

He was so excited he danced a little jig and then pointed over his shoulder at the boat. "Where we off to then, queen of my heart?"

Hela's eyebrows rose. "You have become bold, haven't you?" she murmured. "Very well. Whitehall Palace. Row hard. We don't have much time. And no, I'm not going to kill your queen," she added.

William sketched a bow before gesturing with a flourish towards the boat. Hela couldn't help grinning at his enthusiasm. If only all her subjects were this reliable. This... infatuated.

"How long would you have waited for me?" she asked once the boat was underway and he'd pointed to her basket. She buckled on her armor over her gown. The boy flashed her a grin over the oars. "I'd have nipped off to get some supper at some point, but I'd have stayed out all night if I had to. I'd wait for you forever. I still haven't seen enough magic, my lady. Besides," he added and even had the audacity to wink despite the fiery blush staining his cheeks, "you've quite stolen my heart away. I'll be telling stories about you the rest of my life."

"I expect nothing less," Hela said. William's eyes sparkled. "But if it's magic you want to see, then this is about to be your very lucky day. I can absolutely promise you are going to see wonders the like of which very few people in this world have ever seen. Most would not even believe possible what you're going to witness this day."

The boy whooped and bent over his oars with renewed determination. Hela didn't need to provide any more encouragement and settled back to conserve her strength and puzzle out the shape and feel of the ritual.

Was it Dee speaking the words now, or had the stone got its claws into Sif or Brunnhilde? Maybe both? Maybe even all of them. London slid by on either side, smoky, stinky, and vibrant, its inhabitants unaware of the threat to their queen and their entire way of life.

"Sif, please stop. It's me, it's Brunnhilde: don't you recognize me?"

Hela's mouth curved in a wolfish smile; it appeared the stone had a will of its own and in this, at least, it was aligned with Hela's desires. She and the boy halted in the shadow of a building and stared down into the exposed foundations of what was going to be the new banqueting hall.

John Dee stood in the center on top of a mosaic array that had clearly been designed to Dark Elven specifications. He held the book and the stone in his hands and was walking from point to point along the pattern as he chanted. Nearby, Lady Sif confronted the Valkyrie. No, not confronted: opposed. She was blank-eyed and firmly under the objects' control.

Hela could feel the magic building, the power inching along her nerve-endings as Dee layered spell upon spell within the pattern, focusing them through the stone and the chant to connect Midgard to Svartalfheim and rip open a tunnel between them. It was a clever piece of spell craft and Hela watched in silence, ignoring the two Asgardians posturing and threatening like peacocks while she hurriedly memorized the closest section of the mosaic. She'd need to replicate it exactly if she was to cast it successfully and begin her conquest of Asgard.

"What's happening?" William whispered, his eyes round and glittering above cheeks flushed with delight. And there wasn't even any visible sign of magic yet, at least not to his untrained, human eye.

Hela pointed. "Lord Dee has been influenced by the objects he holds and is now under their control. The book and stone belong to the Dark Elves who live in Svartalfheim and who are trying to break through into Midgard – into this world – in order to conquer it and enslave all humanity."

William's head snapped up so that he could gaze at her with unblinking intensity. Hela's finger moved on regardless.

"The black-haired warrior is Lady Sif and she is great friends with the blonde warrior, Brunnhilde the Valkyrie, not that you could tell at the moment as Sif is also under the stone's power. In her case, I expect it is using her as a slave to defend itself, keeping everyone away until Dee can complete the ritual and the path to Svartalfheim has opened."

"What ... what will happen then?"

Hela shrugged. "The stone will probably absorb the last of their power and life force and they'll die. It's irrelevant. By that point, the armies of Svartalfheim will already be marching through the breach."

The boy was silent, robbed of words for the first time since she'd met him. Hela snorted and put him out of her mind. She needed the Asgardians to be fighting each other so that she had a chance to take the stone and the book for herself. From the tension in the air, the spell was on the verge of becoming self-sustaining. When that happened, the stone would become inert and be safe for her to touch. She picked up a lump of rock from a pile of rubble nearby, took aim, and hit Lady Sif in the face, knocking her back a step. Blood ran from her cheek and nose and she let out a screech of pure fury and flung herself at the Valkyrie.

"Sif, don't!" The shield-maiden ignored Brunnhilde's plea as easily as Hela ignored the William's inarticulate cry of protest. The Valkyrie traced the stone back to its origin and Hela blew her a kiss. Before she could respond, Sif was on her. Hela sidestepped the fray and advanced on Lord Dee.

Despite her impatience and the threat of the Asgardians interrupting her, she approached with caution and respect. She understood part of this magic simply through observation and deduction, but it had proved itself to be wily and she could not afford to lose her own magic again. She hesitated on the edge of the mosaic, extending her senses to brush the edges of the ritual.

Then, taking a deep breath, she stepped onto the pattern and approached the blank-faced man chanting at its center.

"Tell me what you are doing," she demanded and stretched out her hand. Black sparks stung her fingertips as the magic tasted and then rejected her. Didn't hurt, but most importantly, didn't steal.

Interesting. It needed strength to become active but now that it is, it neither wants nor can use my magic. What does John Dee have that I don't, other than being native to this Realm?

Ah.

The ritual to open the path needs to be conducted by someone born within the destination Realm. That's why although it took my magic and that of the Valkyrie to strengthen itself, it chose him to complete the summoning.

Hela's gaze fell on the bleeding, screaming shield-maiden and she narrowed her eyes in appraisal. Yes. Perfect. It seemed as if the candidate to open the path between Helheim and Asgard had already made her presence known. When Hela was back in Eljudnir and her armies were assembled, she would cast this spell herself and it would call to Sif and force her to play the part that was John Dee's today.

And if Sif died here, well, the Valkyrie had a swatch of material clamped between her teeth as a gag – she was as helpless in the stone's grasp as the shield-maiden.

Either one of them would fulfil Hela's purposes when she was ready to launch her invasion and claim the throne destined to be hers. Smiling, she memorized the next part of the mosaic beneath her feet.

TWENTY-ONE

WARRIOR OF HEL

Brunnhilde backed desperately away from her friend, leaping to the top of a half-constructed wall and taking the second's reprieve it gave her to rip off the cuff of her sleeve and shove it in her mouth.

It was less than dignified, but with Sif harrying her relentlessly, she was too distracted to keep a grip on her words. The last thing this situation needed was for her to aid Lord Dee in his attempt to open the path to Svartalfheim. On the other hand, it meant she was unable to plead with the shield-maiden for her to come to her senses and stop her attack.

Even as she thought it, Sif kicked the base of the wall hard enough to shatter the mortar holding it together. The wall collapsed in a crash of rubble and Brunnhilde leapt from among the flying debris towards John Dee. Immediately, Sif threw herself at the Valkyrie with a bellowed war cry.

Brunnhilde danced out of her way, gripping the material between her teeth to muffle the words she could not stop herself from saying. She wished, desperately, for just enough space and time to send a distress call to Heimdall the Far-Seeing. An imminent invasion from Svartalfheim and the presence of the Goddess of Hel were enough to justify a request for reinforcements, not to mention that Heimdall's sister was apparently intent on carving out Brunnhilde's heart.

The building site was littered with unconscious Midgardians and some who, from their unnatural stillness, she knew to be dead. Sif's arrival in Whitehall Palace had been bloody and frenzied and now, despite the echoing clash of weapons as the Asgardians battled across the site, the humans appeared loath to intrude. That at least was good news as far as the Valkyrie was concerned. The fewer innocents she had to worry about, the better.

Sif picked up a masonry block a foot square in one hand and hurled it at Brunnhilde's head. The Valkyrie ducked and heard a piercing scream from behind: spinning around, she saw a teenage boy frozen in the shadow of a wall watching the block tumble out of the sky towards him.

Brunnhilde jumped, not at the boy but at the falling block of stone. She met it in midair and kicked it sideways, sending it off course to smash into the wall several feet along from the cowering Midgardian. She landed lightly, nodded once to the boy, and turned once more to face her friend – and enemy.

For an instant, she was relieved: Sif had taken the fight to Hela, who must have advanced too near Lord Dee. But Hela was a far more powerful goddess than either of them and, unlike the Valkyrie, she had no reason to hold back in their battle. The circlet she'd worn on her brow had transformed into a spiked ebony helm and she twisted and struck out with the Nightsword in a complicated, lethal dance. Her armor shone black and one sleeve of her gown was slit open. The crisp white of bandages showed through. The injury did less to hinder her than her full silver skirts.

This was Brunnhilde's chance to destroy the ritual and the artifacts. Breathing a prayer to Odin to watch over the shield-maiden, she skirted wide around the battling warriors and headed for John Dee.

The beautiful, mesmerizing crystal in his hand glowed like a tiny sun as the words tripped and raced from his tongue and wove arcs of fire in the air around him. Those same words beat in Brunnhilde's brain and blood and chest, the need to speak them growing in strength with every step. She was running out of time and, she suspected so was Dee. So was Midgard.

Clamping her jaws on the cloth in her mouth, the Valkyrie stepped on to the ornate mosaic on the floor. Stepped into the heart of a whirlwind, the heart of a tidal wave, the heart of a battle on the verge of defeat. The cloth fell from her mouth, she flung out her arms, and screamed.

Screamed Elvish.

Hela's rage at how the shield-maiden had spoken to her at their last meeting was compounded by the fact that, while she'd replenished much of her stolen magic, she was still far weaker than she was used to. Her depleted death touch would be ineffectual against an Asgardian, and without this most lethal resource at her literal fingertips, she was being forced to rely on her martial skill.

And in this particular case, against a warrior of Sif's reputation and training, she was only just holding her own.

It also left the Valkyrie free to meddle in affairs about which she knew nothing. Hela needed to end this fight quickly and definitively and she could not.

Once again, her swords met Sif's in a shower of sparks and clang of steel that echoed around the building site and bounced from the walls of the palace. The pair battled back and forth and every time Hela attempted to close on John Dee, Sif found a way to interpose herself between them, even at risk to her own life. She remained blank-faced through it all, her teeth showing only when she exerted herself. The rest of the time, she looked as bored as if she was standing guard over an empty room.

The ritual was entering its final phase when the clank and clatter of armored footsteps heralded the arrival of a score of Midgardian soldiers appeared around the corner. They had swords on their hips and long, wickedly pointed pikes in their hands. There was a long pause as they took in the scene and then, with grim determination, they split into two groups. Half advanced on John Dee and the Valkyrie, who was now standing on the elven pattern beside the lord and chanting along with him. The spell's compulsion had finally overcome her defenses.

The rest of the soldiers came for Hela and her opponent.

She had a moment to wonder what Sif would do before the warrior kicked the closest soldier in the chest hard enough to dent his breastplate and fling him back into the arms of his companions. Well, that was definitive. It might also be just the distraction Hela needed.

She leapt backwards and lowered her sword until it pointed at the ground. "Please help me," she begged the soldiers.

"These women have gone mad, attacked me and my lord Dee without provocation. You must restrain them before they kill us all."

Sif didn't give her time for more, leaping at her with a scream that confirmed her supposed lunacy quite nicely. The air was crackling with power now, and every time metal kissed metal, there was an explosion of black-edged sparks. Hela's long, unbound hair was beginning to float in a halo around her head as the atmosphere charged with magic. Brunnhilde's and Sif's were likewise reacting, and Hela could well imagine how otherworldly they must appear. Yet compared with what was about to arrive through the path from Svartalfheim, they looked positively human.

The soldiers had halted at her appeal, while those confronting the Valkyrie and her charge appeared at a loss for what to do. Brunnhilde was motionless as long as they didn't advance too near, whereupon she drove them back with a flurry of strikes and then, as soon as they reached a distance she deemed safe, she disengaged and retreated to Lord Dee's side. She, like Sif, had become the stone's protector.

Meanwhile, Lady Sif had forced three of soldiers into a running battle. She was evading them with ease, leaping up onto walls and then falling on them from above to snap their weapons and tear their armor. Droplets of blood spattered the building site as more and more soldiers were drawn into the fray.

Their pikes were long enough to keep Sif at bay most of the time, but her Asgardian strength, speed and agility were so far beyond their experience or ability to counter that they resembled nothing more than a group of small children defending desperately against a giant eagle bent on consuming them.

The soldier Sif had kicked was unconscious against the wall and William was crouched beside him, ashen and panicking. Apparently, this was not the type of magic he'd wanted to see. Little fool. What had he expected, parlor tricks? For all his supposed devotion, he'd been unable to see Hela for who she truly was. That ignorance extended to his knowledge of magic and now he was learning some harsh truths. Still, she made sure none of the soldiers were advancing on him before facing the four confronting her.

Despite Hela's plea for aid, the naked steel in her hand had convinced them she was a threat. She backed away in a wide semicircle, further from the shield-maiden and the whirling chaos of the melee surrounding her. She needed only an instant to reach Dee and snatch the artifacts from his hands and break the building spell – or harness its power to Realm-jump home.

Fifteen soldiers and Brunnhilde stood between Hela and the culmination of her plan, the successful conclusion of her outrageous stay in this forsaken Realm. A pike flashed towards her chest and she batted it away with contemptuous ease, but a second was already stabbing for her kidney and she had to sidestep further from the mosaic array to avoid it.

As much as Hela wanted to see Midgard punished for how it had treated her since her arrival, she had no interest in being present when the armies of Svartalfheim marched out of the path between Realms and Dee was shrieking the final incantation. It was now or never. The Goddess of Hel leapt over the heads of two soldiers and sprinted forwards.

The Valkyrie was engaged with three others and had her back to Hela.

Sif picked up a soldier and threw him into three others and the whole group went down in a tumble directly in Hela's path. She tried to leap the tangle of limbs and armor only for one of them to snag a lucky hand around her ankle. She had no idea whether he'd done it on purpose, but it didn't matter when she was jerked out of the air and landed heavily in their midst. Forty feet away, the Valkyrie was sweeping soldiers before her as if they were kindling and John Dee's voice was a hoarse scream of ecstasy, his face twisted with righteous madness.

Hela kicked free, ducked a block of stone thrown by Lady Sif and then picked up a pike and threw it at Brunnhilde. The bladed end punched the blonde warrior off her feet and face down on the stone.

Hela followed the weapon at a flat sprint, her free hand outstretched ready to snatch the stone from Dee's grip. She was two strides away when there was a terrible tearing sound and all the magic concentrated into a point that swirled and writhed in the air above the mosaic, pulling at her core and trying to twist her bones as well as the dimensions themselves.

Soldiers screamed and fell. Their hands clapped over their bleeding ears. The very atmosphere itself split open and there, impossibly distant, were the tall, jagged mountains of Svartalfheim. Also impossibly distant, and yet at the same time impossibly near, waited legions of Dark Elves. There was a pregnant pause in which all movement within the building site ceased, and then Lord Dee and the Valkyrie collapsed as the spell left them.

Hela stopped moving. Lady Sif stood over the downed soldiers, panting and shaking her head to clear it. She stared at her sword and then lowered it so fast the tip clanged off the ground. "What's happening? Why are you threatening me?" she demanded. Everyone ignored her, their eyes drawn to the rent in the fabric of the world. Their eyes drawn to the blue-skinned, white-haired warriors approaching through the air, rank upon rank upon rank with seemingly no end.

The spell was complete and Midgard, all unknowing, was at war.

Brunnhilde groaned and rolled over on the stone. There was a deep, penetrating ache between her shoulder blades. She wasn't quite sure what had happened: something had thrown her face-first onto the stone, bruising her cheek and jaw. Her throat was raw as if she'd been shouting all day and her nerve endings felt scoured and tender as if foreign magic had been sluicing through her veins.

The Valkyrie blinked gritty eyes and attempted to focus. There was a shimmer in the air above her that she couldn't quite make out, while to her right Lord Dee lay in a heap on the stone. The crystal and book he'd been holding had tumbled out of his grip and the former was glittering prettily in the sunshine. Brunnhilde blinked at it some more. There was something important about those objects, she knew, but her fatigue was so great that she couldn't place them.

"God preserve us!"

"Bright-Battle, is that you? Odin's eye, stand up, Valkyrie. We've got company."

The panicking voice was familiar in the same way the book

and the stone were familiar: something she should recognize but couldn't. A shadow fell over her and she squinted up at it. Her, she did recognize. Hela, queen of Helheim and Niffleheim.

Everything came back to Brunnhilde in a sickening rush and she lurched onto her feet and blinked away a surge of nausea. She raised Dragonfang into a defensive position.

"No further, Your Majesty," she rasped. The building site was loud with cries of alarm and the first sounds of a scuffle, but Brunnhilde only had eyes for Hela. She couldn't be allowed to get her hands on the elven stone and the book of ritual that had... Oh gods. The shimmer in the air and cries of fear made even more sense now. She and Lady Sif had failed in the task given them by the All-Father. The bridge was open.

Hela feinted a cut at Brunnhilde's head and dodged the other way, trying to circle behind her. The Valkyrie read the ruse and managed to stay between Hela and the artifacts, but with the Dark Elves' imminent arrival, things were about to go from bad to worse.

"Sif! I need you," she yelled.

"Bit busy calming the populace, I'm afraid. Plan?"

Not as such, the Valkyrie admitted to herself as she countered another flurry of strikes from Hela, backing closer to the artifacts and Lord Dee until she could kick backwards with her heel and catch him in his ribs. The man grunted, which at least meant he was alive.

"My lord? My lord, it's about to get very dangerous here – I suggest you remove yourself immediately. While you're at it, find a way to destroy that crystal or I fear we may all be dead very quickly. And not just us. Your queen, your family, all of London. And that's just for starters."

"No," he groaned. "No, that can't be right. I opened the path to the angels. To Paradise! You... you are one of the angels, the archangel Uriel. Aren't you?" He was wavering on his knees, a fine tremor running through his hands when he appeared in the corner of Brunnhilde's vision. His face was as pale as his snowy beard, and she wouldn't have been surprised if his soul had slipped free of his body in the next moment.

"Enough!" Hela shouted before Brunnhilde could think of a way to respond. The goddess's lips drew back in a snarl and she waved her free hand in a complex gesture.

The Valkyrie felt a tingle of magic pass by her and lunged. Hela parried the strike and then Dee appeared, his eyes blank as he stared up at Hela and waited for her next command.

"Curse you," Brunnhilde snapped and attacked again, harder this time, pushing down the knowledge of who she was fighting and concentrating only on staying alive. Hela merely grinned and defended with ease.

"They're nearly here, Bright-Battle. Whatever you're doing, hurry it up," the shield-maiden bellowed, dragging the reluctant soldiers into formation facing towards the hole in the air. She wore an expression of grim determination that couldn't quite hide her panic. "They can't abide the taste of steel or iron," she shouted. "Just a touch will burn them and cause pain. Use that to your advantage, use anything made of metal. Not just swords but hammers, chisels, your chainmail, an iron bucket for all I care. Do you understand me?"

Brunnhilde didn't see their response because her view was

abruptly blocked by the first dozen invaders from Svartalfheim stepping down out of the sky and into Midgard. They were warriors, taller by far than the humans and clad in highly polished and lacquered wooden armor and bearing blades of glass and bone. They didn't hesitate; their feet touched Midgard's stone and soil and they advanced immediately on Sif and her small and terrified squad of soldiers.

Others turned in the direction of Brunnhilde and Hela, the waiting Lord Dee and the lad with the clever, frightened eyes who clutched at Dee's sleeve.

Brunnhilde pointed at him with her sword and then focused on Hela again. "Get him out of here right now, lad. Go!" she yelled. There was a scuffle as the boy scrambled backwards, paused, and then grabbed Lord Dee around the chest and hauled him backwards. Dee was babbling about angels and heaven and leading an army to conquer the world.

"It's your own world in danger of being conquered now, man," Brunnhilde shouted after them, unable to stop herself.

Hela chuckled. "I never knew you were so petty," she said with malicious approval and something uncomfortable stirred in the Valkyrie's gut. "Now. I suggest you hand over those objects before the elves kill you all."

Brunnhilde backed up until she was standing over the book and the stone and then kicked them both behind her. She glanced back just long enough to discover their location and then faced Hela once more, settling into her stance and her focus. She raised her blade. "I think we have bigger problems than fighting amongst ourselves for possession of the spell items. We need to stop this invasion."

Hela padded forward, as predatory as the great wolf Fenris.

"'We' need do no such thing. What happens in this Realm is none of my concern," she said.

Brunnhilde exhaled and relaxed her shoulders. "As I thought. You simply want the magic for opening a bridge. You want a rival to Bifrost that you control, not the conquest of Midgard, which you've never cared about before. That was the one thing I couldn't understand, you know, that you would side with Svartalfheim to take this Realm." She put her head on one side and grinned. "But you haven't, have you? And I bet you didn't actually plan for the bridge to open while you were all alone here, either," she added sweetly, marveling at her own daring.

Only if Hela was going to kill her, she'd have done it by now. The Valkyrie was fairly sure that the queen of Hel's abilities were in as reduced as her own, though "fairly sure" was still a huge gamble in light of their respective abilities.

There was no time for further talk. Hela screeched her fury and attacked, doing all she could to push Brunnhilde away from the artifacts. At the same time, another wave of Dark Elves stepped out of the pathway. These were not armored but instead clad in long robes and trusting to the warriors around them for protection. They took up a place on each of the points of the recently vacated mosaic and began to chant. Each held a crystal in one hand.

Their words were wholly unfamiliar to the Valkyrie and yet whatever Valkyrior ability was left in her blood resonated with it. They were sealing the pathway, anchoring it to this location and this Realm so that they had a permanent link between them. A gate standing forever open.

"Your Majesty, we really–" Brunnhilde tried and then flung

herself sideways to avoid a blow that would have decapitated her. Hela was done with talking, it seemed. Half a dozen elves interposed themselves between the pair and Brunnhilde found herself fighting three of them instead of Hela.

Thank Odin, she thought and catapulted herself forward to lash out with both her blade and her steel vambrace. She smashed her forearm into the face of the nearest Dark Elf, who let out a terrible, bloodcurdling scream and fell backwards, clutching at his smoking flesh. His companions came on as if they hadn't even noticed what had happened, zealous determination glittering in their beautiful, alien eyes.

Brunnhilde managed a brief glance around in between short, vicious battles: Hela was fighting with ruthless efficiency and cutting her way steadily towards the artifacts. It appeared nothing was going to stop her getting her hands on them, not even a flood of Dark Elves descending upon her. Sif and her tiny squad of soldiers were surrounded on all sides by the blue-skinned warriors, while the elf mages on the array chanted in unison and built more layers of magic to sit heavy and suffocating in the air, pressing down on the Valkyrie's chest until it was a struggle to breathe.

Yet another wave of elf warriors descended, more warriors. They flooded into place around the mages while those that came afterwards converged upon the Asgardians and those few humans still left alive.

"We have to close the path," Brunnhilde yelled. "Sif, Hela, we have to close the path or we all die here!"

The raven-haired warrior raised a gauntleted fist in acknowledgment while the Goddess of Hel gave no indication she had either heard or cared. Sif leapt over the heads of the soldiers and landed in the midst of the elves facing them, screaming a war cry. As soon as she had drawn all attention, a soldier at the rear of the little group slipped out of formation and sprinted away from the building site. The Valkyrie could only pray that he was going for reinforcements.

Half a dozen warriors encircled Sif, and then she saw nothing but flashing glass blades, snarling blue faces, and splashes of blood arcing against the brightness of the sky.

TWENTY-TWO

UNLIKELY ALLIES

Hela snapped the neck of another elf and threw her corpse at two others. In the space she made, she took another step forward – a step closer to the artifacts. A step closer to the power she needed. And, most importantly, a step closer to being able to Realm-jump home.

The Valkyrie's words played again in her head, but without urgency. Hela didn't care what happened to Midgard or its people. She didn't care whether Svartalfheim conquered this Realm. What she cared about was securing the artifacts and the power.

Another elf came at her, his bone blade honed to a wicked sharpness and humming through the air for her throat. She leaned backwards just far enough that it skimmed past her flesh and then punched her own sword through his wooden armor and into his ribs. He fell back kicking, an agonized squeal breaking from his throat, and she twisted the blade and wrenched it free.

Took another step closer and faced another opponent. For every one she killed, a dozen more emerged from the tunnel in the sky. The Asgardians were moving like liquid fire, in and out and up on the walls, leaping down to take out half a dozen enemies at once and flitting away before anyone could land a blow. Still, they could not turn this tide. Twenty, no thirty, Dark Elves flooded between Hela and the book and stone lying abandoned at the base of a stack of carefully hewn blocks of pale marble.

The queen of Hel paused and flicked a glance towards the mages standing on the mosaic. All nine of them had their arms raised and hands outstretched and she could feel the magic building between them as they directed it upwards to the pathway that opened just above their fingertips. Even as she watched, a dozen more elves jumped down out of the opening to join their brethren in the battle to secure the anchor point.

If they managed it, the focal stone and book would have fulfilled their purpose. With the bridge locked between this Realm and Svartalfheim, they'd be useless to her. She wouldn't be able to open her own bridge between Helheim and Asgard. Everything she'd done here, every humiliation she'd suffered, would be for naught. And that was not a risk Hela was willing to take.

With a snarl of distaste at what she was about to do, Hela stepped back from the artifacts and jumped over the elves' heads to the Valkyrie's side. "You have to actually kill them if you want us to win," she grunted, lunging past to cleave an elf's arm off at the shoulder. It fell back with a scream, the steel of her blade eating into its exposed flesh and nerves as well as severing its arm.

The Valkyrie gave her a sidelong glance but forbore to comment. Instead, they fought their way to the small island of beleaguered humanity bolstered by Lady Sif. Hela gave the shield-maiden a sour look and was gratified to see her blanch.

"One of the soldiers has gone for reinforcements," she panted after a pause. "He's under firm instructions to bring everyone he can lay his hands on, not just soldiers. No exceptions."

"Do you think there will be enough?" the Valkyrie asked.

Hela snorted. "It doesn't matter if they bring an entire army, it's the mages we need to stop and I doubt Midgardians have either the skill or the courage for that."

Sif gave her an unimpressed glare, her earlier discomfort apparently forgotten. "Then it's a good job the three of us are apparently friends now, isn't it? We wait for the soldiers to provide backup for this lot–" she indicated the knot of humans battling desperately against an overwhelming number of elves "–and then we take out their spell casters."

Brunnhilde was already nodding. Instead of answering, Hela simply turned back to the fray and began to fight. The sooner this was over, the sooner she could forget it had ever happened. Relying on Asgardians, on *minor goddesses,* for help? Her, Goddess of Helheim and Niffleheim and rightful ruler of Asgard? *Humiliating.*

Perhaps the Asgardians shared her distaste, or maybe they just understood the urgency, because there was no more talk. The three goddesses made exquisite use of their strengths, abilities, and martial prowess – not to mention their steel armor and weapons – to exact a terrible toll on the Dark Elves. There were blue-skinned corpses lying in piles and heaps by the time the tramp of feet and clank of armor indicated the arrival of human reinforcements. *And about time too.*

Hela leapt to the top of a partially built wall and paused there to catch her breath and take in the scene. From this vantage, she could see almost directly into the pathway and the army of Svartalfheim stretching back into the infinite distance. Thousands upon thousands of elves were patiently awaiting their turn to cross into Midgard. Despite herself, Hela felt a flicker of unease at the sight. She told herself it was simply prudence and a desire to return home victorious and let her gaze travel across the rest of the building site that had become a battlefield.

She was genuinely shocked see both John Dee and William crouching at the edge, mostly hidden by a spoil heap of dirt and loose rock. What did they think they were doing?

A column of armored soldiers marched into view and then, a moment later and from a another direction, a second column. Even, to her surprise, a group of burly men coated in a fine layer of stone dust: the masons, she presumed. Instead of armor and weapons they wore heavy leather aprons and bracers on their arms the better to carry stone and wielded heavy, metal-headed hammers and long chisels. They made sure to stay behind the soldiers, but she had little doubt they'd make their presence felt.

Lastly, there emerged a thin stream of noblemen dressed in velvets and furs. Each wore a sword and dagger, but no breastplate or even helmet. Hela would be unsurprised if they changed their minds about fighting pretty quickly. Still, she welcomed anyone – anything – who'd distract the elves and give her a chance to end the mages and, while she was at it, steal one or two of the stones they held.

The ritual requires a focal stone in the location we desire to bridge to, and several back home to focus and channel the power. I won't need that many, but I'll claim them all to experiment with. Who knows what other delicious magicks I might perform with their help.

The building site soon teemed with violence as the Midgardians formed into two lines at right angles to each other and advanced on the invaders, calling out their queen's name as if for luck. The elves surged to meet them with a cry of their own and the name of Alflyse rang from their throats. So that was who was behind this, the ambitious, resourceful new queen of Svartalfheim's Eastern Spires. She was determined to make a name for herself, it would seem. Hela admired both her ingenuity and her determination even as she set out to ensure neither would come to fruition.

Hela and the Asgardians battled their way towards the mosaic and the mages sweating and laboring upon it. Their honor guard was still in place and they leapt to their masters' defense.

Hela ducked the swing of an obsidian blade and slapped the elf wielding it hard enough to knock him backwards into his companion. She jumped into the gap they left but the pair recovered in time and forced her back before she could reach the closest mage and kill him. She was, however, afforded a swift glance at this part of the mosaic and the shimmering, inlaid lines in golden stone radiating outwards from the power node on which the mage stood. Of course. Now that they stood upon it, she recognized the pattern as one that doubled and redoubled power until it became a self-sustaining system. That was how they'd form a permanent link to Midgard.

It was the last piece of the puzzle. Ritual, stones, anchor points and individual spells to bind them all together. Grinning savagely, she shattered an elf's collar bone with her sword and faced the next.

These warriors were exquisitely skilled and while Hela's magic was returning slowly, she didn't have enough to use her death touch upon them. Each of the nine mages had four bodyguards, and although they clearly hadn't been expecting Hela or Odin's little hunters, they knew their duty and didn't hesitate, spending their lives with reckless abandon.

Fortunately for her, that was a coin Hela was well used to reaping.

It was a bit like old times, fighting alongside Sif as they'd done on so many occasions before, though never quite under such circumstances.

To Brunnhilde's right, the queen of Hel spun and hacked and slashed, white-haired warriors falling all around her and none seemingly able to make so much as a touch upon her skin or armor. Brunnhilde herself was slower than she would like, drained of energy and strength. It had been a fortnight since she'd slept more than a few minutes at a time and the rigors and toll of the battle were already beginning to make themselves known, dragging at her limbs as if she had anvils strapped to her shoulders and thighs.

The Valkyrie knew herself to be the weakest link in the chain surrounding the mosaic and its load of spell casters and the thought brought a flush of shame to her cheeks. Gritting her teeth, she narrowed her eyes and redoubled her efforts. On her wrist, one of the jewels in Frigga's bracelet flared and then cracked, but it did little more than add a spark to Brunnhilde's slowing sword. All the jewels working together would do nothing more than give her a few seconds of energy.

Even once the array was broken and the path destroyed, it wouldn't prevent those already here from exacting their revenge. The Dark Elves were known for their cruelty and if their way home was cut off, those marooned here would kill as many humans as they could before being cut down simply out of spite. Brunnhilde knew instinctively that they would never surrender or consent to live out their lives in this Realm. No, they would slaughter indiscriminately and dedicate each death to their queen and her ambition.

The Midgardians were performing better than she had hoped, their lines solid despite the ever-increasing numbers they were facing and despite that those numbers were taller, faster, stronger and, of course, more alien than any opponent they could ever have faced before.

Their courage was a thing of beauty and a sight to behold, one that warmed the Valkyrie's heart. Here were warriors worthy of Valhalla and the urge to Choose their souls when and if they fell rose like the tide within her.

To her left, Sif slipped between a dying bodyguard and another one injured and struck at the closest mage, scoring a deep cut to his shoulder. His voice faltered in the chant, a hoarse scream replacing it, and Brunnhilde felt the magic fluctuate.

"Again!" she roared at Sif, but the elves converged on her and pushed her back. She killed one even as she retreated and this time the Valkyrie felt the magic jolt. Brunnhilde hesitated and then stepped back, back again, out of range, and watched.

The shield-maiden drove her sword through an enemy's belly and the magic jumped. Strengthened. Moments later Hela got close enough to hack down a mage, half-severing their arm. This time, the magic faltered.

"Sweet Frigga," Brunnhilde breathed. She leapt back in, shattering glass swords and hacking those made of bone in two. "The mages, not the guards," she bellowed. "Every guard you kill strengthens the ritual." Sif found space to frown at her in question. There was blood spattered across her cheek. "Death-magic, remember? Everyone we kill just hastens completion of the spell! It's the mages we need to stop – kill them or get them off the pattern! The spell isn't linked to their lives!"

Understanding dawned in Sif's face even as instinct and training saw her duck and then slash backwards, opening an elf's armor and spine. She fell, shrieking, and the shield-maiden winced. It was too late: the magic jolted again.

Again, the Valkyrie didn't know if Hela had heard or whether she simply didn't care. The fact she was fighting beside them was miracle – or terrible – enough. Brunnhilde concentrated on what she could do. Her abilities were still hampered, but she had enough. Probably. It would be a surprise, anyway.

Brunnhilde glamoured herself. There were shouts of consternation from the warriors facing her and she took the opportunity to shove one into another and then leap over their swinging weapons as they flailed about looking for her. She landed beside the closest mage and ripped her sword across his throat.

The mage gurgled and collapsed and the Valkyrie spun away as his bodyguards converged around him, lashing out at thin air and hoping to find her. The magic faltered and she breathed out in relief. She was right: only the guards of the magi were so linked. Selfish, but sensible: they didn't want to risk having to sacrifice themselves to complete the binding and instead could just kill those most loyal to them.

Already, Brunnhilde could feel the glamour faltering. She leapt again, further out of the fray and across the building site, letting it fall as she did and emerging within a knot of Dark Elves. She shattered glass weapons and used the flat of her blade, her fists and feet to incapacitate seven of them, then jumped over the heads of the rest and landed beside Lord Dee and the boy.

"My lord! *What are you still doing here?*" she demanded, real anger limning her tone. Wordlessly, the man thrust something towards her: the book of ritual. On instinct, Brunnhilde recoiled.

"He says it's safe now," the lad said quickly. "He wants you to destroy it. Says it's too... it was too precious for too long for him to do it, but that it's caused such destruction and evil. I don't think he's well," he added under his breath.

Brunnhilde poked at the book with Dragonfang's tip, horribly aware of the raging fight, the dying, overwhelmed Midgardians, and her need to end it. Somehow. Nothing happened, so she knocked it out of his hand and then stood, raised her blade, and chopped the book into pieces. Dee and the boy cowered away, and then ducked at the great roar of sound rising from the mosaic. Part-scream of elf, part-scream of magic. A wave of energy slammed into Brunnhilde. Her stolen Valkyrior abilities. Not just her death perception, but everything that set her apart from Sif and the other minor Asgardian goddesses. Every gift Odin had given her rolled over her and it was power she could use, strength that was her own!

Brunnhilde stared down at the tatters of parchment. "You stole my strength? You stole what makes me *me*?" she demanded, overwhelmed, and then gasped. "Odin's eye, does that mean you've returned...?" She spun around and caught sight of Hela pausing and then taking in a great breath. A manic smile lit her face, and she swept a dozen elves from her path with a gesture. The Goddess of Death cackled and reached out, her death touch shriveling the nearest mage to bone and cinder in an instant.

Every single Dark Elves currently on Midgard – Brunnhilde couldn't even count there were so many – converged on the mosaic. On Hela. On Sif.

Sif, who was still trying not to kill her foes and whose strength, if it had been stolen and then restored, contained no higher power or magic with which to defeat her enemies. She had only her strength and skill and she was viciously, laughably outnumbered.

Brunnhilde staggered. "What have I done?" she whispered. Then she began to run.

Hela's stolen magic returned to her in a great, dizzying rush. She sucked in a draught of air that was suddenly sparkling and golden with power, with possibility.

With it came fury and righteous vengeance and the urge to rend and kill those who had so incapacitated her. It would be so tempting to give in, so righteous and deserved as she took their lives one by one while they cowered and ran and hid from her bloody vengeance. The Valkyrie's words rang in her head: a warning against death. Deaths of the bodyguards, perhaps, but she'd practically encouraged the slaughter of the mages.

Hela took a single second to heal the wound in her arm and then blasted the elven warriors out of her path and advanced upon the nearest mage, her cloak rippling behind her. Her death touch was a thing of awesome beauty and destruction and it stole the mage's life in an instant.

The spell weakened and she laughed. Beneath her boots, another part of the array was revealed and she committed it to memory. She turned to the next mage, intent on sucking out his life, only for every Dark Elf currently on Midgard to abandon their respective battles and sprint to the aid of the circle of spell casters. That, too, was none of her concern. Let the Asgardians and the humans deal with it.

Hela cast an illusion that hid her from plain sight and skipped through the mosaic, memorizing the positions of the mages and the power nodes upon which they stood, the lines connecting them together and how the whole formed an array of immense and self-sustaining power. Once she understood the pattern, she stabbed the nearest magician and seized their focal stone. Its power burnt at her and she dissipated it with a contemptuous gesture – they thought to use death-magic against her? Against her, the very mistress of Death?

With a flourish, Hela brought her sword down upon the mosaic and shattered it, destroying lines and nodes and severing the magic. The mages caught up within the ritual let out terrible screams and clutched at their heads, wavering, falling to their knees and bleeding from the eyes and ears.

Above them, the tunnel began to collapse in on itself and Hela could hear the distant shrieks of Dark Elves caught within the path between Realms. Dozens threw themselves into Midgard, tumbling to the stone and landing gracelessly on top of the magicians who'd enabled their arrival. The rest, Hela suspected, would die as the tunnel fell apart. Lost in the void between Realms.

That, too, was no concern of hers. With the pattern memorized, the ritual understood, and one of the required stones in her possession, Hela slid out from among the flailing elves and sidestepped the panic-stricken Valkyrie racing to her companion's aid. The mages hadn't managed to finalize the spell, and so she could manipulate the magic within the stones and bend them to her will. Victory was still within her grasp. Behind her, Sif fought on doggedly, blades slicing at and into her she was surrounded by so many foes, as Hela made her leisurely way towards John Dee and the boy.

When she was close enough, she dropped her illusion in front of them, eliciting shocked gasps.

"My lady!" William squeaked, his voice breaking and angling high in his surprise. "What is–" he began.

"Have you seen enough magic for one lifetime, young William?" Hela held out her hand. "The elven stone. Now." Her tone brooked no dissent.

John Dee looked up at her with tears running down his face. He held out the crystal in a trembling fist. "What have I done?" he whispered.

Hela took the stone and stared down at him in contempt.

"What exactly did you expect when you meddled with things beyond your understanding? You humans are so puny and so weak. So easily manipulable. It was only a matter of time before someone took advantage of you. Now where is the book?"

"The blonde lady stabbed it to pieces," William offered and pointed. Scraps of parchment blew across the ground or soaked into pools of blood.

Hela's fist clenched on the hilt of the Nightsword. "No matter," she grated through her teeth. "No matter. I heard enough of the ritual to fashion my own spell. And, of course, I have the souls of millions of dead standing ready to power it."

The old man began to sob. "Is that all you came here for, truly? My shew stone and book? Are any of you three creatures angels?" he asked, as if desperate to salvage something, some pride or justification for the slaughter being perpetrated here.

The boy nudged him. "Better," he whispered, with a smile, however frightened, for Hela. "This one, at least, is a goddess."

Dee shook his head, denying the boy's assertion, and Hela contemplated just killing him. Instead, she spared the briefest of glances for William. "You have ambition, young man, and I admire that. Don't let anyone take it from you. Not your ambitions and not your dreams."

"Never, my lady. Your Majesty. Never," he said fervently.

Hela turned away and looked at the carnage of the building site. The tunnel in the air was almost gone and the Asgardians had cut down the last of the mages. They wouldn't be facing magic now, but the numbers opposing them were overwhelming. No one could survive that.

"No more than you deserve for your disrespect of me, your

rightful ruler," Hela muttered. "But if you should somehow make it through this alive, then don't forget the words of the ritual that you learned, shield-maiden and Valkyrie – I shall have need of you and them in the future."

Hela flexed her magic and grinned again at its responsiveness and the limitless depths of her power. She gathered it to her, took one more look at the raging battle, and then glanced back at the boy and winked. "The better part of valor is discretion," she murmured, and clicked her fingers to Realm-jumped home, leaving Midgard and the Asgardians to their miserable fate.

TWENTY-THREE
HOW GLORIOUS

Everywhere Brunnhilde looked, a sea of blue-skinned warriors crowded them, snarling and hating and cutting at them, desperate for their blood and their deaths. Everywhere she looked, dead Midgardians; mostly soldiers, some not. And everywhere she looked, dead elves.

And yet still the living fought, not just the Asgardians but the humans too, with a grim determination that would have made her weep under other circumstances. Made her proud now, proud and pained.

Hela had vanished, which Brunnhilde disliked but wasn't surprised by. The restoration of her power was only ever going to go one way: the queen of Hel was far too selfish and rated the flawless beauty of her skin too highly to risk it in a Realm that meant nothing to her. It left Brunnhilde and Sif to coordinate and lead the dwindling number of soldiers to victory against the fatalistic viciousness of the remaining Dark Elves.

There were still four mages left alive and, between them, they were doing everything they could to restore the tunnel in the sky leading back to Svartalfheim. The Valkyrie didn't think they'd manage it, but her concern was that any spell they wrought might once again pull at her strength. If they could fatigue her again, then not even Sif at her most lethal would be able to defeat the number of enemies facing them.

"We need more soldiers," the shield-maiden bellowed across the battlefield. Brunnhilde agreed but had no idea where to find them. She shrugged helplessly in reply and Sif's mouth tightened. She took a deep breath and then relaxed. Her face took on a terrifying and icy remoteness, an expression Brunnhilde had seen countless times before in her duty stalking the battlefields where Asgardian warriors fell in death and glory. It was the expression of a warrior preparing to die for the cause in which they believed, and the Valkyrie determined then and there that Sif would not die alone, if die she must.

Die for Midgardians? Sif? No. That will not happen. Neither of us will die here and nor will too many more of these brave humans, she vowed. Brunnhilde had no idea how to keep that vow, other than by destroying the elven force arrayed against them, beginning with the mages to prevent them re-establishing the path to their home world.

"I've got this lot. You organize those and I'll meet you in the middle," she shouted, gesturing at the humans nearest her. She swallowed bitterness and then met Sif's determined glare once more open. "No mercy."

It was a phrase she rarely had cause to use and one that went against everything she believed. Even a foe who fought with honor was to be honored in turn. To kill without care or regret was a horror to her. *But the fall of Midgard is worse.*

The black-haired warrior's expression betrayed an instant of shock and then she nodded once, turned away and began bawling orders at the soldiers and masons on her side of the building site.

Brunnhilde got the Midgardians nearest her into a rough square and then glamoured herself and slid between the knots of elves towards the mages. The mosaic on which they'd been standing was mostly destroyed – Hela's handiwork – but she could feel the flickers of magic as they harnessed what they could from it, the raw and untethered ends of spells and ritual, and worked frantically to knit them back together. Strange shapes coalesced and then collapsed in the air above them: the tunnel, being conjured back into existence?

There was no longer time to worry that each death Brunnhilde gifted the elves would be fuel for the spell as had been the case before. She had to believe that there weren't enough mages left alive to direct the death-energy into the ritual in a way that was useable. Because otherwise, Midgard was already lost.

Obeying her own order to show no mercy, the Valkyrie didn't do her enemies the courtesy of dropping her glamour so that they might engage in a fair fight. Though it stained her to her very core, she struck down the first mage from within the cloak of invisibility, giving them no chance to defend themself. She'd had cause to hope before this day that succeeding at their mission on Midgard would take away the dreams that had plagued her. Now, Brunnhilde knew that she'd just replaced one type of nightmare with another – and this, one of her own making.

The Valkyrie made herself look at the dead Midgardians and those battling to stay alive against a force so vastly their superior and reminded herself yet again whose side they were on. The Dark Elves had chosen this. They'd chosen invasion and conquest of a Realm unaware of their existence and unprepared to defend itself. They'd chosen bloodshed and madness and cruelty.

If Brunnhilde had to gift them the same in retaliation – taking a hundred lives to save a million – then she would. She wouldn't relish it, and she'd never stop feeling shame over it, but she was a warrior and she'd been sent by Odin to stop an atrocity.

She just had to commit one in order to do so.

The Valkyrie shoved away the thought and fought on. What other choice was there?

Steel-clad soldiers had come, and with them scores of archers with steel-tipped arrows. Brunnhilde wasn't embarrassed to say that it was they who turned the tide in the end and not the Asgardians' prowess.

Despite their skill and determination, they were just two warriors fighting alongside scores of others. Against hundreds. Their efforts were unremarkable compared with the humans who'd faced and fought Dark Elves, a race far superior to them martially as well as in strength and size.

The last elf fell to Lady Sif's sword and stillness descended upon the building site for one long, disbelieving moment. And then a ragged, exhausted cheer echoed from the walls and buildings surrounding them.

Brunnhilde limped over to the bloody, bruised shield-maiden and dragged her into an embrace. "Still alive?" she asked into Sif's sweat-lank hair.

"Not entirely sure. Have you come to Choose me?"

The Valkyrie managed a wry smile and leaned back. "Think you were brave enough to go to Valhalla, do you?" Sif merely stared at her and Brunnhilde snorted, and then kissed her cheek. "No, I'm not here to Choose you, but yes, I would have if it came to it."

Sif managed an imperious nod and then her shoulders slumped. "Gods, but I'm tired."

It was Brunnhilde's turn to stare in silent outrage.

Her friend winced. "Sorry." She gestured at the building site, at the vacant-eyed soldiers who, now they were no longer fighting for their lives, were beginning to realize just what it was they'd done. Who it was they'd fought. And how they'd triumphed.

"But look what we did. We saved Midgard. Despite the odds, it's done."

Brunnhilde looked, but it was hard for her to find the pride that Sif was radiating. Still, the warrior was right. Midgard was safe, and they'd had a hand in that.

"I know we'll be arrested and tried for treason if we stay, but there's a part of me that would like the chance to explain what has happened," Sif said quietly as soldiers, masons, and noblemen began the long, arduous process of establishing who was still alive and how badly the others were hurt. "These people have dealt with something they've never seen before. Surely someone owes them an explanation. And the way they fought. The courage in the face of such odds. If only we could have saved more of them."

"I agree, Sif. But if Elizabeth does order us arrested, I don't want to have to fight men I've just fought alongside. Contact your brother; let's go home."

"*Make way for Her Majesty the queen!*"

The Asgardians exchanged a glance and then a bark of laughter. Luck wasn't with them after all.

A phalanx of heavily armed soldiers marched around the corner followed by a middle-aged woman in heavy white make-up and an enormous wig. Her gown was of stiff brocade and silk and dripped with pearls and gold.

She wore it the same way Brunnhilde wore her armor, as a protection and a statement of who she was. She came to a halt at the edge of the building site and took in the scene. To the Asgardians' surprise, she nodded coolly at the extravagant slaughter and the alien appearance of the elves. A moment later her hawklike gaze pinned Brunnhilde and Sif in place. She extended one heavily ringed hand and beckoned.

Soldiers ran forward to lead them, though whether as honor guard or prisoner escort, Brunnhilde couldn't say.

"Your Majesty," croaked a wavering voice. More soldiers reacted and the scrape of swords being drawn was loud in the silence. To Brunnhilde's astonishment, it was Lord Dee with the boy still at his side. "Your Majesty, it is I, John Dee. These women, these... warriors, I should say, are all that stood between your kingdom and disaster. I watched every moment of this battle and they fought with as much bravery and, dare I say it, more skill than these glorious soldiers you see before you. Without them, we would have been quite lost. I beg you reward them and not punish them. I had thought them angels, my queen. Now I know them to be England's greatest defenders."

Queen Elizabeth stared between the seated lord and the Asgardians and then at the injured and fatigued soldiers doing their best to stand to attention among the corpses. "Is this true?" she demanded. There was no hint of give or weakness in her voice – this was a woman well used to giving orders and having them obeyed.

"It is true that we were sent here to avert the destruction of your Realm," Brunnhilde said carefully and before any of the survivors could reply. "But we cannot take any credit for what happened here today. Your soldiers are some of the finest we have ever had the privilege of fighting alongside and, I think I can speak for my companion as well as myself, they are of such a quality that I would not wish to face them in combat. I grieve with you for those who were lost in this battle and–"

The elf didn't come screaming his war cry. He came in a silent rush, ignoring the terrible gaping wound in his face and the other that had stolen the life from his left arm. Despite the agony it must be causing him, he carried a steel sword in his good right hand as he sprinted towards Queen Elizabeth's unprotected back.

Brunnhilde leapt left while Lady Sif pivoted right and they burst out through the twin lines of soldiers before those men had a chance to react. Brunnhilde threw herself at the queen and grabbed her up in both arms and spun so that the Valkyrie's own armored back was to the charging elf. Sif sprinted past them as the first shouts of alarm went up. She smashed the sword out of the elf's hand and with the return stroke, she took off his head in a spray of blood. It bounced to a stop by the queen's velvet slippers.

Elizabeth stared down at it from the protective circle of Brunnhilde's arms and then looked up into the Valkyrie's face. "Well," she said softly, "if that was part of your plan to garner our good opinion of you, we have to say it worked. Now if you could just let me go… We are the queen, after all."

Brunnhilde stepped hurriedly away and then froze as cold, sharp metal kissed the back of her neck. She locked eyes with Elizabeth and the woman hesitated just a beat too long before flicking her fingers in dismissal. The blades withdrew.

"What are these creatures?" she asked, poking at the head with her toe as if assassination attempts upon her person were too commonplace to be remarkable. Perhaps they were.

"Dark Elves, Your Majesty," Lady Sif said. "They are an enemy of the land from which we come. They never should have reached you here and we beg your forgiveness that they did."

"What about my lady Helga?" a voice piped up suddenly. "You're all talking about how these two and the soldiers saved the world, but none of you want to mention the lady I served these last days. She was here, too. She did just as much to win this battle as they did." Brunnhilde looked over as Lord Dee whispered furiously into the boy's ear to silence him. "I don't care if she was the queen of Hell," he protested in a vehement whisper. "She was funny."

The Asgardians looked at each other with identical expressions of disbelief. *Funny?* Sif mouthed and Brunnhilde had to look away otherwise she would start laughing and possibly never stop. She was so tired.

He sighed wistfully. "And beautiful and terrible. Queen of the fairies, an Amazon, Cleopatra herself. My dark lady, my eternal muse."

It was too much. Brunnhilde was going to laugh, or scream, or cry, if she had to listen to any more. She interrupted him. "With your gracious permission, Your Majesty, we must take our leave," she said. "Our All-Father needs to know that we are safe and that the threat to your Realm is ended." Sif nodded and the Valkyrie knew she'd be contacting her brother through their mind-link.

Elizabeth looked around the building site once more and then back at the pair of warriors. "Mighty indeed," she said softly. "Truly mighty and glorious. You have England's thanks, strange warriors of a distant land. And you have mine."

The pair bowed deeply and then Bifrost shimmered into existence behind them. There were cries of wonder this time, not alarm, and they stepped up onto its rainbow surface with not a little relief. They bowed again and stepped backwards, and the Realm of Midgard vanished.

They were only a few steps onto Bifrost when Brunnhilde's shoulders slumped. "All right, get it over with," she said wearily.

Sif spun to walk backwards in front of her and shoved a finger in the Valkyrie's face. "I told you. Didn't I tell you? How many times have I told you? I don't like Midgard. Now do you see why?"

Brunnhilde groaned. "You think any of that was to do with Midgard rather than Svartalfheim? Have you forgotten who it was you were just fighting?" She waved her hand before the shield-maiden could respond. "Not now, my friend, I beg you. Can we just get home, get bathed and, please Odin, get a good night's sleep? I will listen to you complain for a full hour once I am well rested."

Sif cut herself off mid-sentence and a thoughtful look stole over her face. "A full hour?" she clarified and then stepped backwards off Bifrost and into Heimdall. Her brother caught her and spun her around and then gave her a gentle push to the side.

"I see you're alive and I'm glad of it," he said with perfunctory dismissal and then turned to the Valkyrie. Sif squawked in indignation and was ignored. "Lady Brunnhilde, I have been authorized to provide you with quarters here in the bridge temple. There is a hot bath and a soft bed waiting for you just through there. Lady Sif can give the All-Father the initial report, yours is not expected for sixteen hours."

Brunnhilde gaped and then stretched up onto her toes and pressed a kiss to Heimdall's cheek. "Sixteen...? Thank you, thank you, thank you!"

Heimdall grinned and pointed again to the bridge temple and the Valkyrie didn't need any more encouragement than that.

"Hey, wait!" Sif began, reaching for her. Brunnhilde evaded her grasp. "An hour, you said. Remember? Brother, how could–"

Brunnhilde slammed the door on the rest of her friend's complaint and then leaned against it, taking in the giant bath wreathed with steam and, through another door, a soft, wide, low bed. She groaned and kicked off her boots, bypassed the bath with only a hint of regret, and threw herself, armed and armored and uncomfortable, onto the blankets. Hela had fragments of the ritual and possibly one of the stones, but she couldn't manipulate them yet. Certainly not within the next sixteen hours, and that was all she cared about.

It didn't matter. Between one breath and the next, the Valkyrie was asleep.

She did not dream.

EPILOGUE

When Hela reappeared in her Palace of Bones, her seneschal, Eirik, and Fenris the wolf both startled and her guards lunged away from the walls. Hela was pleased to see it, pleased that their alertness hadn't slipped during her absence.

"It is I, your queen," she said. Fenris recovered first and lolled out his tongue in lupine welcome, his hackles lowering as he relaxed out of the protective stance he'd taken over her throne. Eirik ordered the guards back into position and summoned servants. Then he hurried to prostrate himself before her.

"Welcome back, Your Majesty. Is all well?"

Hela hesitated. Was all well? She was weary down to her bones despite the restoration of her magic – and its burgeoning now that she was back in the source of her power.

"All is well," she said eventually. "What news?"

"Both Helheim and Niffleheim remain at peace and there has been no unrest during your absence, neither among your subjects nor from threats at your borders. In addition, and as per our last communication, my queen, I have had your generals draw up plans for the conquest of Svartalfheim. They are in their early stages but await only your approval to be fully developed. We can begin preparations for the conquest of Midgard now that you are safely returned from that Realm. We march upon your order." Eirik bowed again.

Hela nodded and then approached Fenris to scratch the giant wolf's muzzle. "He speaks the truth?" she whispered and the wolf blinked slowly in acknowledgment. She smiled. "Good. Then you may return to your wandering with my thanks."

She waved her hand at the colonnade at the end of the vast chamber, relishing the ease with which her magic flexed and bent to her will, once more an inexhaustible well of power and majesty. The columns parted to allow Fenris's huge form to slip out into the wilderness. He vanished with a flick of his bushy tail and Hela held the wall open a moment longer, both to watch him break into a joyful charge up the valley and because she could, because it was no more difficult than breathing.

Hela grinned and drew the building back together again. When she returned to her throne, Eirik was still waiting patiently for her further requests for information or orders.

"You have done well, seneschal. I am pleased. You may take some rest now, but not too long. I will have a need for you later to discuss Svartalfheim's fate. I fear Queen Alflyse is over-stretching herself. Someone needs to slap her back down to size."

"I shall await your summons, my queen," Eirik said. He bowed once more and removed the slender gold torc from around his neck. Hela took it from him and he backed away, before turning and marching out of the grand hall. Once he'd gone, she crossed to the magic alcove and returned his torc and her own to their place within the mountain giant's skull. The slab-like bottom jaw was missing several teeth and Hela retrieved the two elven focal stones she'd claimed and placed them in the gaps. They hummed with alien power but for now they were quiet, sleeping. They would wake when she needed them to and not before.

The queen of Helheim wove the spell that hid the alcove and then made her way to her suite. She cast off her armor and clothes and sank into a steaming bath – a proper bath, long and wide and deep and nothing at all like the wooden monstrosities she had been subjected to on Midgard.

Midgard. As she relaxed in the bath, with her head pillowed on the cloak imbued with her magic, she considered the destruction of the human world for all it had done to her, the indignities it had heaped upon her head. Destroying Midgard would be far easier than the conquest of Svartalfheim – the Dark Elves themselves had proved that just today.

And she had suffered at the hands of the humans to an extent that would enrage her loyal subjects on her behalf. All that was justification enough for that Realm's ending.

A besotted, infatuated smile rose in her memory, a boy's intelligent eyes and his delighted laughter at her threats and her magic. His final words to her, whispered in the instant before she jumped home: "Hear my soul speak. The very instant that I saw you did my heart fly to your service."

Hela ducked her head under the water, wetting her hair. Midgard could wait. Maybe in fifty years or so she'd return there at the head of an army and claim it as her own. Until then, she'd a mind to see what young William accomplished.

ACKNOWLEDGMENTS

Writing is a very collaborative process, so huge thanks to my agent, Harry Illingworth, for his ongoing support, and also the excellent team at Aconyte Books – Lottie, Gwen and Anjuli – for their input and advice in helping me craft this story. Thanks also to Grant Griffin for the fantastic cover art, and to Sarah Singer at Marvel Comics for their editorial support.

As ever, my eternal thanks to the Bunker, who keep me sane in this crazy publishing world and encourage me to challenge myself.

It was a huge amount of fun to write Hela and bring her malice and arrogance into a world where women were allowed neither, and to put Lady Sif and Valkyrie in that same environment and see how they responded to Elizabethan society. Any errors in research around the period are entirely my own, of course.

And finally, thanks as ever to the readers who pick up my work: it's a privilege to get to share my stories with you.

About the Author

ANNA STEPHENS is the author of the Godblind trilogy (*Godblind, Darksoul, Bloodchild*) and the Songs of the Drowned trilogy, which begins with *The Stone Knife*. All are available worldwide. Anna also writes for Black Library in their *Age of Sigmar* and *Warhammer Horror* worlds. As a black belt in Shotokan Karate, Anna's no stranger to the feeling of being hit in the face, which is more help than you would expect when writing fight scenes.

anna-stephens.com
twitter.com/annasmithwrites

LEGENDARY WARRIORS
EPIC BATTLES

MARVEL LEGENDS OF ASGARD

MIGHTY HEROES
NOTORIOUS VILLAINS

AMAZING POWERS
DARING EXPLOITS

POWERFUL STORIES
ICONIC HEROINES